Praise for Jack Stein, Psychic Investigator

Metal Sky

"If it's more adventure and science fiction blended which is of interest, Jay Caselberg's *Metal Sky* is the item of choice. . . . The blend of science fiction with mystery offers satisfying elements of both."—*Midwest Book Review*

"[Caselberg's] storytelling is brisk and accessible; it never loses your interest." —SF Reviews

"Nicely written." —SFRevu

Wyrmhole

"A fun, fast-paced SF mystery." —*Booklist*

"Fascinating and well-imagined . . . a terrific read, combining all the elements of great science fiction: originality, speculation, and consequence."
—Julie E. Czerneda, author of *Migration*

"Complex, layered, black as night, unputdownable."
—Stephen Baxter, Hugo Award–
nominated author of *Exultant*

"Jay Caselberg weaves SF with mystery for a new spin on the PI genre. In a fluid, dreamlike world where everything is changing, Jack Stein, Psychic Investigator, uses sharp-edged dreams to solve a case of miners vanished off a distant planet. An adventurous romp of a first novel, *Wyrmhole* keeps you guessing. The philosopher's stone and alchemy shift into the digital age."
—Wen Spencer, Compton Crook Award–
winning author of *A Brother's Price*

Turn the page for more rave reviews. . . .

Jay Caselberg

THE STAR TABLET

A ROC BOOK

ROC

Published by New American Library, a division of
Penguin Group (USA) Inc., 375 Hudson Street,
New York, New York 10014, USA
Penguin Group (Canada), 90 Eglinton Avenue East, Suite 700, Toronto,
Ontario M4P 2Y3, Canada (a division of Pearson Penguin Canada Inc.)
Penguin Books Ltd., 80 Strand, London WC2R 0RL, England
Penguin Ireland, 25 St. Stephen's Green, Dublin 2,
Ireland (a division of Penguin Books Ltd.)
Penguin Group (Australia), 250 Camberwell Road, Camberwell, Victoria 3124,
Australia (a division of Pearson Australia Group Pty. Ltd.)
Penguin Books India Pvt. Ltd., 11 Community Centre, Panchsheel Park,
New Delhi - 110 017, India
Penguin Group (NZ), cnr Airborne and Rosedale Roads, Albany,
Auckland 1310, New Zealand (a division of Pearson New Zealand Ltd.)
Penguin Books (South Africa) (Pty.) Ltd., 24 Sturdee Avenue,
Rosebank, Johannesburg 2196, South Africa

Penguin Books Ltd., Registered Offices:
80 Strand, London WC2R 0RL, England

First published by Roc, an imprint of New American Library,
a division of Penguin Group (USA) Inc.

First Printing, December 2005
10 9 8 7 6 5 4 3 2 1

PUBLISHER'S NOTE
This is a work of fiction. Names, characters, places, and incidents either are the product
of the author's imagination or are used fictitiously, and any resemblance to actual persons,
living or dead, business establishments, events, or locales is entirely coincidental.

The publisher does not have any control over and does not assume any responsibility for author or third-party Web sites or their content.

If you purchased this book without a cover you should be aware that this book is stolen
property. It was reported as "unsold and destroyed" to the publisher and neither the author nor the publisher has received any payment for this "stripped book."

For Annie

Acknowledgments

As ever, my deep appreciation goes to Laura Anne Gilman for her input and advice. Also, of course, I would like to thank my lovely editor, Liz Scheier, and my agent, Rich Henshaw. And, last but not least, my thanks to Eric Lavalette for keeping me partially sane in *that* place over decent lumps of flesh and good glasses of wine, which can be found if you look hard enough.

One

Jack Stein craned forward in his seat, leaning over the front panel to try to get a better view of the approaching city through the forward viewscreens, though the flier's nose partially blocked the view. He'd heard about the city, but the tales were nothing compared to the sight now becoming clearer in front of the small craft. The small ship was on auto now, banking as it descended, avoiding other air traffic on its way into Balance City's port. Balance City. He could see now how it had gotten its name. A thick rock spire pushed up from the canyon floor, spreading toward the top into a broad, flat surface. Deep cracks and scorings climbed irregularly over the spire's surface, disappearing into the darkened shadow of the overhang. Atop the plateau sat the city proper, a construction of metal and shining glass. Since the city's beginnings, natural urban growth had spread buildings in an ordered grid across the plateau's surface and farther. The area had not been enough, so the residents had simply continued, building out from the city's lip to the opposite sides of the canyon. It looked exactly like the urban spread was simply balancing atop the single spire that sat beneath it.

He'd been slightly nervous when boarding the flier on the orbital platform that served as the changeover point on his journey, but not as nervous as he was now. These damned things were supposed to have pilots, weren't they? Not that Jack had ever been a particularly good air passenger of any form.

The flier banked again, and headed lower. Jack swallowed and frowned, wondering what was happening. It looked as though they were flying too low, moving down beneath the city elevation, and he swallowed again, stretching forward for a better view. Perhaps it was just the approach path. Any moment he expected the flier to swoop up again, but then he saw why and he released his breath. Beneath the outgrown platforms at either edge of the plateau, construction had continued down as well as sideways. Buildings clung precariously to the spire's sides, struts and braces holding them in place, all uniformly colored in green or yellow, varying shades, but giving a subtle patchwork feel.

"Huh," he said to himself. Balance City's port was there, not above, but below. A wide flat area sat suspended beneath the platform, and his flier was close enough now that he could start to pick out individual craft arrayed in neat rows along its length. The order echoed the order of the city above. What the hell did Billie want to come here for anyway? It just didn't look like the sort of place in which she'd really be comfortable. Billie wasn't particularly one for the regimented life, especially not with her origins amongst the dirt and squalor of the Old end of the Locality. She'd lived most of her life without rules, without constraints. For that matter, Balance City didn't look like the sort of place Jack Stein would be at home in either. His comfort level was shaped by dirt and squalor too.

Jack shook his head, not that there was anyone to see the gesture. Billie had had no right to take off like that. Not that he could have stopped her. He had some sort of say in her activities, since they worked together, shared space, but he didn't really have the right to stop her doing what she wanted. Okay, he spoke of her publicly as his niece, but the only bond that had brought them together in the first place was mutual convenience. They worked together. And yeah, the bond of their friendship had grown since then, but even after all this time, he knew that the only authority he had over her was that which she allowed him. She was getting older now, as well, and that didn't help matters.

The flier slowed, easing into alignment with the docks, and Jack sat back. There was no point running over the whys and wherefores. Finding her and making sure she was okay was the important thing. The conversation with Heering had been too thin on detail. All he really knew was enough to suspect that she was in trouble, and if she was in trouble, she needed him. That feeling deep in his guts, that sharp-edged spear of cold that set his senses bristling, had been enough to drive him to scrape together what resources he needed. He'd put the fare together and made his way to Utrecht, carrying what he hoped was enough to cover him for the time he needed to be here and whatever he needed to do to find her. He was a PI, for Christ's sake. How long was it going to take him to find one teenage girl? Okay, that teenage girl was Billie, but still . . .

As the small ship pulled into what amounted to one vast, suspended hangar, Jack scanned the surrounds. Metal walls, neatly marked bays, directional signs placed at even intervals and tracks running between the bays. The varied array of fliers sat within the bays, edge aligned to edge . . . not a one of them out of place. Yellow diagonal patterns clearly marked the acceptable parking placement. Jack slowly shook his head again. Oh, he was going to have fun here; he could already see that. He thought he'd had enough ordered neatness in Yorkstone, but this was much worse than that.

Other than his frayed nerves from the flight, he seemed to have arrived in one piece. The flier nestled to a stop and an automatic grapple locked on beneath without pause. He heard the clunk, felt the smooth transition between the flier's power and the geared traction that started drawing the craft across the hangar floor. There was a slight unevenness as the automated mechanism drew the flier around and off to one side, but the sound of machinery was as smooth as their motion. Gradually, the small craft slowed and eased into an empty bay, perfectly aligned with the diagonals. Jack sat where he was, waiting while the flier powered down, patiently allowing a few seconds to see if anything else was going to happen. Deciding that nothing was, he unstrapped himself and stood, stretching out the kinks from the long flight down.

"Mr. Stein, if you would make your way to the reception area with your luggage please." The voice came from all directions.

"Yeah, but . . ." said Jack, looking around.

"The reception area is clearly marked. Please follow the yellow signs and bring your luggage. Please do not deviate from the directions."

The faceless voice went silent, and a moment later the flier's door whirred open.

Okay, thought Jack . . . if that was the way they wanted it. He grabbed his bags from the back and stepped out of the craft. Immediately in front of him was posted a yellow sign in five separate languages. The words he could understand said RECEPTION. He grunted and headed in the direction indicated. Yellow lines marked the path as well as the signs.

There was something not quite right, something that felt out of place, but he couldn't put his finger on it. He hitched the luggage strap on his shoulder, not even bothering to check that his bag was skimming along behind, dutifully doing as the voice had instructed, although the temptation to break off and examine the place was strong. After a couple of minutes, he noticed exactly what was missing. It had been working at him and he'd been unable to pin it down, but now . . . every port Jack had ever been in was covered in stains, the marks of passage, the smell of fuel and exhaust, and in his line of work he'd spent enough time around ports drinking in their chemical-edged taint. This place was pristine. An overtang of something metallic touched the atmosphere, but the smell was slick and clean, just like the rest of the dock.

Another turn led him through a couple of parked fliers and some neatly stacked crates. A small passageway stretched in front of him, dark, but as he stepped into it lights sprang on and bathed it in brilliance, harsh and clean. The corridor stretched on before him, a single door at the end. With a brief shrug, he headed up toward the end of the corridor. Moments before he reached it, the door silently slid open. It closed again as soon as he and his luggage were inside. There was the slightest warning sound, and then the elevator whisked him upward.

The door slid aside to reveal a drab open space, desks at the end with yellow lines leading right up to them. Jack took the hint and wandered toward the closest desk. Another line showed him where he should stand. Lines everywhere. Things just begging to be crossed. Behind the desk sat a woman . . . at least he thought it was a woman, though the mustache was a little confusing. She/he sat staring down at something concealed from view. Jack cleared his throat. She—he'd decided she was actually female, not that it really mattered; it just gave him some sort of context to work with—did something on the desk in front of her and glanced to one side without looking up in his direction, although he was clearly the only arrival in the place. Jack cleared his throat again. Finally, with a sigh, she beckoned him forward, still staring fixedly down at the desk in front of her.

"Um . . ." said Jack.

"Mr. Stein," she said, at last deigning to look up.

"Yes, that's right."

"I see no authority to travel." She fixed him with a blank, expressionless look.

"Huh?" said Jack. "Authority to travel? I'm sorry, I don't know what you're talking about."

She sighed again. "You come to Utrecht, you need an authority to travel."

"I don't know anything about that," said Jack. It was news to him. "Look, okay, I don't have the proper authority. Can we do something about it?"

She glared at him, hardly what he'd expected. Jack was telling the truth. He'd heard nothing about any authority. He'd gotten the message about Billie and dropped everything—not that there was a lot to drop—to get to Utrecht as quickly as he could. He tried a smile.

"Look, I'm sorry; I didn't know I needed any 'authority.' Can we sort it out here?"

This wasn't good, and Jack was starting to feel distinctly nervous. He should at least have had some warning.

The official tutted and sighed, looking down again at whatever was in front of her. A low partition shielded it from Jack's view. She tapped at the thing, glanced to the side, then looked back at him.

"You know, this is most irregular," she said.

Jack dug around for his handipad and flipped it open. "Look," he said. "All I know is that I received this message from a Dr. Heering at the University of Balance City saying I was wanted here."

She waved his handipad away and shook her head. "This is not proper procedure."

It was Jack's turn to sigh and grit his teeth. Here he was stuck with some petty official, and he certainly had matters that were more pressing. Far more pressing. He fought to keep his voice under control. "Look, I've already said I didn't know anything about it. What do I have to do?"

His growing annoyance simply washed over her. "You must have the correct authority. You must have a formal invitation."

"I've just shown you the invitation. What more do you need?"

The woman got to her feet. She smoothed her khaki trousers, pulled down on the canary yellow shirt with its official insignias, and turned away.

"Hey!" said Jack.

"Wait here," she said, and disappeared behind a partition. He stood rocking on his heels for a good ten minutes before she reappeared.

"Follow me," she said, leading him past the partition into a small blank room with a desk and a couple of chairs. "Sit there."

Jack did as instructed, letting his luggage settle like some strangely inanimate pet. From his chair, he had a partial view of the corridor beyond, but that was about it. The official stood watching him for a few moments, then turned and made her way up the corridor. She was joined at the end by a severe-looking dark-haired man. They both turned to gaze in his direction, talking, their heads close together. There was no doubt about the topic of their conversation. He was starting to understand why Utrecht wasn't exactly a top tourist destination.

Jack kept his face impassive with some effort. He couldn't afford to piss these anal bureaucrats off, not yet.

Nonetheless, he stared in disbelief as the man/woman—
he had decided that he wasn't sure again—took hold of
his luggage and pulled it away. What the hell?

"Hey!"

She/he ignored him. Somewhere, no doubt, some
other uniformed official was about to take it apart, piece
by piece. Luckily, he didn't think there was anything in it
to cause concern. He had wisely chosen not to bring a
weapon along for that very reason. Weapons and border
guards never made very good company. All the same, he
just didn't need this shit.

He was afforded an uninterrupted view of the empty
corridor, the empty room, the blank ceiling, the blank
floor, so he turned his attention to his fingernails. Actually, they could have done with a cleaning. He occupied
himself with picking at them to kill the time. Meanwhile, he tried to suppress thoughts of what might have
dragged him out here, the deep feelings working inside
his chest, the emptiness in the pit of his stomach. Jack
knew better than to ignore those intuitions. Billie had
little trouble looking after herself; she'd proved that on
more than one occasion, and he wouldn't want to be the
person who crossed her. She was going to be more than
pissed with him, no doubt. He shook his head. Whatever
the inner prompt that had been driving him was, he'd
find out as soon as he found her. The only worry he had
was that she'd gotten herself in trouble with the local
authorities somehow. From everything he'd seen so far,
it looked like it was something that would be easy
enough to do.

The androgynous official was back again but without
company.

"Mr. Stein, if you will follow me, please."

Jack pushed himself to his feet, rubbing at the back of
his neck as he followed down the corridor. They were

joined at the end by the man he'd seen before, who beckoned them both into a stark office.

The man indicated that Jack should take one of the simple metal chairs placed in front of a neatly ordered desk. Folders sat stacked on one end. Another neat little desk sat at the other end with a couple of stamps and a stamp pad. Jack's heart sank. This was the true mark of bureaucracy. Actual paper and stamps. Those things were expensive. Well, maybe they weren't on Utrecht, but they were luxury items everywhere else he'd ever been. They told him one thing: They were marks that no expense was spared in support of the regime. All the props — just what he really needed. Beautiful. He barely contained the sigh.

The official adjusted his uniform before sitting on the opposite side of the desk, steepling his fingers in front of his face and fixing Jack with a hard gaze.

"So, Mr. Stein. We appear to have a problem."

"Look," said Jack. "I'm not the one with the problem. I received a message that I was needed here. So I haven't got the proper paperwork. Can't we just sort it out here, now?"

The official continued, ignoring Jack's words. "You see, normally, it is standard for someone to get the relevant authority before they arrive on Utrecht. I am considering whether perhaps we should send you back up to the orbital station, where you can make the appropriate application through the proper channels."

Jack barely suppressed a groan. "No. I can't afford the time that would take. Isn't there anything you can do?" Though it hurt him to say the next, he said it anyway. "Please?"

The official considered him for a few moments. "Exactly what *can* you afford, Mr. Stein?"

Ah, so that was how it was going to be. "Um," he said carefully.

The steepled fingers were tapping together in front of the official's face.

"Um . . ." said Jack again. "Um . . . one . . ." The official's eyes narrowed. "Two . . ." This time the official glanced over at his coworker. "Okay, three. Three . . . hundred."

"Very good, Mr. Stein. I can see that your business in Balance City is very important and we must not delay it. If you can show me your handipad with the appropriate letter of invitation and the associated figures, I am sure we can get the forms processed immediately."

Jack nodded, his lips pressed tightly together, and dug into his coat for his handipad. He thumbed it back on, hit the financial transfer, and slipped the device across the desk. The official whipped out a machine, something big and clunky, quickly took the transfer, and then spirited it out of sight, all the while making a show of poring over Jack's device.

"Yes," he said. "This communication seems to be in order." Without looking up, he waved his companion away and reached across for one of the folders. Jack sat, his hands folded in his lap, resisting the urge to twiddle his thumbs while the man across the desk turned pages in the folder, slowly reading them without looking up. Minutes later the official reached for one of the stamps and thumped it down on the bottom of the form with a flourish.

"There," he said. "Make sure you carry this paper with you at all times. It is not enough to have identity documents in Balance City. This will vouchsafe your authority to be here conducting your business. What *is* your business here, Mr. Stein?"

"It's personal," said Jack. There was no way he was going to tell this guy he was a PI. No way at all. When it had come to the part on the form asking for occupation, he'd said consultant. It was an old trick from his intelligence days, official enough to sound sort of high-powered, but vague enough not to give anything away. And anyway, the guy had seen enough, and Jack had seen enough of him. If he said anything about coming to see family on Utrecht, it was bound to pique the guy's curiosity. Who knew what sort of tabs this place kept on its citizens?

"My luggage?" he asked.

"Yes, certainly. Follow me."

And that was Jack's first introduction to Balance City. He dragged his bags by their leash into an elevator, which zipped him rapidly up to surface level, and he stepped out of a glass box where the elevator terminated, and into the middle of an open plaza.

Two

Digging out his handipad again, Jack tapped up a map of the area and turned it this way and that until he was oriented. His hotel was about two miles across the central part of Balance City. The university was farther out. He checked his credit balance, but he figured he still had enough to get him around without cutting into the emergency supply. But where the hell was he supposed to get a cab?

If worse came to worst he could walk, but he didn't want to waste the rest of the day, and really, it was the last thing he was inclined to do. There was enough time to be able to dump his luggage and still get to the university before things shut down for the night if he got to the hotel soon enough. Dammit, he didn't even know what time things closed around here. He'd just become too used to Billie looking things up for him if they had to go somewhere. And hopefully there, at the university, Jack would find out what was stirring the sense of unease deep inside him. That was the last place he'd heard from Billie, and the place where the odd little university man had spoken from, telling him to come. Billie and he had been in fairly constant touch on and off, punctuated by gaps of a few days, sometimes as much as a week, but nothing as long as this last one. Then, the silence and the call that had brought him here. Still, he should have found out more about the place.

Lazy and stupid, Jack.

He looked around himself, trying to get his bearings. The plaza stretched about him, gray, uniform blocks inserted into one another like the pieces of a jigsaw. Metal seating ran in an even row all around the outer edges. Apart from the seats and the glass elevator booth that he had just stepped out of, the space was empty—empty except for one feature that stuck out, impossible for him to ignore. Standing off in one corner was a ludicrously large cartoon representation of some sort of hopping insect, all done out in bright green and yellow. It could hardly be art; it wasn't even pleasant to look at. Oh, yeah—it probably had something to do with travel, some supposedly cute representation of "hopping" from place to place. There were no other signs indicating what this open expanse might be, so he guessed it was meant as a visual cue. Still, they could have used a bit of taste when choosing their signage, couldn't they?

With a sigh, he let his bags settle and fished around for his handipad again, but not before glancing up at a silvery orb suspended far above the plaza. There was no need to guess what that might be for, and he struggled to suppress the urge to wave at it. Damn Billie again. What *did* she want to go running off to a place like this for anyway?

After a long trudge across the naked stone blocks, not a person in sight, he reached a roadway. He glanced back at the plaza, then first one direction, then the other up and down the road. To the left it ran to open forest; to the right, the start of the urban sprawl, all glass and metal. It was so different from the Locality. The Locality, even Yorkstone, had been contained, growing within their own semiorganic structures and subject not only to the constraints of their inner dimensions, but also to the whims of their programmers. Jack rethought his impression. *Sprawl* wasn't really the right word. Even the buildings stepped gradually taller as they grew closer to the center, not a single one out of sequence to disturb the neat lines. The place screamed order, and he felt like screaming back.

He spotted what looked like a shuttle stop and headed in that direction, towing his bags behind him.

It didn't take long before a compact green vehicle whirred to a stop in front of him, settled to the ground, and twin doors slid open. No driver, no other passengers, but taking the prompt, Jack maneuvered his bags inside and found a place to sit. As he settled back for the journey—at least it was going in the right direction, according to the map—he realized that this shuttle was the only traffic he'd seen. He'd been too busy concentrating on the city's spectacle to notice anything much on the way in, so he had no idea whether the quietness was confined to this particular area. It was almost like stepping into a wasteland. No traffic, no people . . . and, actually, no vegetation either. Perhaps the locals thought that trees might disturb the clean lines of their buildings. The surrounding landscape had been full of trees, but not here. How the hell did anyone find their way around? Where were the landmarks?

As the shuttle moved farther into the city, Jack's concern grew. Not a single soul walked the streets. Not a single vehicle apart from his shuttle moved along the broad roadway in the same direction. He spotted another in the distance heading slowly toward them, but that was it. Glancing down at his handipad, he checked again. There was only about a block to go. This was supposed to be a thriving city. It was one of the main in-system hubs.

There was a stop coming up ahead, so he shifted his bags, ready to alight, and stood. He could walk the rest of the way. Maybe that would give him some idea of what was going on. The shuttle glided into the stop, and the doors slid open.

Jack stepped out onto the empty street, pushing his bags in front of him. He waited until the shuttle drew away, then looked up and down the street, then up above him. Windows, doorways, structures, all spoke of more uniformity and order. There was little variation from one edifice to the others—all neat, clean, and identical. Where were the huge signs above doorways, glittering and scrolling to catch the eye? He shook his head and started in the direction of his hotel.

Window displays held abstract and geometric colored panels. Each doorway had a discreet little sign, similarly lettered, announcing what lay inside the building, either businesses or stores. Jack could do nothing but shake his head. Sure, Yorkstone had been clean, but nothing compared to this place. He just didn't see Billie feeling at home here at all.

Halfway down the next block, he found the hotel. A subtle gold trim was the only thing to set it apart from other doorways nearby. Taking a deep breath, Jack dragged his bags through the doorway and inside.

"Okaaaaay . . ." said Jack as he stood surveying the scene.

It was a hotel lobby, just like he'd have expected to see in any place that he'd been. Potted plants and dried floral arrangements dotted a marbled expanse. Crystal lighting in the ceiling and wide leather couches completed the picture, but that wasn't what caused Jack to stop. The place was full, heaving with people. The noise washed over him along with the smell of food and drink. It wasn't that, though. Every single person in the place was dressed in some archaic garb, flounces and ruffles and powdered wigs. Tambourines lay on side tables or were clutched in hands. Here and there a jester figure danced in and out among the others. If he didn't know better, he would have thought he was in the middle of some bizarre dream.

"Okaaaay . . ." he said again.

This was the last thing he'd expected after the sterility outside. Some sort of convention party. Great.

He spotted a route through the revelers and wove his way to the reception desk. A bright-faced woman stood behind the desk, straight blond hair tied tightly back into a bun, a big smile slipping into place with his approach.

"Welcome, sir. Can I help you?"

"Yeah, Jack Stein. You have a room for me."

"Certainly, Mr. Stein. Just one second." The smile stayed firmly in place.

She fiddled around with a terminal and then looked back at him. "Yes, Mr. Stein. We have you down for six nights. Welcome to Balance City. You have come at a most fortunate time."

"Okay. Six nights is right for now. I might be staying longer. I don't know yet."

The woman nodded. A slight frown flitted across her face. "Have you your paperwork, please?"

Jack frowned. "Paperwork?"

"Yes, your entry permit. I will need to see it. Then if you could sign here and here . . ."

Jack dug around in his coat and withdrew the slip of paper he'd received from the official earlier. Again it struck him as weird that a place would still be using paper. "Is this what you want?"

"Yes, that's it. Thank you."

She nodded congenially and took the proffered form, gave it a quick look, then slipped it through some kind of reader. After glancing at a screen, she handed the paper back. "Please make sure to inform us at least a day in advance if you wish to vary your stay, Mr. Stein. It is important to be able to make the proper arrangements."

"You said it was a 'fortunate' time . . . ?"

She said something, but the background noise made it hard to hear. He leaned forward as he asked her again and caught a glance at the screen beside her. His picture, stats, details, were all there on display.

"Festival," she said. "The Balance City Festival. On this day everybody has parties."

Oh, great. He'd managed to arrive right in the middle of some local excuse for letting their hair down. From what he'd seen so far, it looked like they needed it.

"It is a pity you don't have a costume," she said.

"Um, right," said Jack.

"Oh, well. I'm sure you will enjoy our festivities all the same."

Jack gave another quick glance around the lobby. Somehow, he didn't think so.

As he headed for the elevator, he played the circumstances over in his mind. He and Billie had met Dr. Antille out on Mandala during the quest for a stolen artifact, a piece of technology that had been found in the alien ruins on the exclusive resort planet, and Dr. Hervé Antille had been one of the archeologists assigned to the site. Antille had taken a quick shine to Billie, and she had responded in return. Since the case, she and Antille had kept in touch, until he had finally made the offer for her to come and visit, do some work with him as experience. She had leaped at the opportunity, and who was Jack to stand in her way? Billie always had a deep hunger for knowledge and pursued it with a kind of obsessive want. Sometimes he wondered whether it had been a reaction to the way she'd grown up, filling the hole that the absence of a normal life had left. Despite Jack's discomfort with her whole relationship with Antille, he was pretty sure it was just a meeting of like minds, but with Billie's past, he couldn't help feeling nervous. Back in the Locality, she'd been involved in . . . No . . . he didn't really want to think about that either. He'd dragged her out of that ring of child prostitution and criminal hackers. But even now, somehow, what he'd done then still wasn't enough. Jack always seemed to be letting her down in some way. He grimaced at the thought. Occasionally he even wondered if she was setting up the guilt he felt on purpose, some subtle little game. He wouldn't have put it past her.

Dammit, she wasn't his responsibility, not fully. Not anymore. She was starting to be old enough to look out for herself; at least he'd thought she was. In the current circumstance, though, he was really beginning to wonder if he shouldn't have tried a little harder to talk her out of it.

Sixth floor. All the way up in the elevator, Jack was confronted with mirrored images of himself, looking haggard, old. Travel always took it out of you, but somehow he was looking more wasted than usual. Maybe the healthy life wasn't so good for you after all. Well, healthier than it had been. Billie had seen to that, registering her disapproval at the various patches he had used. Somehow, she'd made him disapprove of himself too. It was no sort of example to set for a young girl.

He would have looked away, but there were mirrors on every side, so instead he concentrated on the changing display indicating what floor he was on. He spared a thought for the uniformed bellboy at the front desk who had looked visibly disappointed when Jack had denied him the possibility of taking charge of the luggage and leading him to his room. Well, he'd get over it. This was a place for Jack to stay, nothing else. He didn't want the fuss and the trimmings.

A slight bounce as the elevator came to a stop, and the

doors whirred open. He stepped out into silence, only the sounds of air-conditioning and machinery undercutting the quiet. At least the noise of the downstairs revelers didn't reach up this far. Jack puzzled out the signs listing the room numbers and headed down the corridor, his bags trailing behind.

The room wasn't vastly different from countless rooms in countless hotels across the populated worlds. It was different from what they'd experienced on Mandala, sheer top-of-the-league luxury, even down to the peacocks, but that had been a whole different ball game and something that seemed a long time in the past now. He shoved his bags into the closet, not even bothering to unpack. First, he wanted to find out how to get to the university and track down this Dr. Heering. Heering knew something, and Jack was damned well going to find out what it was as soon as possible. The pale-faced academic's last words in the call echoed in his head.

"I think you'd better come," he'd said, in a too-quiet voice.

Jack felt the chill rise within him again, but he pushed it back. Maybe he was just overreacting, looking for something to give him that hard edge he'd been missing for the past few weeks. Somehow, he didn't think so.

He gave the room a quick glance — bed, bathroom, small table, standard stuff. He could investigate the rest of the facilities later.

"Front desk," he said, looking around for a blank wall.

Nothing happened.

Jack stood there feeling sheepish for a moment and looked around the room again. All of the walls bore some sort of decoration. No space for a wallscreen at all. There was a small flat screen on a stand in one corner of the room, but every one of the walls was hung with unfortunate abstract paintings. No wallscreen? What kind of place was this? He walked over to the screen in the corner and said, "Front desk."

Still nothing.

Only then did he notice the other little anachronisms around the room. A small pile of glossy magazines sat on the table. Actual magazines.

"Hunh," he said to himself. No library call function on the room screen. No room screen, if it came to that. It had been years since he'd seen a magazine that didn't appear on a screen or as a download. He thumbed through them. There was a fashion and style magazine, one to do with local current affairs, and a guide to local escort services. He gave a slight frown at the last. Strange. Jack flipped through that as well. One or two of the entries were circled. He shook his head and dropped it back on the table with the others. He left them where they were, looking for other signs. There, finally, he spotted another piece of old technology sitting unobtrusively on the bedside table. He crossed and picked up the handset.

"Front desk," he said.

At last, there was some response. "Yes, Mr. Stein. How can I help you?"

"I need to find out how to get to the university."

"Oh, I can explain that to you easily, but it will be better if you come to reception and I can give you a map and show you."

A map? An actual map? Damn, this place was like living in another century.

"Haven't you got some sort of download?"

"I don't understand what you mean, Mr. Stein."

"Forget it. I'll be down in a while."

He spent a short time poking around the room, checking out the rest of the facilities, working out how limited the place really was. There was a handset to control the screen, piping vids directly from the hotel network. There was an information channel, and he flicked through looking for other services. Okay, most of the stuff was pretty standard, but still, it wasn't anything like the level of technology he might have expected. That could present its own problems. He rubbed the back of his neck and grimaced. He should have guessed when he had to use an actual swipe card to get into the room.

Back down to the lobby and he was immediately bombarded with noise as the elevator doors slid open. Someone in a far corner was bashing a tambourine, and the surrounding group was clapping along with the beat and laughing. Jack shook his head, stepped out of the elevator, and headed for the desk.

"Ah, hello, Mr. Stein. Here is your map."

He leaned in closer to look.

"Here is the city, you see. If you follow this route here, it takes you out to Summergarden. That is where you find the university. There is a technology park out there too." She turned the map over to show a broader map of the surrounding area, pointing to a region well outside of the city. "This is Summergarden. There is a public shuttle out there. Number D-twenty-four. It runs right outside here." She looked up at him and smiled. "But it will not run today."

"Well, how do I get out there?"

She nodded. "You could hire a private transport, but that is quite expensive."

"Hmmmmm."

"But there really is no point today."

"What do you mean?" Jack frowned.

She waved her hand in the direction of the people crowding the lobby. "It is Festival."

"And . . . ?"

"There will be nobody there. Nobody works on Festival."

Jack sighed. "You're working."

She looked disappointed. "Yes, I know. It is a pity, but I have to work. Later, when I have finished, I will go out." Her face brightened. "But you will be able to have a good time tonight."

"Yeah, thanks." He took the map, folded it, and slipped it into his pocket. Somehow, he didn't think so.

"Is there anything else I can do for you, Mr. Stein?"

"No, that's fine. Thanks." He left the desk and headed straight for the elevator, his lips pressed into a thin line.

Back in his room, he tried to put a call in to Dr. Heering at the university, but there was no answer. It looked like the receptionist had been right.

He ordered a plain room-service meal and spent the rest of the evening half watching piped entertainment channels on the small screen in the corner of the room, flipping from channel to channel, but his mind wasn't on it. Later in the evening the outside noise grew, and he went to the window. From buildings the length of the main street, people had spilled out onto the roadway. Drums had joined the tambourines, and the revelers were dancing in the streets. A few blocks up, Jack could see a band playing, people clustered around a stage. The noise thumped through the area, almost below the threshold of hearing, stirring vibrations deep in his guts. He growled under his breath and closed the curtain, hoping to cut some of the noise, but it was there and it persisted. Jack sighed again. He really should have done some research on the place before coming in totally unprepared, but that was it: When someone you cared about was in trouble, you didn't think; you went and you did.

He took a few moments analyzing that thought. He did care about Billie. He cared about her a lot. And she was in trouble. He could feel it deep inside along with the vibration stirring the depths of his stomach. He thought about doing some of his exercises, inducing alpha, that half-awake, half-asleep state between unconsciousness and wakefulness, to try to grasp the clues from semi-dreamstate, but dismissed the idea. He had none of his equipment here, and the circumstances weren't exactly ideal for that state of mental relaxation he needed. Better to try to get some rest and get into time zone so he'd be sharp.

It took a long time for Jack to fall asleep. It wasn't the unfamiliar room, the unfamiliar setting, or even the noise intruding into his awareness. He could deal with all of that. It was the simple sense of disquiet working in the back of his head.

Later in the night, he dreamed anyway.

Three

Jack knew immediately he was dreaming. The familiar sense of place, of personal identity that went with a true waking state, floated in and out. He was standing in an open field, the landscape gently undulating around him and the tang of something sharp undercutting the breeze. Sour, like sweat. He knew this place. He'd been here before. There was no sense to it at all. The artifact case was long gone, so what the hell was he doing here?

"'Allo, Yack." The voice came from behind. There was no one talking. He turned, heading toward the place where he thought the voice had come from.

The smell grew sharper, and was suddenly touched with the taste of something burning. He didn't want to think what it might be.

"Yack Stein."

Yeah, he knew that voice. It had appeared in his dreams before. And as a final confirmation, a ruined figure lurched over the hillside, half its face burned away, the disfigurement unavoidable. Jack grimaced.

"Talbot. What are you doing here? This is my dream, dammit. You shouldn't be here."

Carl Talbot had been present in Jack's earlier dreams about the stolen artifact when he'd been working on the Landerman case, but there had been a reason for that. Talbot had been one of the victims of Landerman's gang. Jack had solved that case long ago. Talbot's presence now made no sense. Could you have a ghost from a dream in a dream? This guy was haunting him, like the ghosts of his past.

"You not finish yet, Yack," said Talbot.

Jack tried to will him away, but the maimed figure stayed where it was. When that didn't work, he tried to will himself away, away to somewhere different.

"Not finish."

He tried to drag his attention away from the ruined face, but it was as if he were compelled to keep looking.

Then, in the next instant, Talbot was gone.

"What the . . . ?"

He was awake. He sat up in bed, a runnel of sweat crawling from his forehead to his cheek. He rubbed his face vigorously with both hands and then sat there in bed for a few moments, collecting his thoughts and working his eyes properly open.

Throwing back the covers, he swung his legs out of the wide bed and padded into the bathroom to pour a glass of water. He drank it in large swallows, then stood staring into the mirror, propping himself up with his hands against the sink. A bleary, shadowed face stared back at him, hair sleep-tousled, eyes slightly bloodshot. Damn, what he'd give for a stimpatch right now. He pressed his eyes firmly closed, then opened them wide. Jack, you're getting past it, he thought to himself. You're losing your edge. No stimpatches, though. Not since Billie. Anyway, what the hell had *that* been about? Stupid dream.

He'd spent plenty of time dealing with that particular dreamscape while dealing with Landerman's lot. He often used his dreams for psychic prompts, clues to lead him down the right path in a case; that was normal. But

this? Okay, so Billie was working with Antille, and Hervé
Antille had been linked to the case too, and to the City of
Trees back on Mandala, as the archeological site had
been called, but that didn't explain Talbot's presence. He
scratched the back of his head. Bits of it made sense, but
the rest didn't. Forget it for now. Sometimes he just had
to wait for the dreams to fall into place, and sometimes
dreams were just dreams. For the moment, there was
nothing concrete to tell him otherwise.

He glanced at the wall, forgetting for a moment. No
time display there, and his handipad was in his coat. No,
wait. There was a small clock by the other side of the bed,
its numbers glowing red.

Six thirty. He groaned. Damn, just what he needed.
Mornings were bad enough without being awake this
early. If he was lucky, most of the parties from last night
would be over by now. Still, being awake at this hour
should give him a chance to get started, and the sooner he
tracked down Heering, the sooner he'd have some answers about what was going on, about what had happened to Billie. A steaming hot shower and some coffee
and he'd be ready to face the rest of the day. He hadn't
even bothered to check if he had coffee. Pulling open the
cupboards, he found a small bar full of local wine and
beer, and not much else, prompting a low sound in his
throat. He'd have to go downstairs for coffee. Great. He
really *was* beginning to hate this place already, not that
there were many places Jack Stein didn't hate.

After coffee and, unusually, something to eat—the
coffee was normally enough—Jack felt he was ready at
least to give the semblance of functioning. There had
been only a few people at breakfast, and a number of
them looked positively the worse for wear. Balance City
had certainly turned it on last night. Somehow he sus-

pected they didn't do that sort of thing often. It was almost as if they had been orchestrated to have fun, and they weren't really used to how they should do it.

As he finished the last of his coffee — surprisingly quite decent — he pulled out the map and studied it. The university was a full ten miles outside the edges of Balance City. He had no choice but to take the local transport. He grabbed his coat from the nearby rack, patted his pocket to make sure his handipad was there and he'd forgotten nothing, and returned to the table for a last swallow of the coffee before heading to the front desk to inquire about the shuttle schedule.

It appeared he was in luck. They ran about every hour, and the next one was in about ten minutes' time. He thanked the girl and headed out into Utrecht's day, feeling as if he were walking into a landscape even more alien than the one he had visited in his dreams last night. But then every cluster of humanity gathered together was like an alien landscape, glossed with the sweat and dirt and odor. Balance City was no different.

Outside there were traffic, people, noise, in complete contrast to how it had been when he'd arrived. The empty streets from yesterday were now fully without a trace of the celebrations of the previous evening. Whoever ran this city did so efficiently, by the looks of things. Maybe too efficiently for Jack's taste. He spent a moment getting his bearings; then, following the directions he'd been given, he headed for the shuttle stop, weaving in and out of smartly dressed commuters. There was something not quite right about the way they looked to Jack, and it took him a while to puzzle it out. Finally, it clicked. The colors were all wrong. The clothes were conservative in cut and style, but the color combinations were deep greens, yellows, blues, even reds. Primary colors, most of them. He was adrift on a sea of rainbow humanity, his own drab

hues—the plain brown coat, the dark top and trousers—
setting him clearly apart from the rest of the crowd. He
hadn't really noticed because *he* was the different one.

Damn. The last thing he wanted to do was draw attention to himself, but there was no way he was going to be
following their particular fashion sense anytime soon.
The residents of Balance City could have it. A bit of research, that was all it took. A simple bit of research. Stupid, Jack. If Billie had been with him, she'd have done
the research, even down to the local fashion and style. It
was really starting to hit home how much he had grown
to rely on her. But she wasn't with him, and that was why
he was here. The simplest bit of preparation . . . He was
suddenly more aware of the curious glances that kept
shooting his way as people passed, and then he caught
himself. Dammit, Stein. You have better things to worry
about.

He found the shuttle stop, making a show of peering at
the neat little notice showing the times, ignoring those
who walked around him, but keeping one eye on the
passing traffic and the street. He felt edgy this morning,
as if something were plucking at his sensory nerves,
thrumming subconsciously within him. He kept his eye
out, checking the people, but there was nothing there to
set off any alarms. Just the locals, heading off to their
pristine jobs. The problem was, how could he tell if he
was being watched when everybody seemed to be watching him? He glanced up and down the street feeling the
familiar stirring deep in his guts.

The shuttle was there before long, and he climbed
aboard, thankful that there were only two other passengers. One was a kid, about the same age as Billie, and the
other was an older man. Both ignored him. Jack took a
seat, glancing at the kid, thinking about Billie. Kids. Kids
were trouble. His gaze lingered on the youth as he

thought. The doors were just sliding shut when a man forced his way through them, brushed down a long yellow coat, and also took a seat. Jack glanced at him with a frown, but the man avoided his look, just like everybody else in this place.

Jack nodded to himself, and turned his attention to the window as the vehicle whirred into motion. The shuttle was larger than the one he'd taken in from the airport, but was propelled by the same sort of almost-noiseless drive.

As Jack looked out through the window as the urban landscape passed, it was clear that the day in Balance City started early. People were already disappearing into buildings, and the crowds and traffic were dwindling rapidly. Jack had never really thought about consigning himself to such a life, the daily routine, uniformity, and conformity that went with a steady job. Maybe he should have, but really, he thought he would have gotten bored in no time flat. His drifting from the military, to intelligence, to freelancing had taken away the boundaries and the uniformity rather than adding to them. Sure, there was uncertainty about what he did, but that was half of the attraction. He had no one to answer to but himself and, in a roundabout sort of way, the occasional client. Well, apart from Billie, that was. No, the life of a psychic investigator suited Jack Stein just fine.

Balance City's layout puzzled him. It was even, ordered, all hard angles, but he hadn't seen a single shop, not a department store or convenience outlet or anything. Block after block of glass cubes stretched to the sky. Where the hell did these people do their shopping? He was still puzzling as they crossed the great span over the canyon leading to the city's edge. There had to be somewhere, right? He was almost tempted to ask one of his fellow passengers, but thought better of it. Billie would have done so in an instant, he was sure. Still, it was supposed to be a guy thing, right? You didn't ask other people.

As they reached the edge of Balance City, Jack grunted to himself. There was no transition, no gradual thinning of buildings. One moment there were walls of steel and glass, and the next, nothing. Open fields stretched before them, broken only by the clear line of the roadway. One or two vehicles moved along its length in the distance, but it could have been a flat, unpopulated plain, except for the marks of agricultural activity. Clearly it was before planting season. He guessed they were farms, and the even tracks crisscrossing the dusty brown ground attested to that fact. He glanced behind to see a wall of reflective glass staring back at him. When the sun was at the right angle, Balance City must simply glow with golden light across the flat plains in front of it.

He turned back to face the front, and narrowed his eyes at a white band that was starting to come into view above the skyline. There was no way it could be another city. Whatever it was, it stretched from end to end of the horizon.

It wasn't till they were much closer—the kid and the old man had gotten out by that stage at a stop that appeared to be in the middle of nowhere, leaving him alone in the shuttle with Yellow Coat—that Jack had a true appreciation for what he was seeing. Spread at even intervals, great white blades turned, stirring with the breeze, line after line of windmills. There were hundreds, thousands of them stretching away to either side and beyond. The tall white poles supporting them were broader at the base, narrowed, and then broadened again, reaching up to a cylindrical housing that Jack guessed held the main mechanism being activated by the motion of the blades themselves. A small green and red light blinked at the back end of every cylinder. Stuck inside the shuttle, Jack couldn't hear, but he bet those vast blades made a sound as they cut the air. His fellow passenger seemed unfazed by what he saw, but Jack sat there openmouthed as they neared, then passed within the ranks of turning propellers, his head turning as he tried to trace the extent of the lines, but they carried on right into the distance until they all merged into one another.

Jack was impressed. Damned impressed. That was one hell of a wind farm. He'd never seen anything on such a scale. He guessed that Balance City must have a voracious need for power. A wind farm like this must provide enough to keep Balance City ticking over and then some. There were no factories, no industrial centers as far as he'd seen, but then he'd completely missed this lot on the way in from orbit. In fact, he'd missed more than a lot, being too damned worried about that little flier.

The wind farm held his fascination for only so long. After about a mile it was behind them, and they were back to open fields. The other man who rode with him had still not made eye contact nor acknowledged Jack's presence. For the moment, that suited Jack just fine.

Small clusters of neat dwellings appeared on either side of the road, and at long last, off in the distance, he could see trees. Not one or two, but whole stands of trees. Jack guessed it had to be more thick forest of the kind he had seen on the way down from the orbital. A mere ten minutes later, long, low buildings grew in the distance. Off to one side, broad dishes pointed skyward. More glass and metal. Clearly this was the technology park of Summergarden, in the center of which sat the University of Balance City. The place was large enough to be a small town, and he wondered how many people worked or studied here and how many lived nearby. His fellow passenger alighted and disappeared down a side road. As the doors slid shut, the man turned, looked over his shoulder, and watched as the shuttle pulled away. Just for an instant, Jack thought he saw him talking into something concealed within his palm. Jack frowned. He tried to watch the guy, see what he was doing, but the shuttle pulled around a corner and the man and his canary coat were lost from view.

Moments later a clear sign marked the start of the university, and at the next stop he stepped out. He spent a couple of seconds orienting himself before heading into the complex proper. Technology park? More like a technology wasteland. Low blocky building after low blocky building studded with small glass windows. They reminded him of barracks. Not a memory that he particularly wanted right now. Here too was the strange absence of trees he'd noticed in Balance City itself. What did the Utrechtians have against trees anywhere near urban construction? He shrugged to himself and headed for the main building. Taller than the rest, it stood in front of a broad quadrangle, paved instead of grassed.

Neat little signs out in front pointed the way to various departments. He glanced around the quadrangle again, frowning slightly. Where were all the people? Still recovering from last night? He looked up at the sky and then dug out his handipad to check the time. No, it was late enough that he would expect some sign of life by now.

It didn't take him long to find the department buildings. A small white sign in front announced ARCHAEOL-OGY DEPARTMENT. The main door was set right in the building's center, and he headed up the steps.

Inside there was a small lobby covered with notice boards, just as he would have expected. A glassed-in reception desk sat dead in front—unattended. He glanced down the corridors left and right, hesitating. Should he just wander in? There was nothing else for it. As he turned into the corridor to the right, he noticed gold-lettered signs hanging from the ceiling, and he followed them down, reading them one by one. Right toward the end he found the one he was looking for, and he entered. Another long corridor stretched before him, doorways with signs on them announcing who or what lived within. DR. A. ALBUS . . . DEMONSTRATION LAB 1 . . . SEMINAR ROOM . . . DR. H. ANTILLE—he paused for a moment at that door—DR. K. FRANCIS . . . PROF. J. LEAMING. He followed down one side of the corridor, stopping at the door at the end. RESEARCH LAB 1. No luck. There were no sounds either. He worked his way up the other side, finally located the door that said DR. A. HEERING, and paused outside and thought for a moment. The urge to investigate had returned. Maybe he should just take a quick look at Antille's office.

He took ten steps back down the corridor and opened the door. It was a small office with two desks. A comfortable leather chair sat behind the larger of the two, and books and journals sat in profusion on shelves behind. Pictures of various bits of stone and artifacts were pinned up all over the walls. A pair of screens sat on each desk, their displays lifeless for now. Jack took a step inside, his senses alert, seeking some trace of Antille or Billie in the cluttered empty office. He was just feeling a slight stirring deep in his abdomen, the tug that gave him direction toward something that he could use as a psychic cue, when a voice stopped him in his tracks.

"Hey. You. What are you doing there?"

Jack turned slowly. A pale-faced young man with thin dark hair stood in the corridor, his hands shoved into the pockets of a white coat, a nondescript shirt and trousers on underneath.

"Um, nothing," said Jack. Good opener, Stein. "I was looking for Dr. Heering."

"Well, you won't find him there. This is not his office."

Jack nodded. "Yeah, well, it didn't seem like anyone was at home in Dr. Heering's office."

"No, of course not," said the young man. "Dr. Heering is in the labs. I am his assistant. And you are?"

"Sorry," said Jack. "I'm Jack Stein. If you can take me to Dr. Heering . . ."

The young man looked Jack up and down skeptically. "And you want to see Dr. Heering . . . ?" He let the words trail off.

"Because he *asked* me to come and see him," said Jack pointedly.

The assistant gave Jack another suspicious look, and then turned reluctantly, beckoning him to follow down to the end of the corridor.

Damned if Jack was going to give him the pleasure of offering up any more information than that.

Behind the door stretched a long laboratory, one that Jack had seen before. This was the place where he'd dreamed Antille, seen him with the artifact, seen the machines. He paused for a moment, adjusting as dream memory was suddenly overlapped with reality. The young man was standing at the door, waiting for Jack to pass, and he cleared his throat.

"Right," said Jack. The long, low benches, the lights hanging over them, the pieces of archeological artifacts were all too familiar.

"Dr. Heering is over there."

Jack nodded and walked to the end of the lab. Heering's assistant stood at the open doorway, watching.

Jack made the connection; the young man had every right to be suspicious, what with the Outreach activities concerning the artifact in the first place, but that had been almost two years ago now. Outreach had made concerted attempts to "acquire" the tablet, as had the questionable group the Sons of Utrecht. People attached to this particular department would have taken the brunt of most of that. Did the suspicion last that long? Or perhaps there had been other incidents since then.

He recognized Heering from the call immediately.

"Dr. Heering?"

The owl-eyed face looked up at him, blinking rapidly, dragging its attention from a piece of stone sitting in front of him on the bench. Heering frowned.

"I'm Jack Stein."

Heering drew his breath in quickly and then seemed to hold it. "Yes. Of course you are. I am Aaron Heering. You came sooner than I had thought you would."

"So what's this about Antille and Billie? And where is everyone?"

Heering paused and then waved his assistant away. The young man lingered at the doorway for a few moments, then nodded slightly and withdrew.

"Of course," said Heering. "I understand you are anxious." He draped a cover over the piece of stone and stood. "We had better go to my office. You are right: There is no one around, but it is vacation time right now, between semesters. All the students are away, and many of the staff take this opportunity to have a break as well. I, on the other hand, have pressing research to continue, and Donnelly there is assisting me in my work. That's the reason we are here, but you never know who might just pop in. It will be better to talk in my office."

Jack wondered briefly what Heering was working on, but then decided that it probably wouldn't mean anything to him anyway, and the doctor seemed eager to get him to follow away from the lab.

Heering's office was much more ordered than Antille's. Neat stacks of paper and journals sat boxed on the shelves. The desk was clear. Heering indicated a seat, waiting before shutting the door.

"You don't look very much like your niece," he said slowly. "There is not much family resemblance."

Jack frowned. "And what's so unusual about that? We come from different sides of the family." He found the instant suspicion interesting. "Look, what do you want me to say? You're the one who suggested I come. Remember? Now it's my turn to make a suggestion. Tell me what's going on. Where are Billie and Antille?" He leaned forward in his chair, his jaw set.

"I'm not so sure that I can do that, Mr. Stein. Your concern seems genuine, but how do I know that I can trust you?"

Jack got to his feet then and took a step forward. "Of course it's damned well genuine. Listen, Heering, you'd better start telling me what's happened to Billie. . . ." He could feel the anger and frustration growing in him like the filling of a well.

Heering lifted a hand. "Threatening behavior will get you nowhere, Mr. Stein."

Jack took a deep breath and sat slowly back down. "I'm waiting."

Heering nodded and spoke, almost as if to himself. "You do seem worried about them."

"Look," said Jack. "Why do we have to go through this shit? We've established that. I was involved with Hervé Antille in that whole Landerman affair. He must have told you about it. Billie was there with me on Mandala. It's because of us that those bastards were taken off Antille's back. Since then, I think they might have left you guys alone. Alone to get on with your 'pressing' research. Or am I wrong?"

Heering pinched the bridge of his nose between thumb and forefinger, looking down at the floor. "I keep fairly well to myself. We have work to do here, but yes, Dr. Antille may have mentioned something of that sort. It is true, we are working on similar avenues. Our paths clearly . . . how do you say . . . overlap."

Jack sighed, barely managing to keep his impatience under control.

"All right. I just can't be too careful," said Heering, and finally took the chair opposite. "Let us begin."

If Jack didn't know better, he would have thought that Heering was gearing up for the start of a lecture.

Four

Jack leaned forward in his chair, a feeling of nervous chill deep in his gut as Heering started to speak. The archeologist held his fingers steepled in front of him and gazed into the middle distance through and over them, his wide eyes unfocused.

"Dr. Antille has been doing some startling work with the alien artifact. You know all about the artifact, obviously. And quite frankly I'm rather jealous. Significant progress. I, myself, have been working on pieces from another site—one we believe is related—but Dr. Antille's progress has been outstanding. He received some research help, I believe, from the young woman. She's quite talented, you know."

Having Billie referred to as a young woman was a little strange in Jack's ears. He still thought of her as a girl. She hadn't even been twelve when he'd first met her, but now? Was sixteen a young woman?

Heering didn't wait for any response. "Dr. Antille believed he had found the correct mappings to be derived from the symbols on the artifact's surface. Clearly he could not release these results until he'd done more investigation to verify his assumptions. And, of course, there is nothing to cross-reference against."

Heering spread his hands. "So there you are," he said.

"Where am I?" said Jack. "I don't get it."

"Empirical observation," said Heering. "It's the only true way to test a theory."

"I'm sorry, I . . ."

Heering sighed. "He had to test the calculations. The only way to do that is to verify that they worked. How else could he confirm his results?" There was a hint of exasperation in Heering's voice now. "Of course, he was virtually convinced that he was right, and I believe he had good reason to be so, having looked in detail at his findings. But that was about two weeks ago now."

Jack frowned. "Test the results? How?"

"By using them, of course," Heering said. "He had to use them in an actual demonstration. Thought experiments are well and good, but truth lies in the practical application of the theory. If they pointed the way to the alien homeworld, then he had to go to the alien homeworld and see. It should have been quite easy. He just had to use the coordinates in reverse to return home, or so we believed. . . ."

Jack picked up on the *we* and noted it. Heering was far more deeply involved than he was letting on.

"Of course, the university has access to some ships provided by our sponsors. He had to use one of them, because obviously the drive is essential. That goes without saying. One cannot make a jump without a jump drive."

"And he took Billie with him?!" Jack was out of the chair again.

"I believe so."

"Shit."

Jack rubbed his cheeks with one hand, pressing his lips together, thinking fast. "Shit," he said again. "How could he . . . Never mind . . ." He shook his head. Nothing would stop Billie going with him. Nothing at all. Once she had her mind made up . . .

"And there's been no sign of them since?"

Heering slowly shook his head. "Not a . . . how do you say? . . . peep."

"Damn." Jack paced over to the window and looked out over drab, featureless walls. Blank as his thought processes right now. "I have to go after them. That's the only way." How the hell was he going to do that?

He spun to face Heering again. "I'm going to need your help. Hervé must have taken notes, right? Must have recorded what he was working on. You said you'd checked his findings. Do you have access to them?"

Heering was watching Jack pace back and forth with an interested expression, as if he might be observing some intriguing research subject.

"Dr. Heering!"

"What? Oh, yes . . . I probably do. Dr. Antille entrusted backup copies of his work to me. But I don't know what—"

"What else? I'm going to need a ship. But how the hell do I get a ship out here? Christ. In this goddamned anal place, there are going to be rules and regs, aren't there. How the hell do I get a ship in Balance City?"

He had to think this through. Billie was out there somewhere, maybe on the other side of the universe for all he knew, and there was no way even to get in touch with her. Or was there?

"Is there any sort of communication with this ship?"

Heering blinked. "Quite impossible. Conventional communication means would be impractical anyway. The ship would likely be back before any message sent from it would arrive. Subspace communication is well and good in the appropriate circumstances, but the distances involved . . . Do you not think we would have been in touch if we could have?"

Think, Jack. Think.

He had to use what he knew.

"I'm going to need access to Antille's office, see if there's something there I can use."

Heering looked at him quizzically. "I'm not sure I understand."

"I'm a detective, Dr. Heering. A psychic detective. *Psychic*. Get it? There may be something there of Antille's or Billie's that will help. Work with me."

"All right. All right. There's no need to raise your voice."

"I'm not . . . dammit." Jack took a deep breath. "All right. Can we go to Antille's office now?"

"If you think it might help. It is essential that Dr. Antille is returned safely. His work is important. If you knew the true implications of his findings . . ." Heering stood. Jack was out the door before him and down the corridor toward Antille's office.

Jack couldn't care less about Antille or the importance of his findings. Billie was what really mattered.

Again, Jack paused at the doorway of Antille's office, but this time Heering hovered behind him, watching with a kind of detached interest.

Taking a slow step inside the cluttered room, Jack reached within himself, seeking that pull, that tautness. Nothing. He took a slow, calming breath, held it, and then let it out just as slowly, seeking the balance that would release his inner senses.

"Mr. Stein—"

Jack thrust a hand up for quiet, and Heering subsided.

Concentrate, Jack. He knew he had felt something when he'd been in here before. It had come from the direction of the desk he presumed was Billie's. He turned his focus toward that side of the room. There! He felt the pull. One step, two, and he narrowed his senses, feeling for the thing that was creating the spark. He had it. A small stone shard lay on a pile of drawings, holding them in place. Tentatively he reached for it, dreading the rush, but as his fingers made contact there was nothing more than a slight tingling sensation at his fingertips. It meant he would have to work with the piece, see if he could get it to give up its secrets.

"I'm going to need to take this with me," Jack said, looking back over his shoulder at Heering.

Heering frowned and gave a slight shrug.

Taking the shard and placing it deep in his pocket, Jack concentrated again, refining his senses further, reaching out to the room. He could feel faint traces, markers of Billie's presence, probably Antille's too, but there was nothing strong enough to draw him closer. The piece of stone in his pocket was there, present, pulling against his awareness, but he blocked it, shutting it out from what he felt from the rest of the office.

"That's it," he said finally with a sigh.

"So tell me what you have found," said Heering.

Jack turned slowly to face him. Heering wasn't a client, but he was the closest thing he had to a client right now, and to be fair, the academic was proving useful. He rolled out the rehearsed explanation. "No, it doesn't always work like that. That piece has something, but I don't know what it is. Energies seem to accumulate in certain objects, and either they give me cues immediately or I have to dig deeper. I'm going to have to work with this one."

"Energies?"

"Yeah. I don't know how else to explain it. Marks of events, people, that sort of thing. Power finds its way into surrounding objects. Sometimes it's the rooms themselves; sometimes, like this one, it's an individual object. For some reason I can read them, pull clues out of those energies and work with them."

"So it is imprecise?"

"Oh, you bet it's imprecise. As I said, I have to work with them. Sometimes that means putting a whole lot of different clues together to come up with a complete picture. If I'm lucky, then they all work together. Otherwise . . ."

"I see."

"Yeah," said Jack. "Now, what about these notes?"

"We will need to go back to my office."

Jack nodded. "Okay. Let's go."

He followed Heering back up the corridor. Just before they reached the door, Jack had another thought. "What about the artifact itself?"

Heering stopped and turned, looking troubled. "I do not know."

Jack frowned. "What do you mean, you don't know?"

"I do not know where it is."

"How can you not know? Antille was working on the damned thing, wasn't he? You have to have some idea where he would have kept it."

Heering shook his head. "Dr. Antille was very careful about the object. After all the trouble we had with it . . . Well, you understand."

Jack did understand. The artifact itself had already been the cause of a couple of deaths, and very nearly his own. At least two separate groups had enough interest in the thing to involve large sums of money and complete disrespect for anyone who might get in the way. Antille was probably wise to have stashed it somewhere, but it did little to help Jack's current dilemma.

"Fine. I'll just have to make do with what we've got."

Heering nodded and stood back to let Jack walk into the office before him. Heering followed, closing the door quietly behind him. He stood with his back to the door, watching Jack with that detached scrutiny, looking as if he were waiting for Jack to do something.

"What is it?" said Jack.

"Perhaps you will find something here?" said Heering.

"Oh, I get it," said Jack. "What do you want to do? Test me or something? It doesn't work like that. Now, can we get on with it?"

Heering looked disappointed, but nodded and stepped into the room, taking up the seat in front of his desk. He pulled out a keyboard from a compartment just below the surface and tapped a couple of keys. The screen sparked into life. Jack was still having difficulty coming to terms with this old technology. In some ways Utrecht was completely modern; in others . . .

"I have the items under a strong encryption routine. It will take a few minutes for the material to unpack."

Jack took a seat and sat back, prepared to wait. Whatever Antille had passed on to his colleague was crucial. Jack knew that much.

While he was waiting, Heering tapped another couple of keys and started scanning other notes on the screen. Jack could make little sense of what he could see over the archeologist's shoulder.

A good five minutes later, a small bell-like tone came from the screen, and Heering turned to beckon Jack forward. "Here we are."

Jack crossed and peered over his shoulder, standing just behind him. On the screen was a page of notes. It was a picture of an actual page, handwritten formulae and arcane symbols spread across it. Heering hit a key and another image replaced the first, then another and another.

Nothing. There was nothing there Jack had a hope of understanding. "How am I supposed to work with this?" he said.

"Perhaps if we go to the end," said Heering. He hit another couple of keys and the images flicked past one after the other, finally stopping on a single page. "These are the concluding notes. Most of the previous pages relate to explanation and the steps to reach those conclusions with some background material. I believe this page relates to the coordinates that Dr. Antille believes will lead to the relevant world."

Jack squinted at the screen with a slight frown. It contained line after line of what looked like formulae. Whatever information the page contained, it was completely opaque to him.

"Dammit. It's useless. I don't know anything about astronavigation. What am I supposed to do with this?"

He stood straighter, rubbing the back of his neck with one hand.

"I suggest you find someone who does," said Heering.

"You said you'd looked at the conclusions. Why can't you help?"

Heering shook his head. "I have looked at the translations and the derived projections. I too know very little about astronavigation, Mr. Stein. I know about deriving the relevant formulae and coordinates, but to actually put them to practical use . . . I am a theoretician."

Great. The true academic in the ivory tower.

"And how exactly am I supposed to find someone who can help? Here? I need a ship and I need someone who can navigate it. I'm sorry, but I didn't see much evidence of anywhere I was likely to find that in Balance City."

Heering spun his chair slowly to face Jack.

"As above, so not below," he said.

"Huh?" Jack looked down at him blankly.

"I thought that would have had relevance for you, Mr. Stein," said Heering, a slight smile for once appearing on his lips.

"I don't get it." He remembered some phrase like that, but he couldn't see the connection.

Heering continued to look amused. "Your niece spoke often about the notes, the ancient alchemical texts that you had used on a previous case. Being, as you are, a psychic investigator, I thought that phrase might mean something to you. As above, so below . . ."

That was what it was. "Yeah, yeah, I've heard it before. What of it?"

"I am sorry," said Heering, the smile slipping away. "It was my little joke. Balance City is not all as it seems. Clearly you have seen only the surface levels. There are levels below. It is quite different down there. I suggest you go back and investigate the lower regions. You might just find what you are looking for."

Damn. Of course. That was why he hadn't seen any shops or facilities in the city. All of them were out of sight in the lower levels. He should have remembered the way the city grew downward as well as up. He'd seen it clearly enough on the way in, but his mind had been on other things.

"But can't you help at all?" asked Jack.

"I am sorry," said Heering. "Transportation is not my area of expertise. If you want to engage in space travel, I suggest you find someone who knows about such things. I truly cannot help you."

Jack grimaced. Heering was right, of course. "Okay, I'm going to need a copy of that page, if it contains what you say it does." He pulled out his handipad. "Can you send it to me?"

Heering looked troubled. "I'm not sure that I can—"

"Dammit, Heering. I need that stuff."

"But I cannot do that. I don't think we are equipped for that. The best I can do is give you a print of the page."

"A print?"

"Yes, a reproduction on paper."

Paper? "Damn," breathed Jack. This place was full of anachronisms. Back home, a reproduction on paper would cost a fortune.

He nodded slowly. "There's one last thing, Dr. Heering."

Heering looked up. "Yes?"

"I need access to the rooms where Billie was staying. I need to see if there's anything of hers that I can use."

Heering pursed his lips and shook his head slowly.

"What?" asked Jack.

"I would have no idea about where the young woman was staying. It is unlikely we could find anyone to assist in that at the moment. The accommodations are not very well attended at this time of year. I'm afraid to do so would take some time, and there'd be explanations and authorities."

Of course there would. This was Utrecht. Jack sighed. "Okay, it was a thought."

Heering nodded his understanding. "I'm sorry," he said.

Five

All the way back on the shuttle, Jack was turning options over in his mind. Despite what Heering had told him, he thought it doubtful that he'd find what he needed in the lower levels of Balance City. He'd seen what sort of people lived here already. Regardless of their little party time, there were the marks of rigidity everywhere. The sort of person he'd need would be a little freer than the mind-set that pervaded the upper reaches. He just couldn't imagine that it would be so much different.

Maybe he should call for help, but he couldn't think who there might be who *could* help. Typical. He'd rushed into this without thinking things through. Billie was missing, and here he was charging in like some ancient knight in armor, except he didn't have a horse, he didn't have a weapon, and he didn't quite know where he was going.

He reached into his pocket and reassured himself with the crinkle of paper shoved into his pocket. It was thinly coated with some sort of protective gloss, it was true, but that would protect it for only so long. He'd just better not lose it in the meantime. If he was lucky, he might be able to find some way to transfer it to the handipad, but everything he'd seen of Utrecht so far made him doubt that. Next to the paper sat the small stone shard. He felt the tingle as his fingers brushed its edge. He hadn't had time to look at it properly, and he didn't want to yet—not until he was in the sort of setting he needed. The hotel room wasn't ideal, but it was close enough to what he wanted. He could set the door to DO NOT DISTURB and then see what he could get out of the stone itself.

The wind farm distracted him for a few minutes, the giant blades turning, flashing with light, the lines of white support poles stretching on to infinity. In unison, all along the lines, the small green and red lights continued to blink. It must be a bizarre sight late at night from the other side. A wall of winking colored eyes staring back at you. There was only one word for it: alien.

Funny that he should think of that particular word. Alien. That was what it was all about—the hunt for the alien homeworld, if it was the homeworld. Jack had had previous dream contact with these strange beings, or at least it was possible that he had. He had dreamed them, and in some way, devoid of speech, they had communicated with him. Silvery bodies and featureless cylindrical shafts that led to whatever sensing faculties these creatures had. For all he knew they had been a mere construction of his subconscious mind, filling in strange details to make up for the void of his own experience. Well, maybe Billie and Antille knew the truth of it now. That was where they'd gone—seeking the homeworld. There was no way he could tell on his own.

Mercifully there was no one else on the shuttle on the way back in. Nor was there any sign of his erstwhile fellow passenger, which gave Jack some comfort. What Heering had said about being between semesters was working to his advantage. It was only a small thing, but a good thing all the same. These stuffy Utrechtians made him distinctly ill at ease.

And he was back to thoughts about how he could possibly find what he needed in this place. An entire people who used one day in the year to break free from their cultural rigidity. That was what Festival was all about. It had to be. Then there was the whole experience with the officials when he came in, and yet they'd allowed him to buy his way out of the situation. There was a contradiction there, but not one that he was equipped to puzzle out right at the moment. And Billie—Billie with her complete distaste for authority—how the hell had she put up with it for so long? Two and a half months wasn't too much time, but for Billie . . .

Damned if he knew what his place was as far as Billie was concerned.

Here he was on a foreign world, completely out of touch with his people and customs and devoid of his regular contacts. Anyone he could have possibly approached was days, weeks away, and he doubted they had the skills he needed anyway. He didn't move with pilots and navigators. Most of his contacts were strictly ground-based. It looked like he would just have to make do with what he had himself.

He sat back to watch miles and miles of empty brown fields slip by as the shuttle headed back into the city.

Fifty minutes later he stepped back into the hotel lobby, only now really noticing the contrast from the previous evening. The wide leather sofas and small chintzy tables and chairs were virtually unoccupied. A local businessman was sitting on one of the couches. Jack knew he was a local. The bright green suit and purple shoes gave it away immediately. Jack nodded in the man's direction, but he was fixedly ignored.

Shuffling around in his pocket, he retrieved the map given to him by the girl at reception and headed for the front desk. Another young woman stood there, smile slipping into place automatically.

"Yes, sir. May I be of some assistance?"

"Um, yes," said Jack, as he spread the map out on the desk between them and smoothed out the crumpled paper with the flat of his hand. "One of your colleagues gave me this map yesterday, but it doesn't seem to have everything I need."

"I don't understand, sir. What are you looking for?"

"I can't see any shopping facilities. Other things. Where would they be?"

The young woman blinked a couple of times, then smiled again. "The hotel shop has many things you might need. Anything else you can order through the hotel system and it will be delivered to your room. Perhaps there's something I can help you with."

He wondered if there was some way of cutting through this shit. "Look, have you got a map of the lower levels, please?"

The smile slid away. "It is not recommended that visitors to Balance City visit those areas. We can accommodate all your needs here."

Jack shook his head. "No, not good enough. Have you got a map or don't you?"

The receptionist pursed her lips. "Yes, we have such a map."

"Well, can you give me one, please?"

Her expression became even more severe, disapproving, but she ducked below the desk and came up bearing a folded glossy piece of paper. Jack slid it from her grasp and proceeded to unfold it on the desk. It had several interconnected leaves. Jack examined the first. A large empty space, vaguely oval in shape, sat at the center, what Jack presumed must be the central spire upon which Balance City was built, and all around the edges of it were districts marked out in different colors. He flipped over to the next page. Another level was shown, again with the central blank space, but this time the level's

diameter was smaller. Again, color-coded regions spread
out from the central oval, but not covering as much area.
Flipping rapidly through the remaining pages, he found
similar maps, each decreasing in size until the last and
smallest one. Each one had a written key along the outside edge, and grid references. He folded it roughly back
up and slipped it away in his pocket.

"Thank you," he said.

She merely nodded.

"I don't suppose you have a digital version of this?"

A flicker of a frown and she shook her head, her face
still registering disapproval.

"No, I didn't think so."

He could feel her watching him all the way to the
elevators.

"Damned stupid tourist," she was probably thinking to
herself, but why anyone would want to come to Balance
City as a tourist for any possible reason escaped Jack for
the moment. As the elevator doors slid shut, Jack noticed
the parrot-clothed businessman watching him too. He allowed himself a wry grin as the elevator climbed toward
his floor. So Jack Stein was the odd one out. Okay. He
could live with that.

Back in his room, he shrugged off his coat and hung it
on a hook behind the door, reaching into the pockets to
retrieve both maps, the paper covered in calculations
given to him by Heering and the small stone shard. Pressing the indicator to be sure he wouldn't be disturbed, he
dropped all but the stone shard on the small table and
drew the curtains. The power from the fragment still tick-
led at his fingers, which gave him some comfort. The object's importance hadn't been an illusion. Stripping off
his trousers and shirt, he moved to the bed, lowered himself to lie in the center on his back, cupped the stone piece
between his hands in the middle of his chest, and began

his relaxation routine, maintaining concentration on what he held while his breathing slowed. He had none of his tools here, the inducer pads, the sterile surrounds—he'd just have to trust that he could force himself into sleep state with his practiced techniques. He had to be able to force the dream and control it rather than just let it happen.

Little by little, Jack felt himself start to drift down through alpha, deeper. Awareness started to slip away, gently rocking him into the edge between wakefulness and dreaming. The stone, he thought. The stone. Billie. Concentrate on Billie, on Antille. He conjured their images in his mind, trying to link them to the stone chip held warmly between his palms.

There was light. Blue-white light picked out details of a familiar landscape. Jack stood in a pretty field, squinting against the glare. Grass, wild and tangled, sprinkled with tall wildflowers, stretched out toward a low hill in one direction, and what he presumed were trees in the other. They didn't look like trees, but they grew out of the ground and were clustered together. In place of trunks, four large branches stuck into the ground, and they were slick, reflecting back the bright light. A single spire reached skyward on each one, making it look like a cluster of framed cathedrals. The air carried a tang. Jack wrinkled his nose. It was a bit like old sweat. He turned slowly, looking for some clue that might tell him where he was. Which way was he supposed to go? He thought about heading for the trees, but there seemed to be nothing prompting him to go in that particular direction. For a moment he tried willing himself upward, but in this instance he seemed confined to the ground. No flying here. Pity. With a shrug, he started walking in the direction of the low hill.

As he neared, a figure crested the rise, silhouetted with

glare so he could not make out the features. He stopped walking and waited. The figure stood at the top of the rise, seeming as though it were looking down at him. Jack couldn't quite tell. The figure started down the gentle slope and gradually grew more distinct. It was a man, and as he drew closer Jack could see exactly who it was. Carl Talbot was heading down the hill in his direction, wearing a pale suit and half-open shirt, his hair slicked into place like something out of the old vids. Talbot took his time, and Jack waited. He glanced behind him once or twice, but the cathedral trees were still there, so he turned his gaze back to watch Talbot's steady approach. When Talbot was about ten feet away, though distance was always deceptive in the dream landscape, he stopped.

"Hello," said Talbot.

"Hey," said Jack.

There was a silence, followed by a slight buzzing in the air, like the sound of insects.

"What are you doing here?" said Talbot.

"I guess I'm looking for you," Jack answered slowly. But that couldn't be right. He forced himself to concentrate, but his willpower kept slipping away.

Talbot nodded. The sweat smell was joined by the hint of ozone.

"Where are we?" asked Jack.

Talbot shrugged. "I wish I knew. You wish you knew." But Jack did know.

Sometimes dream statements weren't quite what you expected, but Jack just accepted it for what it was.

"Who killed you?" he asked.

Talbot frowned, puzzling over the question. "Am I dead?"

"Yeah, sorry."

Talbot's eyes widened. The buzz had grown louder, pounding in Jack's ears.

A bright flash lit the landscape, a sizzling rush, and then the buzzing was suddenly gone. The sharp smell of burning filled the air. Talbot still stood in front of him, but half his face had been burned away, and one arm was gone, leaving just a blackened stump. His remaining eye was still wide.

"See wha' you done," he said with what remained of his mouth.

"I've done?" said Jack. "That wasn't my fault. I'm not responsible."

Wait! He'd dreamed this dream before. He was simply replaying an earlier dream sequence from an earlier case. That didn't make sense. Talbot had nothing to do with what was going on now.

"Stop!" he shouted.

He looked down at his hand, but it was empty. He closed it and opened it again, willing the stone shard back. When he opened his hand this time, it was there. He channeled his attention down, staring at the rock chip, focusing his concentration. Then he willed his thoughts to Billie. Billie was closest to what he needed. Billie, he thought, calling to her in the void.

But when he looked up, the landscape was the same. Talbot still stood there looking at him out of his half-ruined face.

"Yack Stein," said Talbot.

Jack tried to look away, past the blasted features, trying to determine where they were. Above him lay a broad ceiling. No, it wasn't a ceiling. It was farther away than that, far, far above. It was . . . it was sky, but dark, leaden gray. That was all he could see. They were standing on nothing, floating. Quick traceries of light shot back and forth below them. Jack tried to look everywhere but at the face that was speaking to him.

"You . . . haf . . . to go."

"What is it, Carl? Where do I have to go?"

Talbot tried to wave his arm. His remaining eye looked surprised. He gestured with the other, good arm. The sky disappeared. The lights in the darkness disappeared. Blankness remained. They floated in nothing. Jack peered into the nothingness, trying to work out what he was supposed to be seeing. There, over Talbot's maimed shoulder, something was forming, far away now. Jack concentrated. Quad shapes. Quad shapes like four thick, stocky legs, joined to a central spire that reached up into the sky.

"'Ere!" said Talbot emphatically. "You haf to go."

"Why do I have to go there, Carl? Tell me."

Talbot drifted into vaporous wisps and blew away, saying nothing more. Jack was left with the structural image in front of him. He stared at it, imprinting it deeply.

Then he was somewhere else. He was standing on a plain. Silver shapes flashed above his head, almost too fast to follow. One zipped silently past, whipping his head back as he tried to track it.

He turned to track it into the distance.

Something was standing behind him. It was tall, four legs, spaced evenly around a thick central body. It seemed smooth, featureless, shining slightly with a silvery slickness. At first he thought it was some sort of sculpture, the same sort of structure as the other things he'd seen, but on a smaller scale. And then it moved. Jack took a step back. Again, one of the four legs swung forward, repositioning the body. The top of the thick central shaft tilted forward. The whole thing looked ponderous, awkward. About halfway up the shaft something slowly bulged, then separated. A section folded down and then another. Behind one of the sections, there was a hollow. Jack shook his head. This was just weird, and the weirdness was working in his chest, making his heart pound faster. There was something in the hollow. Despite the fear starting to rise within him, he looked closer. There was a shape in there, something flat, rectangular. He recognized that shape. It was the artifact.

The sections that had folded down swung back up, and the hollow was concealed once more. The bulging torus slowly merged back into the shaft, and then the thing was gone.

Jack swallowed back his frustration.

"No, dammit!" he shouted at the empty plain. This was the same dream. The same dream over again. Almost instant by instant, scene by scene, he had dreamed this very same dream over two years ago.

He was alone on the plain, and then he wasn't. Talbot was back.

"What do you want?" said Jack.

Talbot winked with his one remaining eye. "We know you are 'ere, Yack," he said.

And Jack was awake.

Six

Jack had been expecting more. Something else. Something different. He knew there was no point trying to go back into dreamstate, though. He sat up and checked the time display. An hour. Nothing he could use there, at least not that he could see yet. He just couldn't work out why Talbot kept reappearing. The dead guy had been a clue in the earlier case, but how could he be a clue now? It made no sense, unless it was because the dream back then had been linked to the aliens. Both of them had the strange quad alien beings, and both had Talbot. Those last dreams had been more about Talbot himself, but now it was about the aliens. Maybe that was the link. Anyway, it appeared he'd have to use his other avenues of investigation, and meanwhile, time was ticking past and he was no closer to finding out what had happened to Billie.

He dressed, then reached for the map that the woman had given him. Sitting at the small glass table, he spread it out, then flipped through it, peering one by one at the misshapen colored ovals representing the various levels, knowing that really it was a pretty pointless exercise. He knew nothing about Balance City and the way things worked here. Maybe this place had some sort of life going on somewhere, but damned if he'd seen any sign of it yet. Heering had been pretty pointed in his direction, though. He folded the map away with a frustrated sigh, grabbed his coat, and, after shrugging it on, shoved the map into an inside pocket. That was one thing he'd learned over the years: You didn't wander the streets of a strange city with a map on full display, even the handipad variety. It screamed *victim*. And as it was, he stood out without even trying. Not that he had any intention of purchasing any of the rainbow outfits that would let him fade into the crowd.

He patted his pockets, more out of habit than anything else, but apart from his handipad and the map, there was nothing to check. All it did was remind him of another thing he was missing—a weapon. Where the hell was he going to find a gun? You never knew when you might need that little added bit of security, especially in Jack's line of work. Dammit, Stein. Preparation. He should have learned that by now. He was right not bringing one with him, with the security he'd seen on the way in, but at least he should have searched for where he might be able to find one.

Checking his room, and then making sure the door was firmly locked, he headed back down to the lobby to have a word with the concierge. That should at least give him a steer in the right direction. Hotel staff were supposed to know things.

A woman he hadn't seen before stood behind the desk. Dark hair was tied back in a severe bun, and high cheekbones accented slightly almond, dark eyes. The hospitality smile flashed into place as he approached. When he dug the map out of his pocket and spread it flat in front of her, the smile rapidly slipped away.

"Maybe you can help me," he said, flipping over a couple of the map leaves.

"I will try," she responded in a flat voice. "Of course . . ." she added, almost as an afterthought.

"Okay," said Jack, meeting her blank expression and prepared to play out the charade. "This map is pretty good, but it doesn't give me a lot of information. If you could give me any pointers about areas that I should really avoid, I'd appreciate it."

There was the barest pursing of her lips and a narrowing of the eyes. "I'm not sure I understand."

"I'm a foreigner here. I don't really know the city. I would guess you might be local." It wasn't a given, especially not in a hotel, but she had the look and the attitude. "Every city has areas that you might want to stay out of at night. Right? Even in the daytime. I just want a couple of pointers. Could you do that for me?"

She barely restrained a sigh, then gave a reluctant nod. She leaned forward and turned over two of the map leaves, looking at them and moving them back and forth, then laid one of them flat. With one finger she traced a line around the edge of the purple-hued oval on that page. The level—Jack guessed it was about four down—was uniformly shaded, except for a squarish green projection at one edge, not too far from where her finger now pointed.

"This level, Algol," she said, briefly pointing to the name at the top before returning to trace the western edge again, "is not so nice. Here, especially, I would advise care. In fact, you'd be better off not going there at all, particularly alone."

"I see," said Jack.

"Not advisable at all," she said with a brief nod, as if confirming it to herself.

Jack gave a half smile. So that was likely to be one of his first stops.

"Okay," he said. "Anywhere else?"

"Well . . ." She turned another couple of leaves. The page now showing was a mosaic of regular pink and light blue squares. Their oval was quite a lot smaller than many of the others. "This area, Carlton, is . . ." Here she paused. "Where some of the . . . local politicians, and others, make their homes." Again the pause. "They tend to like their privacy and security."

"Security?" Jack picked on the word, feigning innocence. You generally didn't need security unless you had something to be secured *against*.

"It's just," she said, moistening her lower lip, "they don't exactly welcome visitors."

"Hmmmm." Jack tucked the information away. "All right. One more question and then I'll leave you alone. Do people hunt here?"

"Yes, of course," she responded.

Jack nodded. Lots of forest, a certain type of population. It was the classic environment for hunters. He had thought they might. "So," he said. "Where might I buy some hunting equipment?"

Her expression lightened a shade, and for a moment her gaze flickered across his face and body, as if she were reassessing. She gave the briefest nod, then turned her attention back to the map, flipping back to one of the higher levels. "Here," she said, taking a pen and circling a yellow area. "This is a shopping district. You will probably find what you are looking for here. But, really, if you wish, we could arrange something for you. Perhaps you'd like to engage the services of a hunting guide?"

"No, that's fine," said Jack, reaching for the map and folding it away, back into his inner pocket. "I prefer to do these things myself. You've been most helpful. Thank you."

And she had, but perhaps in ways she didn't expect.

"Let us know if we can be of any further assistance, Mr. Stein," she said.

Oh, that was good. She knew exactly who he was. He might have guessed they were keeping tabs on him. How much exactly did they know? Somehow the idea didn't exactly make him feel comfortable.

More than half a dozen separate spots gave access to the city below, each marked on the map with a clear red circle. Jack had already decided that he'd try the area on the westernmost side first, if only to get a feel for the place and work out if there was any chance of finding what he needed. Equipping himself properly could come later, if he absolutely felt the need for some hardware. A quick glance at his map of the upper level gave him a clear idea of which way he should be heading. It didn't seem to be too far from the place he'd first emerged from the port and into the glass-and-steel sterility of Balance City.

As he left the hotel's front doors, his senses tingled with the old familiar feeling of being watched. Someone was observing him. Perhaps it was just the concierge, perhaps it was only the hotel's own surveillance equipment, but the sensation was clearly there. He was suddenly struck with the knowledge that right now it would be a bad move to let anyone know that he knew.

By the time he reached the shuttle stop, the feeling was gone, but the unease wasn't, and he stayed vigilant, using the old tricks to keep a watchful eye: the casual glance, the use of his peripheral vision, even that feeling of certainty that grew in his gut and reached out to the world around him. Partly from stakeouts, partly from the old intelligence and counterintelligence days, when it was wise to make sure the watcher wasn't the watched as well, the habits were almost autonomic. For now, though, he seemed to be in the clear. It did prompt another thought. He looked up and around at the surrounding buildings. Their clean, hard surfaces were unblemished, no protrusions, nothing that didn't look purely functional. He did wonder, however, if somewhere in Balance City there was not a group of observers watching the comings and goings of its populace, keeping tabs and storing it all away in neatly filed archives ready to be recalled at a moment's notice.

The expected shuttle cruised to a halt, and Jack climbed aboard, squeezing between a packed group of colorful locals, each of whom studiously avoided eye contact. Grabbing a handrail, he simply avoided them back, though he was slightly amused to catch one or two of them giving him the full head-to-toe when they thought that he wasn't looking. Okay, so he wasn't one of them. They could live with it. With a slight snort to himself, he turned his attention to the passing streets, keeping an eye out for where he was supposed to alight. With Balance City's complete lack of useful signage in the city proper, he needed to keep alert.

He shouldn't have worried. The shuttle pulled to a stop right in front of a small open space that proved to be just what he wanted. If it had had any vegetation, it might just have been a park, but it was bare, empty, apart from one obvious feature. No words, nothing but a big blue sign bearing one thing—a big white arrow pointing down. This way lies madness, he thought, then shook his head. Where the hell had that come from? He squeezed past a couple of his fellow passengers and stepped down, waiting for the shuttle's doors to close before turning and entering the square.

A boxed glass structure similar to the one he'd stepped out of when he'd first arrived stood to one side of the sign, and on the other side was what looked like a staircase, descending into darkness.

Jack pulled out the map, flipping through the leaves, checking. He needed to descend a full four levels to get to Algol. He guessed the stairs were practical. The elevator could hold only so many people, maybe ten, twelve people max, and if they had a rush . . . But if they thought he was going to walk down that many flights of stairs, they had another think coming. Not Jack Stein. He wandered over to the top of the metal staircase, frowning a little at the number of steps, the metal walls and ceiling descending into gloom. Even from here, he could feel a vague breeze blowing up from the levels below, touched with the scent of machinery and damp. He took two more steps, and as he neared, a pink light flashed on at either side of the entrance. One by one, banks of lights sprang into life, sending a wave of illumination down the tunnel as far as he could see, and the whir of machinery throbbed beneath his feet. The damned thing was an escalator! Only then did he notice the hooded structure paired to this one and facing the opposite direction. Okay, that wasn't so bad. He had to give the Utrechtians grudging credit for their engineering, at least.

Jack was torn now. He could take the elevator all the way down to Algol, or simply ride the escalators level by level, stopping briefly at each stage to get a feel for the districts that populated the spaces below. He had no idea how far down it might be, but the escalator was moving at a fair clip. The idea was tempting; everything he'd seen of Balance City so far had been surface level, in more ways than one. In the end, though, he decided he'd better take the elevator. He wasn't here for sightseeing, and the longer he delayed, the greater the chance something might happen to Billie in the meantime, if something hadn't happened to her already. As he walked toward the elevator booth, behind him the machinery subsided into silence, leaving him with the chill sound of his own last thought echoing in his head.

It didn't take long for the car to arrive. He stepped inside, giving one last check to see if there was anyone else around. The doors slid soundlessly shut, the barest lurch, and he was whisked rapidly down to the level below. The glass walls had shown him it was no farther, giving him a clear view of building walls and the approaching street that rose up to meet him. There were no controls, just a single stop at the bottom. He stepped out, wondering if there was an express version somewhere that took you all the way from top to bottom, bypassing the intervening districts. Jack took stock for a second. Another booth stood right next to the one from which he had just emerged, but this one had a small blue and white arrow above it, pointing down.

Far above, about 150 feet by his reckoning, was a lumpy, dark ceiling, covered with pipes and conduits. A narrow street stretched to the left, blocky, dark buildings extending all the way from ceiling to floor and lost in the maze of service channels above. The perfectly straight roadway led off into a dark blur at the end, illuminated by harsh orange lighting, fading into oneness in the distance. At the end, Jack guessed, lay the spire's walls. The other direction was similar, but off in the distance Jack caught the hint of what he presumed was daylight. In that direction, the buildings seemed also to become paler as they neared the source of the light, but that could have just been a trick of the eye. The air itself tasted oiled, and the hint of ozone prompted a brief, unwelcome flash of the Talbot dream in Jack's head. He was uneasy enough as it was without that particular memory.

A green-and-orange-garbed local chose that moment to walk past, looked at him curiously, then stopped and turned back.

"Ick du last," said the man.

Jack just stared at him.

"Cand I hef?"

Jack shook his head. "I don't . . ."

"Oh," said the man. "I am sorry." He paused, seemingly collecting his thoughts. "Are you lost?" he continued after a moment. "Do you need some directions?"

"No, thanks," said Jack. "I'm fine. Just looking."

The man hesitated, looking doubtful, but when Jack said nothing more, he nodded and went on his way.

Some local dialect. Okay, Jack had noticed the accent before, but he hadn't even thought that there might be a regional variation of language. Everybody pretty much spoke the same thing these days, as cultures and nations, planets and colonies had blurred, one into the other, even more over the last few years since the ease of travel that the jump drive had introduced. The seemingly careful, almost stilted word choice of everyone he'd encountered up to now suddenly made more sense.

He noticed a couple more brightly daubed locals farther down the street upon which he stood, clearly visible against the drabness of the surrounding architecture. Their fashion choices suddenly made more sense too. The whole place had a sense of the drab, an ordered, monochromatic life—it was almost like being in one of those old black-and-white vids. The feeling of being watched all the time too couldn't help, though maybe that was just Jack.

He grunted to himself with grudging acceptance and, not wanting any other encounters, turned for the elevator to take him down. Once upon a time, in the early history of this place, he guessed that much of the residential space had been on the surface, up on the plateau above, but as it had been subsumed by business and offices, the people had spread below, clinging to the safety of the spire for some reason. Their growth had drawn the lesser people below, down into this giant suspended parking garage of a city. Why hadn't they spread across the landscape? There had to be a reason, but he knew little enough about the history of the place to know that any such speculation would be no more than a guess. Same as the rest of this world.

Seven

Algol was slightly smaller than the districts above. It had taken Jack three quick elevator rides from the place he'd first stopped, and then he'd wandered out toward the western edge. The buildings were paler in color than the — what did he call it? level minus one? — but they still had the same sort of square sameness to them. He'd had little trouble working out which way to go. Head toward the light, Stein. Head toward the light. And so he had.

He was barely prepared for the view from the edge either. Tall glasslike barriers marked the district's edge, strangely clean, no smudges, finger marks, or any sign of human contact. The glass walls bellied outward, wider at the bottom than the top, allowing a clear view not of the buildings below, but of the brown, craggy canyon wall opposite and down, down into the canyon's depths. Jack stood there, looking into that abyss, feeling a deep unease inside him. It was as if nothing were keeping him safe from that plunge. Sure, there were the glass walls, but it was an illusion, as if he were suspended above the drop. Heights like that made him uncomfortable. He swallowed and stepped away from the edge, turned away from the view, and started getting his bearings. Up that way lay the port, and if Balance City worked like any other, that was the way he should be heading. He stood for a couple of seconds, willing his sense to kick in and to guide him, but nothing. He growled quietly, deep in his throat, randomly picked a street from those on offer, and started walking, hoping to run into a bar or something along the way. The districts of Balance City might be different in their own way, but there were fundamentals about any place humanity clustered together. Some things operated the same way wherever you were.

Five stops later, four stiff and mannered bars behind him, he found what he thought offered some promise. Sure, there had been watering holes along the route, but so far they'd been typical of this place, showing all the regimented order of everything else he'd seen. And the district was quiet. A few locals sat around drinking, laughing, the normal early-evening workers and others winding down after their day. One after another, Jack had entered, gotten a whiff of the feel of each place, shaken his head, and wandered on. This one, however, was different. He could feel it in the place in his gut that sparked and pulled, alerting him that he needed to pay attention. He stood out in front on the street, looking at the place, trying to seek a clue why he was drawn here, to this bar particularly.

A neatly lettered sign arched above a wide doorway. FARLEY'S. Okay. Tinted bubble-glass panels made up the top half of the doors, and light filtered through the yellowish glass, painting the street outside with the washed-out hints of jaundice. He could catch glimpses of shadowed movement inside, but that was about it. Two broad windows sat on either side of the door, the bottom two-thirds of them curtained. He thought about stepping up to the window and peering inside over the top of the curtains, but then decided that wasn't such a good idea. With a quick nod to himself, he headed for the double doors.

The bar smelled like a bar. That was a good start. Jack gave the room a quick scan with a slightly cautious eye, but saw nothing unusual, nothing that would draw him here. A couple of interested glances from the current occupants, he noted, but there was anything but hostility there, and he sauntered over to the bar.

"Hey, there." The barman was a tall guy with a shiny shaved head. "What can I get you? And if I'm not mistaken, this is your first time here, right?"

Again Jack nodded. "Bourbon, neat," he said, and turned to lean back on the bar to give the place a better look while he waited for his drink. Pale furniture, some hunting trophies on the walls, dark wooden booths. There was nothing particularly unusual about the bar, but at least it seemed a little less sterile than the other places he'd seen. Why here? That was the question. That place deep in his gut had told him that there was something here he needed to know, but, as often happened with these things, he had no idea what it was supposed to be. He turned back to the barman as he returned and placed the drink — a healthy measure — on the bar in front of him.

"Nice place you have here," said Jack.

"Thanks," said the barman. "Hope you enjoy it."

Jack reached for his handipad, but the barman held up a hand. "The first one's on me. You need anything, just give me a shout."

Jack thanked him, nodded, and headed for one of the booths, his drink in hand. He slid into the bench seat and positioned himself, elbows on table, leaning slightly over his glass, one hand around its slick surface, his other bunched into a fist and supporting his chin. The old watching stance. Looking but not really looking.

The wooden fixtures might have been pale, but the bar's lighting was dim. Pools of dusky yellow light centered over round tiled tables. What looked like stone bowls sat on each of the tables across the central area, half-full of something—Jack couldn't quite tell what from his position. He turned his focus to a pair of what looked like businessmen at a table near the bar. Definitely not from the city: drab gray suits, conservative shirts, large glasses half-full of some dark, cloudy brew, possibly local, sitting in front of them, beads of moisture on the outside of the glasses. Jack let his attention drift into their conversation.

"Yeah, and I let this guy line up and take his best shot. I said to him, I said, 'Give me what you've got.'" The man was overweight, tanned, deep shadowed eyes set into his fat face. A sweat sheen was visible on his forehead. He licked a plump, purple bottom lip before continuing. "I said to him, I said, 'You just try.'"

"Yeah," said his skinnier, graying companion.

"Yeah," the fat one said, nodding his head. "Man, I'm telling you, I was ready for him. Lock and load. I'm telling you . . ."

Jack hated that sort of bullshit, the sort who dished it, knowing almost immediately with that brief exchange that there was nothing of use to him with this pair. He let his focus slip away from them and around the bar, casually observing, his eyes half-hooded, leaving his deeper senses open and receptive.

Ones, twos, and threes were clustered around the bar and scattered among the tables. There *was* something different about this place, but he couldn't quite put his finger on it. Then, suddenly, he realized what it was and why it had been so hard to pin down. Most of the people in this particular establishment wore clothes that Jack would view as normal. Subtle colors, conservative styling. The normality was the abnormality. Everyone in the place was from somewhere else—somewhere other than Balance City. Okay. Maybe there was some promise here after all. He took a healthy swallow and gave a satisfied grimace as the burn took his mouth and throat, then settled in his stomach. The problem was, none of the bar's current customers looked like they might have means to own a ship, particularly not the sort of ship he needed. Sure, one or two of them might have access to one, but somehow he didn't think so. And he was convinced, for the moment, that he needed a ship.

One by one, Jack checked out the other patrons, sized them up, reaching out with his deeper senses. One by one, he drew a blank. He took another big swallow, draining the remainder of his glass, and placed it down on the table with a heavy sigh. This was getting him nowhere. And as far as he knew, right now that was where Billie was. Nowhere. Nowhere he could get to, anyway. He pushed his glass back and forth on the table surface with his forefingers, glancing up now and again to make sure he wasn't missing anything. Once again, it was starting to look like his intuition had led him astray. Bloody useless, Jack. It was no use berating himself, but old habits died hard. With a sigh, he grabbed his glass and headed for the bar.

Jack nodded to the bartender and tilted his empty glass meaningfully. The bartender simply nodded in return and moved off to pour his drink. Nice. Jack had his handipad out and ready by the time the bartender returned. As he was paying, he decided to do some probing.

"So what do I call you?" asked Jack.

"Ah, thanks," said the bartender, putting his reader away again. "Call me Rufus."

"Is this your place?"

"Yeah, mine, all of it."

"So you're the Farley on the sign?"

"Well, no, actually. I bought it from Mick Farley about six years ago."

Jack nodded. "You're not from here originally, are you?"

"No, you're right there." Rufus grinned. "Few of us are in Farley's."

Jack gave an amused little snort and glanced around the bar. "I could sort of tell."

"Well, you know how it is," said Rufus, reaching for a cloth and starting to polish some glasses. "Every big city has its load of expats. Most of them wind up kind of hanging together. Farley's just happened to be the place that served that community. I liked it. I liked the atmosphere. So I ended up buying the place, you know? In a way I guess I'm providing a service."

Jack nodded.

"So what brings you to Balance City?" Rufus asked.

There was nothing forced about the question. Rufus seemed genuinely interested rather than simply making conversation, and Jack found himself warming to the guy immediately. He imagined that Rufus had his crew of loyal regulars and would keep doing so.

"A bit of business of my own," said Jack.

Rufus simply nodded, not pushing the question. Jack liked that too. He leaned on the bar, feeling a little more comfortable in the place.

At that moment the doors opened. A couple of people around the bar looked up, but then returned to their drinks. Rufus tilted his head in recognition toward the new arrival. He was a younger man than Jack, dark hair hanging long around his face, wearing a calf-length black coat, leather or something like it. A dark red shirt sat underneath, and utilitarian casual black trousers . . . and . . . spacer's boots. Jack narrowed his eyes, not because of what he saw, but because there seemed to be something awfully familiar about the young guy's face. What would he be? Very early thirties? He had his arm draped around the shoulder of a young woman, raven hair and pale skin offset by ruby red painted lips. Large hologramatic earrings dangled from her lobes. She scanned the bar and its occupants with an expression approaching bored disdain. The young guy held up two fingers as he approached the bar.

"Come on, Rufie. You know what I want."

"And the same for your lady friend?" said Rufus.

Undraping his arm from the woman's shoulder, he placed both hands on the edge of the bar. He leaned in, across the bar, before speaking again. "Well, what do you think?"

Now that he was closer, Jack could see a dark mark across one cheek, roughly concealed by the curtain of hair.

The young guy saw him looking, and looked straight back, unashamedly assessing, peering through the hair, checking Jack up and down and then fixing on his face. His eyes widened a fraction, then narrowed. A slight frown creased his brow, barely visible under the hair.

"Hey, don't I know you? Didn't we have a fight once . . . ?"

"Dog . . ." There was a cautionary note to Rufus's voice.

Was that his name? Dog? Well, Jack was about to find out. The guy brushed past his companion and took two steps toward Jack and peered into his face.

"Wait a minute. I *do* know you." He pressed his fist against the side of his head and closed his eyes. A second later they opened again. They were brilliant blue. "Got it. Stein. That's it. Lucky Stein." He pointed his finger at Jack's face several times in succession. "Yeah. Yeah. That's it. Dammit. Lucky Stein. I'm right, aren't I?"

It was Jack's turn to be baffled. Nobody called him that anymore, hadn't in years, not since he'd been working for someone else. But there *was* something familiar about this guy, something he thought he should know. He looked at the face, tilting his head to one side as he tried to make out the features, in his mind's eye pulling away the long strands of hair, smoothing out the mark on the cheek, and then he had it. . . .

"Danny Boy? Danny Boy McCreedy?"

"Heh. But nobody calls me *that* anymore." McCreedy grinned. With the grin came more familiarity. Jack recognized that grin more than anything. "Not if they want to live." He reached out and grasped Jack's hand. "Lucky Stein. Well, I'll be damned." He turned to his companion. "Stella, this is an old mate, back from the military days. Finish your drink and I'll see you later. The old Dog's got some catching up to do."

She gave a sniff, looked at Jack with a bored, dismissive expression, reached for her drink, knocked it back, and headed for the door without even a backward glance.

Jack frowned. "But what about . . . ?"

McCreedy waved his hand dismissively. "Don't worry about Stella. She can look after herself." He grabbed Jack by the shoulder and steered him toward a booth. "Sit. Dammit, man. What brings you to this godforsaken hole? Lucky Stein, eh?" He shook his head, looking at Jack with a foolish grin, reached back to one of the empty tables, and snagged the bowl that sat there, placing it down between them as he slid into the booth to join him.

Well, at least Jack's gut had been accurate about something. Right place at the right time, Stein. Timing was everything.

Eight

"Yeah, so I spent some time basically drifting after I quit the service. I dunno. Nobody really leaves, you know. It stays with you, or you stay with it. I'm not sure which one it is."

Jack nodded, knowing exactly what McCreedy was talking about. There were echoes of your past clinging to the darker places of your mind, awake or asleep. He watched McCreedy—he wasn't ready for the "Dog" name yet—as the younger man ran his fingers through the long strands of his hair and then thoughtfully traced the burn mark on his cheek.

"I guess I never really got over being a shuttle jockey, you know? That stays with you too. Shuttle, ship, pilot, it's all the same shtick. And here? This place? It just sort of happened. I spent some time as a station rat up there on the orbital, but that got boring after a while. It's too much of a hollow community." He gave a brief laugh at his own witticism. "Anyway, I was down here doing some work, found a few like-minded souls, and . . . well . . . I'm still here. How about you?"

"Pretty much the same," said Jack. "Pretty much. The drifting. I hear you. After that, well, you know, fate pushes you one way or another."

McCreedy nodded sagely. "That it does." He grabbed

the bowl, took a pinch of the green powder, held thumb
and forefinger beneath his nose, and took a healthy sniff.
He reached for his drink, and took a big swallow to follow it.

Jack frowned. "What is that stuff?"

McCreedy pushed the bowl toward Jack. "Kreff. Local
vegetable matter. Sort of lends a nice clarity to proceed-
ings. Have some?"

Jack shook his head. "Maybe later."

"It goes really well with a drink . . ." said McCreedy,
but Jack held up a hand.

"Damn, but things happen in a funny way. Things
were always pretty weird around you, Stein, anyway."
McCreedy shook his head.

"Yeah, well . . ." said Jack, not willing to dwell on
anything that happened back then. He'd excised way too
many of those events from his consciousness, those missions where McCreedy was along. "So you're still piloting?" asked Jack.

"Sure," said McCreedy. "What else am I going to do?
Nothing else like it. Got my own ship too. A little beauty
it is. Own ship. Own boss. That's all you need, right?"

"Uh-huh," said Jack. He'd decided he wanted Mc-
Creedy to feel a little more relaxed before he pushed on
the ship front.

"So what about you, Stein?"

"Mmmm, long story in many ways. I'm sort of a PI
these days."

"PI? Yeah, might have guessed it . . . What do you
mean, 'sort of'?"

"Well, I'm a psychic investigator. The P stands for
'psychic,' not 'private.'" He let the statement hang between them.

McCreedy looked at him with a blank expression for a
couple of seconds, then nodded, reaching for another

pinch of kreff. He closed his eyes after the sniff, opening them slowly only to reach for his drink. He wiped his mouth with the back of his hand, took another deep sniff, then nodded again. "Mighta guessed," was all he said.

"Jack Stein," he said after another pause, and shook his head.

"So why here?" asked Jack. "It seems pretty sterile to me."

"Oh, yeah. It might look like that on the surface, and the rules can drive you crazy, but there's something about the place. There's a lot of good business here. The expat community looks after each other. Like Rufus, my man behind the bar. You know? We stick together. There's good money on Utrecht. Good money to be made, good business, and if you know your way around, then you can do all right."

Jack nodded slowly. "Hmmm, okay."

"So you haven't told me yet," said McCreedy. "What brings you to Balance City?"

"I'm on a case. Well . . . no, I'm not." Jack grimaced. "It's kind of personal. . . ."

McCreedy pushed back some stray strands from his face. "Come on, Stein. Give."

Jack sighed. He thought he could trust McCreedy. They went back a long way. Young Danny Boy McCreedy had saved Jack's ass not once, but a couple of times. Jack owed him for that, but who knew what had occurred in the interim. He flashed back briefly to the jungle, half his body aflame and McCreedy dragging him through the vegetation, the dark uniform around his shoulder darker with the wetness of blood. Yeah, Jack owed Danny Boy McCreedy.

"Okay. My niece . . . well, she's not really my niece . . . but that's a long story. Anyway, she was involved in some stuff at the university out here. They were doing some research—alien civilization, that sort of thing. They thought they had clues to the position of an alien homeworld." Jack rubbed his hand across the table surface, carefully formulating what he was going to say next. "It looks like they took a jump. Nothing's been heard from them since."

"You said 'them'?"

"Yeah. This professor at the university whom Billie was working with."

"Well . . ." said McCreedy. "That's pretty interesting stuff. Aliens, huh? What are you going to do about it?"

Jack fixed McCreedy with a hard look. "I'm going to find them."

McCreedy sat back, draping his arms over the back of the bench. "Come on. These university guys are going to know what they're doing, aren't they? They're old enough and smart enough to know what they're about."

Jack's gaze didn't falter. "Billie's sixteen, Danny Boy. Sixteen."

McCreedy narrowed his eyes. "Shit, okay, then. I thought you said they were working together."

Jack nodded slowly. "Yeah. Like I said. It's a long story."

McCreedy glanced around the bar before looking back at Jack. "So, *really,* what are you going to do about it?"

Reaching for his drink, Jack took a couple of moments to frame his thoughts. "Well," he began slowly, "I thought I'd track down a pilot, work out where they might have gone, and bring them back. . . ."

McCreedy grinned. "The old search and rescue, hey? Easy enough. We've been there before. Both of us."

Jack grimaced. "Yeah, nice and easy. It's a little more complicated than that, though. I don't know if you've ever heard of a place called Mandala. It's this resort world. Full of the rich and famous with more money than sense. You know the type of place, very upmarket, very exclusive. Part of the attraction there is this archeological site. Alien ruins, though I can't really see what the appeal is—a bunch of empty old buildings all falling apart." He rethought where he was going with that. "Anyway, that's not important. There was this alien artifact that came from there. It was part of a case I was working on. This stone, or whatever it was, was supposed to have the co-ordinates of the alien homeworld or something like that. That's where they went. Looking for this alien home-world. The thing is, the directions are in some sort of alien code. I'm no scientist. I'm no navigator. I don't know how the hell anyone can work out where it's sup-posed to be. And besides, you need the right kind of ship."

McCreedy was nodding interestedly.

"What do you mean, 'the right kind of ship'?" he said.

"It's got to have one of those jump drives. Any old ship isn't going to do." Jack shook his head.

McCreedy's grin widened. "Uh-huh."

"What do you mean, 'uh-huh'?"

McCreedy leaned forward, placed his hands on the table, looked up at Jack, peering through the strands of hair that had fallen forward over his face, his expression suddenly serious. "Things have been kinda quiet around here lately." Then he grinned and reached for another pinch of kreff before leaning back again.

Jack stared at him. "I don't—"

"Old Dog's your guy, Jack. You need a ship. You need a pilot. Dog's up for a bit of excitement." He took a big snort from between his pinched fingers and put his head back with his eyes closed.

Jack could see traces of the youthful pilot he had once known, more than traces, but time had worn heavily on Daniel McCreedy's face. There was more than that burn

scar written on his features. Slowly McCreedy opened his
sharp blue eyes, staring up at the ceiling.

"Yep. Old Dog could do with a bit of excitement," he
said, almost as if talking to himself. Underneath, there was
a deep weariness in his voice and traces of something else.

Jack wasn't sure how much he could trust the younger
man, but for the moment, he had to take McCreedy at his
word. Besides, their past association gave Jack confidence. He knew he could trust McCreedy in a tight spot.
They agreed to meet again at the bar the following day in
the early afternoon and take a shuttle up to the orbital
where McCreedy said his ship was berthed. No alarms
went off in Jack's stomach as they shook hands, and that
was a good sign too. Jack turned for the door. Absurdly
formal, but Balance City seemed to bring that sort of
thing out in people. Jack had just about reached the door
when he had another, sudden thought. He turned and
walked slowly back to the table.

"Do something for me, McCreedy?" he said as he
stood there, deliberately shielding them from the rest of
the room.

"Hmmm?" said Dog, with a brief raise of his eyebrows
and a tilt of his head.

Jack almost had second thoughts, but then considered
that he ought to know by now to trust those gut feelings,
and there was a gut feeling working away right now
telling him what he had to do. Despite his conscious
reservations, he dug inside his coat and pulled out the
small sheaf of papers Heering had copied for him. "Look
these over for me. See if you can make anything of them.
The guy I've been talking to says they give the coordinates. Let me know if he's right, okay?"

McCreedy reached for them, but Jack drew them out
of reach.

"Not here," he said. "Overnight. And keep them safe."

McCreedy took them this time and slipped them from view.

Jack nodded. "They're important. Don't lose them."

McCreedy narrowed his eyes slightly, clearly at the possibility that Jack had even thought to suggest such a thing. Anyway, if something should happen to them, Jack could always go back to Heering.

"Okay. Tomorrow," said Jack, giving another brief nod and turning for the door. He could feel McCreedy watching him all the way out.

Outside, he stood just in front of the bar and took stock. He was tired. Way too tired. Different time zone, different planetary cycle. It was taking its toll. He grimaced. Maybe some sleep. Or maybe a lonely drink in his hotel room. Either way, he didn't think he could achieve much more that evening. Another blank night in yet another blank and faceless city. He didn't really feel like taking in the sights, such as they were. If anything, that was likely to depress him more. He wondered what Billie was doing. . . .

Shaking his head, he shoved his hands deep into his pockets and, head slightly bowed, walked back down the way he had come.

He'd barely reached the end of the street when he became aware of a presence by his side. A quick glance showed dark green clothes. Some sort of suit. He tried to ignore whoever it was and kept walking, his head down. A moment later the presence was joined by another on his opposite side. Oh, great. What now? He shot a look the other way and it was another green suit. The green suits moved in close on either side. Jack stopped walking. So did they.

"Can I help you?"

"There is someone who would like to talk to you," said a voice to his left, no hostility, calm and polite.

Jack turned to face the speaker. The man had a square jaw and ice blue eyes. Short-cropped gray stubble covered his head.

"And who might that be?"

The man looked left and right. "If you would come with us, I am sure all will be explained." He fixed Jack with an expressionless gaze.

Jack turned to look at the other green suit. Thick torso, broad shoulders, baldhead shining in the artificial light. The other man held his gaze impassively.

Jack wanted to take issue, but he didn't. What would be the point? *What if I don't want to? Sorry, but I have somewhere else I've got to be.* He could tell already that none of those was going to work. He sighed. "Okay. You'd better lead the way." It might have been different if he'd managed to arrange some hardware, but these two looked like they'd be carrying too.

The one who had spoken held out a hand signifying their direction. Jack inclined his head.

"So what's this all about?" he asked, as he stepped forward on the indicated path.

"As I said, all will become clear," said the speaker. And that was it. There wasn't going to be any more conversation until they had reached wherever they were going. Jack had been through this all before. He suppressed his next sigh, knowing full well that it would not do a bit of good.

Flanked by the two green suits, Jack was shepherded toward the elevators. He refrained from conversation, refrained from giving this pair of hired lackeys any pleasure by reacting. He simply watched where they were going. An open hand gestured him into the glass elevator booth, the one leading down. The two followed him in and turned, facing the doors as they slid shut and the elevator began its descent. Jack was left staring at the backs of their heads.

He barely had time to take in the new level before he was ushered into another down elevator.

And so it went, level after level, until they had descended a full six. Jack wasn't sure, but it seemed to him that they must be pretty near the city's base. That suspicion was confirmed by the absence of a further elevator leading down. Okay, rock bottom. Well, not quite rock bottom, but it was pretty close.

Now he had a chance to look around. He was steered down a broad street with large white buildings flanking either side. Struts and beams of exposed shiny metal crisscrossed the ceiling and ran between buildings. Within a number of them, flat illumination panels shed clear light across the street and the building fronts, casting crisp, angular shadows. Nothing gloomy about this district. Jack chewed that thought over for a moment. You'd expect something quite different in the bowels of a city. He sniffed and glanced at his companions, but they seemed oblivious. Heering's words came back to him again. *As above, so not below.*

"Down this way," said one of his companions, giving him a gentle touch on his shoulder. They headed down a narrow side street that opened into a round open space. In the center lay a slight depression and some sort of plinth, looking like it had been carved in polished granite. Jack narrowed his eyes and gave a slight involuntary shake of his head. None of this was making sense. He remembered the words of the woman back at the hotel, about how the people in the lowest level of the city liked their "security." Well, that much was starting to become apparent.

Gray Stubble reached out a hand and pressed it firmly on the top of the plinth, fingers spread. A second or two, and the next instant Jack understood. A broad semicircle of what had looked like paving in the depression slid back, revealing a set of metal stairs descending into the

ground. Gray Stubble gestured with his chin, and Jack
took the cue. Slowly he walked down the staircase, glancing up behind him as his two companions followed. Almost soundlessly the covering plate slid back into place,
plunging the stairwell not into gloom, but into bright
light. The panel's entire undersurface was covered with
its own lighting panels.

As he reached the staircase bottom, a hand on the top
of his shoulder halted him in his tracks.

"Stop. Wait here."

Gray Stubble disappeared through a doorway, while
Square Jaw patted him down, removed his handipad and
the map, and seemed slightly disappointed when there
was nothing else to find. He narrowed his eyes at Jack
and tossed the map and handipad on a nearby side table.
Jack returned the look flatly. He didn't know how many
times he'd been through this routine, and there was nothing different about it this occasion. He wasn't going to
make a fuss about it now.

He glanced at the map and handipad sitting on the side
table and just felt thankful that his intuition had told him
to leave the other papers with Dog McCreedy. He could
trust him a hell of a lot more than he could these guys.
Square Jaw was standing by one doorway watching him,
his hands clasped behind his back, a posture that accen-
tuated the breadth of his shoulders and the thickness of
his chest. Was he enhanced? The guy was big. Too big.
Jack shoved his hands into his pockets and looked at the
floor. Anything but having to face that impassive, broad-
faced stare. He twitched one cheek as he realized he had
just been on the verge of starting to whistle and rock back
and forth on his heels. Better not to appear too comfortable while he waited for whoever or whatever was waiting for him.

Nine

He didn't have too long to wait. It was almost a relief when Gray Stubble reappeared and beckoned him to follow down the corridor from which he had just emerged. Jack shot Square Jaw a look, gave him a deliberate smile, and tilted his head. Square Jaw simply watched him, without even so much as a blink. Jack suppressed a sigh, shook his head, and dutifully followed into the corridor. The passageway opened into another circular open area. The room was empty apart from another metal staircase that spiraled downward. Jack took the hint and descended first, his green-suited shadow following close behind.

When he reached the bottom of the staircase, Jack caught his breath. The descending spiral had obscured his view of what lay below. What lay below was . . . nothing. . . .

A vast emptiness yawned beneath his feet. He caught himself at the bottom of the stairs, his hand gripping tightly to the cold metal banister. What the hell?

A chuckle behind him brought him back to where he was. Still gripping tightly to the handrail, Jack looked again. Stretched below, what seemed like miles down, lay sharp crags and a rocky canyon floor, from what he could make out in the fading light. Fissures traced the sides of an opposite canyon wall, or patches of deeper shadow; it was hard to tell. Smudges of olive spattered against the rock wall. Probably vegetation, some sort of bush clinging to bare rock, but the light wasn't good enough to be sure.

"Move. In there," said the man behind him.

Gingerly, Jack put out a foot, expecting to find empty space, but instead the toe of his shoe tapped against something solid, something transparent. He withdrew his foot.

"Go on," said his companion. "It's perfectly safe."

It damned well didn't look it. Jack again took the step, allowing his weight to transfer to his outstretched leg. He then followed with another step. He was standing on nothing, suspended above a vast drop. He felt cold. He took another tentative step. What was this, a scenic panel, or something else?

"I see you are enjoying my view," said a deep, rich voice from across the room. Jack looked up, for the first time seeing the other presence. How he could have missed him, Jack didn't know. Across the broad, rock-strewn maw stood the voice's owner: a large black man in a powder blue suit with a purple shirt held together with an ornate gold clasp at the throat. He was balding, his skin shiny, with a round-jowled face and virtually no neck to speak of. Large gold rings decorated the hands crossed in front of him. There was a yellowish tinge to the whites of his eyes.

"Hell of a thing to do to someone," said Jack.

"Oh, don't worry about it," said the man, taking three steps into the room, looking for all the world like he was walking on air, and taking a seat on a virtually transparent couch. Now that he looked properly, ignoring the distraction of the scene below him, Jack could see several other pieces in the room, made of the same transparent material. "You soon get used to it," he continued. "But not at first." He chuckled then. Jack somehow didn't find the whole thing very amusing.

"Come, Mr. Stein. Have a seat."

Jack stood where he was, though he desperately wanted the feeling of something more solid beneath him. "What's this all about? Who the hell are you? It's only fair. You seem to know who I am."

The man leaned forward, clasping his hands in front of him. "This is no way to behave. Sit down." His voice had the commanding tone of someone used to being obeyed. "I am Maximilian Aire. I do not expect you to have heard of me. And you are correct; I know who you are, Jack Stein. I know all about you. Now sit."

Jack hesitated for a moment, then with a grimace stepped toward one of the virtually invisible chairs, finally taking a seat. The yawning emptiness below him was still distracting. He shoved it out of his mind and tried to concentrate on the man across from him. "Okay, Mr. Aire, what do you want?"

"I should be asking you that, Jack. Why are you here in Balance City? What is your business on Utrecht?"

"I think that's my business, as you say. Can I call you Max?" He said the last with the slightest trace of a sneer, countering Aire's dismissive familiarity with his own. His mind was racing, trying to come up with some reason why this man, this complete stranger, would be interested in what he was doing. It had to be the aliens. "Anyway, how do you know who I am? How did you even know I was here? Maybe you have me confused with someone else."

"I don't think so, Jack."

He sat back, fixing Aire with a hard glare. "Well, even if you don't, it's none of your damned business what I'm doing. My business is my own."

Aire shook his head. "Now that's where you're wrong." He stood, levering his large bulk upright, then turned away, staring down into the growing gloom below. "Why do you think I would rate a basement apartment like this? I earned this view. And I didn't do so by not being interested in what happens in my city." He whirled with a speed that took Jack off guard. "Yes, Mr. Stein, *my* city." Slowly he lifted his hooded gaze and fixed Jack with a hard stare, as if daring him to challenge the statement.

Jack shrugged. "I'm sorry. I still don't get it. I don't know what you're talking about or what you want from me, and I'd appreciate it if you'd let me get back to my hotel. It's been a long day, and the time difference . . ."

Aire waved his hand dismissively. "All right, Stein. If you are going to play stupid, so be it, but it's a mistake. It would be a lot easier for you if you were to tell me exactly why you're here."

Jack sighed. "I'm here to see my niece. I'm visiting. That's all."

Aire blinked and seemed to be digesting that, as if the answer had taken him by surprise. "And what's that got to do with the University of Balance City?"

It was Jack's turn to digest. He had been right. That feeling of being watched . . .

"She's studying there."

Aire narrowed his eyes. "We can check, you know."

Jack nodded slowly. "Check away."

"You know, Mr. Stein, as soon as you arrived on Utrecht, several flags went up. We were immediately aware of your presence. I would be very careful if I were you. We *will* be watching."

"Who the hell are *we?*"

Aire turned away again. "That doesn't matter. I think we are done here. For now. But I expect we might see each other again. It would be wise not to meddle in things that don't concern you."

Jack frowned and stood, biting back a reply.

Aire didn't bother to turn around as Jack left, escorted by the green suit who had been waiting patiently at the staircase bottom.

All the way back up to his hotel—and it was a long way back up to the surface—Jack was running the encounter through his head. He didn't know who the hell this Maximilian Aire was, but he was clearly someone with resources at his disposal. Someone who was used to dishing out orders as well. Had he made a mistake mentioning Billie? Okay, that could wait. The real issue was that whoever *they* were, they knew exactly where Jack was, whether or not they knew precisely what he was doing. That level of interest was strange. Who was Jack Stein to them? The other strange thing was that his extended sense had given him absolutely nothing on Aire. Not a shred. If this guy was important, Jack should have felt something. Weird. Weird, and more than a little unsettling.

He was almost stumbling by the time he got to his room. Never had a hotel bed looked so inviting. He barely had the energy to strip off his coat and remove his shoes before collapsing on the bed. Maximilian Aire and his green-suited lackeys could wait.

Jack was on a ship. It felt like a ship. It smelled like a ship. That vague odor of oiled machinery and something else . . . plastic. Old air, as well. Old air touched with the taste of stale humanity. He sniffed at himself, the front of his top, his armpits. No, it wasn't him. He got up off his bunk and looked for a viewport, something to see were he was, but the room—cabin—gave him nothing but metal walls. He ran his fingers through his hair, trying to force himself to full wakefulness.

"Jack, aren't you coming?" Billie had stuck her head through the door. She looked like she'd been awake for hours, and she had that expression of disapproval on her face she always got when Jack wasn't doing what she thought he should be.

She stepped half into the cabin. Propped on one hip she held a large rifle. She cocked it and stepped back out. "Come on, Jack."

He turned to check that he hadn't forgotten anything and then went to follow. The door was gone.

That was strange.

He pressed his hands against the flat metal wall, looking for the door.

Somewhere in the distance, muffled, he could just make out the sound of Billie's voice. "Come on, Jack! What are you waiting for?"

"I don't know," he muttered, searching for the mysteriously vanishing door. He looked down, wondering what had happened to the floor. He was standing on nothing, suspended, and below him water, dark water, moving with a low swell, stirred. Something pale slipped past in the depths, a vague shadow, and he looked away.

There was another smell now. A smell of . . . cactus? Succulent and green. How did he know what cactus smelled like?

Dog McCreedy stuck his head through the wall, looking at him with an impatient frown, then withdrew. The dark strands of his hair took longer to vanish, trailing after the disappearing face as if stuck within the substance of the wall. He watched them in slow motion, thin snakes of hair.

He sensed movement below him too, and looked down. The pale blur stirring in the water moved back into view, becoming more distinct. It was human. He could see that much now. It was a man's shape. One pallid arm reached up, breaking the oily dark surface, and beckoned to him. Come, Jack. Come here.

"Dammit! I'm coming," he said to the wavering shape.

Pain worked up his neck and across one shoulder. The thick taste of bad sleep made his mouth feel like it was full of dirty old feathers, and he worked his eyes open with difficulty. Shreds of the dream were already starting to fade. He lifted himself upright and winced as the action turned his head and shot a new arrow of hurt across his shoulders. Damned unfamiliar beds. He growled and gritted his teeth. He felt like crap, and he was still in his clothes. There was some sort of smell. This time he sniffed, and the smell was Jack Stein, or Jack Stein's clothes, slept in, worn too long and abused, nothing like cactus.

God he hated mornings, especially mornings like this. Dammit, he didn't even know if it was morning. He sat up on the bed, trying to get his thoughts straight, and glanced at the time display. Yeah, it was morning. With a groan he levered himself upright and swung his legs off the bed, taking another couple of seconds to sniff heavily. His head felt full. Great.

Last night's events started coming back to him, including an image of Maximilian Aire's fleshy features, big, round, and dark in his mind's eye. No, though he tested it, there was nothing familiar about the man. Nothing at all. Sometimes a dream might give it to him. He shook his head. So what had that all been about?

Dammit, he needed coffee. Badly. He looked at the display again and did a rough calculation in his head. Allowing time for getting down to Algol, he still had a couple of hours before he had to leave to meet McCreedy. It was probably just as well.

Stripping off his clothes, he stumbled more than padded into the bathroom and emptied his bladder, closing his eyes and trying to work some of the stiffness out of his neck. He spent a couple of fruitless minutes searching for coffeemaking facilities, then remembered, growled at the room in general, and stepped into the shower, thinking about how much his life had changed over the past few years. Mainly because of Billie. Maybe coffee would do something to ease his mood. That last thought was almost enough to make the prospect of the breakfast buffet semitolerable. Almost.

Jack headed straight out from breakfast, his handipad and the map already shoved in his coat pocket. The muscle at Aire's place had been kind enough to return his things, at least. He thought he could find his way back to Farley's without too much trouble. There was nothing particularly complex about Balance City's layout. Hopefully, he'd see no further sign of his erstwhile greensuited companions. He could do without them this morning. His senses still prickled with the prospect that there might be someone watching him, and he felt the tightness in his shoulders, only complicated by the stiffness of how he had slept. He was not in a good mood. Not at all. He just hoped to hell McCreedy wasn't going to keep him waiting.

It was pretty easy to find his way back to the bar. He stood outside for a few moments, checking both the street and his sense for anything out of the ordinary. The street was relatively quiet. In fact, he wondered if the bar was open—it wasn't even midday yet—but then why would McCreedy have suggested meeting there if it wasn't going to be? He guessed it was near enough to the docks to have its own schedule, especially as it seemed to cater mainly to expats. City ports tended to have comings and goings at any time of the day or night. Why should this place be any different? A couple of locals walked farther down the street, nearer to the intersection, but there was nothing about them, nothing that suggested they were at all interested in Jack Stein, obvious foreigner. He dismissed them and headed for the door.

Just inside he paused, checking the interior. Rufus was in place behind the bar, cleaning a glass, and the barman gave him an affable nod. Apart from that, it was virtually empty. Jack glanced around. There was no sign of McCreedy at all, but then he *was* a little early. He wandered across to the bar.

"Rufus, isn't it?" he said.

"Yes, that's right. And bourbon, isn't it?"

Jack sighed and grimaced. "Nah. It's a bit early."

"Rough night?"

Jack gave a wry half laugh. "You could say that. Do you do coffee?"

Rufus nodded. "Sure. How do you like it?"

"Short and nasty," said Jack.

"Just like your women . . ." Rufus waved his hand at Jack's questioning look. "Sorry. Old bartender's line."

Jack nodded. It was just too soon after waking.

"Seen any sign of McCreedy?" he asked.

Rufus shook his head. "It's a little early for Dog to be dragging himself out into the light. More than likely to shrivel up in flames. Why do you need him?"

"Oh, he was supposed to meet me here."

"Uh-huh. Well, if he said he'd be here, he'll be here. Dog's pretty good like that. He has to be. Couldn't run his business if he wasn't."

Hearing that was a relief.

Rufus busied himself with a coffee machine and came back a moment later with a small cup half-full of black, tarry liquid. The smell washed up into Jack's face.

"Hope it's nasty enough for you," said Rufus, and grinned.

Jack took a small sip and pressed his lips together with satisfaction. "Oh, yeah. That'll do the job." It wasn't a stimpatch but it would run a close second. Damn, but it was times like this that he still missed the things.

"So what are you doing with Dog?" asked Rufus. "Tell me to mind my own business if you don't want me to know. I'll understand. Lots of folk hereabouts don't like talking about their stuff."

Jack shrugged. "Nothing much. I'm just looking for someone." He thought he liked this guy, Rufus, but that didn't mean that he was going to spill the details to him.

"Anyone special?"

Jack declined to answer.

Yeah, it was someone special. Someone really special. He wouldn't be here if she weren't.

Rufus took the hint.

"Hey, Rufus," said Jack after another quick sip of the evil brew. "There may be something you know, though."

"Sure, if I can help." He'd gone back to cleaning glasses.

"Ever come across a guy called Maximilian Aire?"

Rufus sucked air through his teeth. "Phew. Old Million Aire. Now what do you want to go asking about him for? You're not mixed up with that crowd, are you?" He'd stopped his glass cleaning in midwipe.

"Um, no, I don't think so." Jack paused with his cup halfway to his lips.

Rufus gave a short laugh. "Well, he's not called Million Aire for nothing. He's into everything, that one. Politics, import-export, real estate. You name it."

Jack slowly lowered his cup. "Politics?"

"Yeah. You may not have heard of them—in fact, I can't see why you would have—but there's this group here. Million is rumored to be tied in with them. Radical lot. Many people aren't very happy with the sorts of things they're into. If you're mixed up with that crowd, I'd be careful."

"Okay," said Jack. "So what are they called?"

Rufus snorted. "They call themselves the Sons of Utrecht."

"Hmmmm," said Jack. He had more than just heard that name before, and it suddenly explained a lot. A lot more than Rufus could possibly imagine.

Ten

Jack spent a couple of minutes mulling that discovery over. He'd never actually managed to draw a clear link between Outreach Industries and the Sons of Utrecht. He was sure, back then, that he'd put paid to the Sons of Utrecht when he was instrumental in Christian Landerman's being put away, but that had probably been naive. An organization like that just didn't shrivel up because one of its key players disappeared from the scene. For all he knew, Landerman was still directing things from inside. Anyway, Jack had never really known how key Landerman was. This Max Aire might be higher up the food chain. Regardless, it meant he still had to be careful and remain careful, at least while he was still in Balance City. The Sons of Utrecht didn't particularly like outsiders, and especially not those of foreign extraction.

He finished the last of his coffee and gestured to Rufus for another one.

It was about a half hour later, a half hour in which Rufus left Jack alone with his thoughts, that the doors opened and Dog made his entrance.

Dog strolled up to the bar looking troubled, dressed in dark, tight-fitting synthetic trousers and a short leather jacket. Dark stubble shadowed his face. "Stein," he said.

Jack nodded. "McCreedy."

"Let's find a booth."

Jack took his cup and slid into the booth opposite him. McCreedy sat, slightly hunched, his hair obscuring his features, not saying a word.

"So," said Jack, when it was evident that McCreedy wasn't going to say anything else in a hurry. "Have you still got those papers I gave you?"

"Uh-huh," said McCreedy with a slight nod. He reached for the inside pocket of his dark leather jacket, then stopped. "Yeah, I've still got them."

"Well, did you manage to look them over?"

There was a pause. "Yeah." Finally, he looked up. "There's some pretty weird shit there, Stein. How am I supposed to make any sense of it?"

Jack sighed. He had been worried about that. "I think you've probably got more chance of doing that than I do. What's your problem?"

McCreedy chewed at his bottom lip before answering. When he did, his jaw was set in a firm line. "I know where they're going, but I don't, if you see what I mean."

"That's the point," said Jack.

McCreedy sat back, draped his arms over the back of the bench, and stared blankly at Jack for a few seconds. "Listen, Stein. I'm interested, okay. That's not it, though. I sort of get what's going on there, but I'm not sure. When it comes to piloting, I like to be sure. I've worked hard for that ship. I'm not going to fuck it up just on a whim."

"I'm not asking you to," said Jack.

McCreedy shook his head. "I don't know. You need to give me something more."

Jack nodded slowly. "Okay. Then tell me someone I can rely on to do it. Give me that much." Already he was getting a sinking feeling growing in the center of his chest.

"Look," said McCreedy, leaning forward. "Last night

I was a little . . . relaxed. I've had some time to think things through." He flicked a stray strand of hair out of his face and narrowed his eyes. "How do I know this isn't some elaborate setup? That stuff you gave me had coordinates, jump locations. I can see that much. I don't know, Stein. You could be lining me up. Who are you working for, Jack?"

Jack sat back with an exasperated sigh. "Dammit, Danny Boy . . ."

McCreedy's eyes narrowed even more. His jaw remained firmly set.

Jack shook his head, stood, and held out a hand. "Give me back the stuff then. I'll try to find someone else."

McCreedy leaned back.

"Come on. Give."

"Nah. Sit down, Stein. I just need to be sure. We go back a long way. I've got no reason to doubt you for the moment. I just need more information. You don't go off on a mission with no intel, do you? Especially if it's going to risk everything you've worked for."

Jack stood looking at him for a couple of seconds, then slowly lowered himself back into the booth. "What do you need?"

"Start at the beginning. Fill me in on the details."

Jack spent the next twenty minutes talking about Billie, Antille, the artifact, everything that went with it. McCreedy interjected with the occasional question, but for the most part he just sat back and listened.

"Okay, so you think that this Antille has cracked the key. These are his notes, right?"

Jack nodded.

Dog sat back and scratched the back of his neck. "So this kid . . . your niece . . ."

"Well, sort of . . . but that's not important. What is important is that she's okay. And time's running out. I don't know. How long can you last on a ship before things start shutting down?"

"Good question," said Dog. "It depends on the ship. Mine . . ." He shrugged. "Three weeks, maybe four. I've never had to find out."

"That's what I mean," said Jack. "We don't know. I don't know. We don't even know if they're still on this ship, but even if it's a long shot, I have got to find out."

McCreedy suddenly looked suspicious. "There's nothing else?"

"What do you mean?" said Jack.

"Well . . . maybe there's some other reason you want to find this ship apart from the girl. Maybe they were carrying something. . . ."

"Damn, but you've got a suspicious mind, McCreedy."

"And? Sometimes it pays."

"Nothing," said Jack.

Dog paused for a second, studying Jack's face, assessing. "Okay."

"Okay, what?"

"Okay, let's do it. I need some more work on this stuff to make sure what we need to do. That might take me a few hours. There's not a lot to cross-reference against. Maybe we can go to this academic you've been talking to. Get him to help. It would sure as hell make me a little more comfortable."

Jack nodded. If the kid thought he needed time to verify Antille's calculations, then who was Jack to question? Christ, and what was he doing thinking of McCreedy as a kid? Old habits died hard. Just because the last time Jack had really known McCreedy, he *had* been a kid . . . A lot had clearly happened to Dog McCreedy in the meantime. A quick image of a fresh-faced young pilot looking back over his shoulder, dark glasses obscuring his eyes, and a wide grin, the sound of rotor blades slicing through the air above them, flashed into Jack's consciousness. That had been a long time ago. A *long* time.

McCreedy was watching him. "What?" he said.

"Nothing," said Jack. "Shall we?"

"Yeah," said McCreedy, sliding out of the booth.

Outside the bar, McCreedy headed in the opposite direction from that which Jack expected. "Hey, where are you going?" he said after McCreedy's leather-clad back.

"This way. One of the reasons I drink around here. Makes things easy," he said without looking back.

Jack shrugged and followed. McCreedy led him to the end of the street, down a side street, then another. He stopped at the entrance to a narrow metal passageway leading into darkness. Jack swallowed, not liking the look of it at all. There was that metal smell and darkness in front of him, nothing else. McCreedy inclined his head.

"Go on then."

Jack swallowed, grimaced, and stepped forward—to be bathed in sudden brilliance. Illuminated walls showed the passageway leading down to a set of wide metal stairs at the end. Feeling foolish, Jack headed toward them, with Dog following close behind. The stairs were clean and unmarked and rang hollowly with each footstep. They went up a long way.

"Where's this take us?" asked Jack.

"The docks, of course. We're going up to the orbital, just like we said."

Jack was suddenly nervous again, remembering the performance he'd been through with the customs officials when he arrived.

"Um . . . what about paperwork?"

"What about it?" said Dog. "You're with me."

"It's just that . . ."

Dog put a hand on Jack's shoulder, stopping him. Jack turned and looked back down at him. Metal stairs ran behind him, white stripes glowing where the wall lighting caught their surfaces.

"Listen, just take my lead," said McCreedy. "Most of the entries and exits are automated. City systems look after that. Anyone coming up this way is local or with a local. Balance City has its reasons for letting people come and go without much fuss."

"Uh-huh," said Jack dubiously. "So explain that whole charade I went through when I arrived."

McCreedy gestured upward with his chin and Jack took the cue, turning to climb the rest of the way. McCreedy continued talking as they climbed.

"Balance City looks after its own. They'll know we're leaving. But then they always know." He gave a short laugh. "So they gave you the treatment, did they? It doesn't surprise me."

Jack filed that away, feeling like more of an idiot. He wondered briefly if it would have happened if he'd been with Billie. No. There was enough self-deprecation going on in his head as it was.

They stepped out into the now-familiar dock area with its even lines and clear directions and markings. A gentle hum moved through the vast echoing space, almost below hearing. McCreedy scratched the back of his head, grimaced, then nodded to their right.

"Down this way."

Together they walked past line after line of sleekly maintained shuttles and small personal craft. Only one or two were in less than optimum condition. Sharp lines, bristling fixtures—they all looked top-of-the-line.

"Here we are," said McCreedy.

Jack might have known. There was nothing sleek or

new about this particular craft. McCreedy shrugged, half
as an apology, but more, Jack suspected, as a "so what?"

"Nothing like the birds we used to ride around in," he
said.

"No, you're right there," said Jack, trying to keep any
feeling out of his voice.

"Yeah, well, wait till you see my baby," said Mc-
Creedy, slapping on the flier's side with one hand.

Jack was starting to feel more and more dubious. How
did someone like Dog McCreedy come by a ship with the
most up-to-date technology anyway? It had been *too* long
since he'd known Danny Boy McCreedy.

He was starting to have second thoughts about what
they were doing. "Do we need to do this?" he asked.

"What do you mean?" McCreedy paused with his
hand resting on the craft's side.

"Well, why do we need to go up there?"

There was a brief pause before McCreedy answered,
the slightest flicker of doubt on his face. "It's a matter of
trust, Jack. You show me yours; I show you mine. You
know how it works. Besides, I've got a couple of contacts
up there who might prove useful. If your friends left here,
the only place they could leave from is the orbital. We
need to check it out."

It did make sense. Jack nodded.

McCreedy opened up the craft and gestured Jack inside. He climbed in after. "Don't worry about the crap,"
he said. "Just shove anything out of your way."

A number of empty water bottles lay scattered around
the floor, with food wrappers of various colors lying here
and there amongst them. "I'll get around to cleaning it up
one of these days. This old hulk doesn't really warrant the
attention."

He strapped himself in, ignoring Jack's apparent discomfort, and started hitting control pads above his head

and in front of him. With a grimace, Jack strapped himself in too, trying to keep his eyes away from the floor and focus on the routine McCreedy was going through. It was almost as if he were back there, back in the old military transport, waiting to be ferried to wherever they were going to be dropped on that particular day. McCreedy caught him watching and grinned.

The clamps engaged under the flier, and the craft jerked. Jack thrust out his hand, but then quickly pulled it back. There was nothing he could reach anyway. He held one hand tightly in the other in his lap. They were drawn back out of the docking space in a wide arc, the docking clamps disengaged, and another set took over. The craft lurched as their direction changed and the mechanisms drew them forward.

A couple of minutes later and they had crawled toward the hangar lip. All thought of what McCreedy was up to or the state of the craft left Jack as the canyon vista crawled into view in front of and beneath them. What he'd seen from Max Aire's basement apartment was now revealed in its full daytime glory. Aire had been right: It was one hell of a view. McCreedy slapped a couple of places on the panel in front of him, and the drives kicked into life, pressing Jack back into his seat so that it creaked around him. He caught his breath. A bit of warning might have been nice. He shot a look at McCreedy, but the other man was busy doing things on his control panel and glancing out of the front viewscreen. With a sound deep in his throat, Jack decided to make the most of it, turned his attention away from McCreedy, tried to ignore the shuddering and rattling around him, and craned forward to drink in the view as they swept up and out, away from Balance City.

This was Jack's first real view of the orbital station. When he'd come in before, it was in the sealed expanse of the jump ship that had brought him to Utrecht. He'd had a brief period inside the station itself, in a transfer lounge, before being whisked into the staging area for the planetward shuttles. Now, despite the shaking and variety of noises around him, and McCreedy's lackadaisical attitude to it all, Jack was captivated by the view in front of them. McCreedy still had his feet up on the front console and his hands linked behind his head.

The orbital platform was basically flat, stretching thinly from end to end of the viewscreen. A central cylinder rotated gently at its center. From the platform, bristling outgrowths reached in every direction, with no apparent order, all of them tacked on like afterthoughts to the entire structure, as they probably were. Within the bristles, bubbles and cylinders, ovoids, and squares made lumps among the spars. Jack guessed that some of those spars were passageways to carry people from the central environment out to the various stores or workspaces attached to the orbital. All around the edges of the platform lay ships, nose in, butting up against scalloped depressions. From this distance it was hard to judge the dimensions, but it looked like most of the craft were smaller—personal transports, yachts, whatever you wanted to call them. A larger vessel sat near one corner. Jack guessed this was one of the major jump ships servicing this particular platform. Another larger ship, a freighter, sat close by, stretching out and back like a cubist dragonfly.

McCreedy sat forward, touched a few points on the console in front of him, then settled back. The rattling around them subsided slowly, and their craft banked, then aligned with the flattened top of the platform.

"Nearly there," said McCreedy. "You can remove the finger marks from my seat now."

Jack glanced down at the place McCreedy was looking, noticing for the first time the white-knuckled grip he had on the edge of his seat. He cleared his throat, looked back out of the front screen, and pulled his hand back into his lap. Okay, so he didn't travel well off-planet. He glanced back over at McCreedy, but his companion was concentrating on landing procedures, or so Jack assumed. Either that, or he was being polite, and somehow Jack just didn't think that was the case.

They bounced to a stop and Jack sat where he was, waiting. A slight vibration shook the craft; then there was a firm clunk from the side. Jack looked at McCreedy.

"Give it a couple of seconds," said McCreedy. "I never really trust the seals on these things." He checked the panel in front of him, then nodded. "Okay."

"Wait," said Jack.

"What?"

"Those papers I gave you . . ."

McCreedy frowned, flicking a strand of hair away from one eye. "What about them?"

"I just . . ." Jack grimaced.

"Look, if it will make you feel any better . . ." He dug inside his jacket and drew forth the bundle of papers, creased and crumpled now, then reached down to his feet, pulling aside a piece of flooring and sliding back a metal cover. He waved the papers at Jack before shoving them down into the hole in the floor that had been revealed and sliding the panel back in place. He kicked the piece of flooring back over it with one foot. "See? All safe and sound. Sometimes I need to keep things away from prying eyes."

Jack looked at the place beneath McCreedy's feet dubiously. Surely that would be the sort of spot someone would look for if they were doing any half-thorough search. "Yeah, okay," he said finally. The request had been just as much to see that he still had them in his possession.

McCreedy nodded and reached for something above his head, and the door slid back, revealing a shiny plastic tube with steps leading down. This part was familiar. Jack had boarded the craft that had taken him down to Utrecht through a similar arrangement. He eased himself out of his seat and descended. Jack guessed there had to be other loading mechanisms for the larger ships that traveled up and down between the orbital and the surface. The Balance City hangar, though, had shown no evidence of anything larger. But then, he was getting used to the fact by now that much of what Utrecht had to offer was kept hidden from general view . . . Balance City itself not the least of those.

The stair led down to a passageway that circled off at one end, lines of entrances evenly spaced along its length. McCreedy paused at the bottom of the stair, looked in both directions, and then gestured to the right with his head.

"Down this way. As usual, we end up with the cheap seats. We've got a bit of a trip ahead of us." He glanced up at their berth number and nodded to himself. "We can enter the main station only from the ends. Allows us to synch with the rotation." Jack knew that, but he made a slight sound indicating he understood. They traveled the rest of the way to the main junction in silence, pulling themselves forward in the lighter gravity by conveniently placed handholds along the length. Jack wondered that it wasn't completely weightless, but perhaps that was just the way things worked.

There were a number of questions he wanted to ask McCreedy, but they could wait until he had more of an impression, more of a feeling for the man. Well it was more like a reacquaintance than getting to know him, and he reminded himself of that. There was something he wanted to test, though.

"McCreedy," he said.

"Uh-huh," came the answer, McCreedy concentrating on where they were going more than anything else.

"You ever run into a guy called Maximilian Aire?"

McCreedy snorted. "Aire. Jesus. Where did you come across that name?"

"I ran into him yesterday."

McCreedy stopped and turned. "You don't just run into Max Aire. What happened?"

"We had a little chat," said Jack.

McCreedy was frowning now. "I wish you'd told me that earlier."

Jack returned the frown. "What's the problem?"

"Max Aire has fingers in everything. If he's interested in you there's a reason, and in Balance City, if Max Aire is interested in you, then you had better keep your head down. I would have taken a couple of precautions had I known."

"Okaaaay," said Jack slowly.

"No. I mean it," said McCreedy. "Why do you think he's interested?"

Jack sighed. "I'll fill you in on the details later. I have a couple of ideas, but it relates to an old case of mine."

"Well, there's nothing we can do about it. We can worry about that later. We've things to do now. Meanwhile, I'll think about our options."

They made quick progress up the accessway and were soon through the rotationals and into the station proper, or at least onto the central spine, where they were whisked downward to the outer ring by a rapidly moving transport platform. When they'd reached floor level, McCreedy led them through a series of portals and into the main environment, looking completely at home. The structure was large, not as large as a city, but large all the same, and Jack felt slightly lost, staring up at the

metallic ceiling far above him. The orbital was broken into
several commercial regions, and residences clustered in
discrete locations along the length. The cylinder's outside
was broken alternately with ground space, slightly leveled
to hide the curve—it was supposed to be psychological—
and broad expanses of windows. McCreedy took a couple
of minutes to get his bearings while Jack waited patiently,
then pointed them to a moving walkway.

"This will take us to where we want to go," he said,
beckoning Jack to follow.

Ten minutes later, having traveled through a district of
hotels and restaurants, and past a gaudy shopping mall,
they stepped off the walkway, and McCreedy walked past
a few nondescript buildings and through a colorful illuminated archway set into a flat expanse of wall that di-
vided one section from another.

On the other side sat a reasonably flat, grassed area, a
line of benches set at discrete intervals, in front of one of
a broad set of windows. Jack paused, looking at the grass.

"Is this real?" asked Jack.

"Nah," said McCreedy. "But it looks real, doesn't it?
All the comforts of home. You get tired of the plastics
after a while, though. You start to notice the smell. True
station rats like it. Me, I don't. I guess I spent too much
time in the jungle."

He waved Jack forward eagerly. "Here."

Tall railings separated the pseudo-glass from the window display, but they were cunningly constructed with
connecting bars allowing you to lean or sit as you chose,
giving an uninterrupted view of the orbital's bristling ex-
tensions and, where you could see it, the darkened space
beyond.

McCreedy was leaning forward, staring across the
struts and nodules. "This was one thing I never got tired
of, though," he said. "Imagine what this was like before

all that shit happened. Just take a second to imagine what it would have looked like without all of that crap in the way."

Jack tried, leaning his own elbows on the railing, mirroring McCreedy's position. Yeah, he could see the attraction. At that moment the flat platform swung into view, slowly creeping across the viewing area. Watching it, Jack had to remind himself that it was they that were moving, not the platform.

"That's it there," said McCreedy, pointing.

Jack hadn't even noticed the ships. His attention had been completely absorbed by the moving platform. He followed McCreedy's outstretched hand. A sleek white shape projected out from the platform edge, its slightly bulbous nose snuggling into the depression.

"That," said McCreedy, "is *Amaranth*. Beautiful, no?" He seemed captivated by the vision of his own craft.

The ship slowly swung past, and McCreedy's gaze tracked it as it went, gradually slipping out of sight below and behind them, finally obscured by the lip of the viewing area.

It looked like McCreedy had been telling the truth. That bulb toward the front could mean only one thing: McCreedy's ship had the needed drive.

There was one more thing it meant, one more thing about Daniel McCreedy, but it was something Jack wasn't sure he wanted to deal with yet.

Eleven

Jack was suitably impressed, but he made a note to hold the obvious question forming in his head until later: How the hell had someone like Dog McCreedy come across a ship like that? Being here, staring out at the starscape, had given Jack another idea. He wasn't sure how these places worked, but there was bound to be someone who knew where Billie and Antille's ship had been headed. Wasn't there?

"Dog," he said.

McCreedy pulled himself away from the railings, still looking thoughtfully at the place where his ship had just slowly swung past. "Hmmm?"

"Do they keep records of departures and arrivals here somewhere?"

Dog tilted his head to one side and grinned. "Great minds think alike. Well, the answer is, they do and they don't."

"I'm not sure I understand."

Dog leaned back on the railing, propping his elbows up behind him, and grinned. "Think about it, Jack," he said. "This place maintains itself by being a convenient safe haven for ships. Half of Utrecht's business comes from import-export. Sometimes you don't want people to know what you're carrying and where you're carrying it to, if you know what I mean." He tapped the side of his nose.

Jack looked around and then leaned over to stare at the green-white arc of Utrecht just swinging into view. "I don't see what they have to export. I didn't see many signs of real industry down there."

"Well, you wouldn't."

Jack frowned and looked sideways at McCreedy. "What do you mean?"

"There's a lot of high technology. Production in small plants hidden in places throughout the forestlands. They keep it politely out of the way so people don't have to think what they're doing."

"But where do they get their materials?"

"Some of it here, but a lot of it is where the import part of it comes in. Like that freighter we saw on the way in. You did see it, right?"

Jack nodded. "Yeah."

"There are a few cash crops produced on Utrecht too. One or two in particular, and they're either shipped off-world directly, or wind up in the pharmaceutical plants. There's big business in all of that. You can guess how many people are dependent upon those products, either directly or indirectly."

Jack stood there thinking about that for a couple of seconds before pushing himself back from the railing and turning to face McCreedy. "So when do we get to see this famous ship of yours properly?"

Again Dog grinned. "Now's as good a time as any, right? I was getting tired of waiting for you to ask. Wait a minute while I get our bearings."

He turned and faced the viewing area, linking his fingers behind his neck. "Ah, here she comes." The platform edge swung back into view. Dog nodded as he marked the place where the *Amaranth* was berthed, then inclined his head away from the direction they had come. "We're better off going this way. It's longer, but it'll give you a chance to see a bit more of the orbital as well. There's someone I need to see on the way, and maybe, just maybe, we might be able to help you out with your little question."

"My little question?"

"Sure. You want to find out if anybody knows the logged coordinates of your niece's ship. Don't you?"

Jack cleared his throat. "Yeah."

Dog grinned again and tapped at his temple with one finger, shaking his head before turning and leading the way along the edge of the wide viewing port.

Jack suppressed the sound he wanted to make deep in his throat. McCreedy might just get annoying before this whole thing was over.

They crossed the short swath of parkland in a couple of minutes, coming to another arched doorway in the dividing strut wall that segmented the orbital's cylinder into sections. The next area was purely utilitarian, broad, undecorated metallic spaces broken only by connecting conduits, wide struts, and tall stacks of metal containers. Various logos and marks and numbers identified each of the containers. Within the stacks sat loading machinery, all currently idle. Their footsteps echoed from the container walls, and though the place was well lit, shadows crisscrossed their path. Dog barely even looked at the containers, picking his path between them naturally, for although there was no straight route between the stacks, always in front of them stood the next dividing wall, stretching up and above.

"So how do they get this stuff up and down from the surface?" asked Jack.

McCreedy answered without looking back. "Oh, they have heavy carrier shuttles as well. You wouldn't have seen any of them at Balance City, though. There's no call for them there. BC's more involved with administration and finance. They only need people carriers for that. This stuff"—he slapped one of the containers in passing—"gets deposited elsewhere. Mustn't clutter the capital." He gave a wry snort.

He led Jack into the next area, and this, right near the orbital's heart, was more functional. Pseudo-streets and small square buildings made up the bulk of the inner surface, broken again by a large set of viewing windows. Psychologically, Jack guessed it made sense. It was far better to see a sky on either side of you rather than buildings and people at right angles to where you stood. He could just see the edge of another set of buildings hanging above the viewing area, which was a bit unsettling. He had a vision of someone dropping something from above and it falling to impale him as he walked below. He knew it was stupid, but he couldn't help the impression, and he glanced nervously upward, feeling his shoulders tighten. He resolved to keep his attention focused on where they were going.

Dog led the way down a small side passageway between the buildings and stopped outside a door. CENTRAL RECORDS, said the sign.

"Yeah," said Dog as he caught Jack studying the sign. "Even though they're discreet about it, they still have an unhealthy dose of the Utrecht spirit about them." He shrugged and knocked.

"Yes," said a voice from inside. Jack noted the building had no windows. Nor did any that surrounded them. Bureaucratic heaven, thought Jack. Little cells within a hive. Another sign behind him said LADING. Farther down the alley, he thought he could see FUEL TAX, or at least something that looked like it.

Dog opened the door and stepped inside. Jack

followed after. A man, his beard obscuring most of his face, wearing thick glasses and a rumpled shirt, looked up inquisitively.

"Can I— Dog McCreedy! The last man I expected to see alive." The speaker pushed back his chair and stood, reaching out a hand to grip Dog's, his other hand reaching automatically for Dog's elbow.

McCreedy laughed. "Hey, Steve. Yeah, the old Dog's still alive, hard as it may be to believe."

The man called Steve chuckled. "Well, apparently the alcohol poisoning or the kreff hasn't gotten you yet."

"Yeah, yeah. And I see you're buried in your burrow. Still down the rabbit hole."

Steve retook his chair and gestured to the edge of the desk. "Take a seat." He barely glanced at Jack. Meanwhile, Jack looked around the small office, searching for somewhere to put himself. He resorted to leaning back against one wall.

"So, Dog. How have you been keeping down among the planet-huggers?"

"Yeah, I've been doing okay," said Dog, propping himself on the edge of the desk. "How about you?"

"You know what it's like," said Steve. "Work, the clubs, the occasional brawl. We have to keep ourselves amused."

"Heh," said Dog. "Yeah, I know."

"How about planetside?"

Steve leaned back in his chair and reached up to toy with a graying area of his beard at one side of his chin as he waited for the response. Dog rubbed the back of his neck. "Well, you know. They keep their heads firmly up their own asses, so they can't see little ol' me. Utrecht's still Utrecht. BC's just the same. How long since you've been down?"

Steve looked thoughtful. "Nearly two years, I think. You can have it."

"Ah, it's not that bad. We keep each other sane, and it has its own advantages."

"You can have them too," said Steve with a snort.

Jack was getting a little tired with this back-and-forth and wished McCreedy would just get on with it. Somehow they seemed like an unlikely pair, but who could tell in a closed community like the orbital? Enclosed environments made for unusual bonding. Just like the military. Jack cleared his throat.

"So who is your friend?" asked Steve finally.

"Old pal from the services," said Dog. "We go way back."

Steve nodded without looking at Jack. There wasn't going to be a great deal of conversation there. Jack was clearly along for the ride. He scanned the office. A broad screen sat on the edge of the desk, still with lists of figures on it. Shelves and shelves of memory cubes took up the wall space behind Steve, some with hastily scrawled tags in an illegible script. One wall was completely blank. A couple of empty disposable food containers lay on the floor behind Steve's chair, and a writing block and stylus lay in front of him on the desk. Jack guessed this man didn't have much interaction with other people in his day-to-day work. He continued propping up one wall while Steve and Dog talked, still small talk.

"Okay," said Steve. "Why are you here, Dog?"

"I've got a favor to ask."

"Tell me."

"Jack here's looking for a ship."

Steve glanced over and gave Jack a narrow-eyed look that was barely discernible behind the thick lenses. "Hmmm," he said.

"Listen, Steve. Jack's okay. Put it like this. I'm looking for this ship too."

Steve returned his gaze to Dog's face. "Okay. Because it's you. No other reason. Name?"

"Jack?" asked Dog.

Jack shook his head. "No idea."

Dog sighed. "Well, that's a lot of use."

"Wait," said Jack. "It was a ship associated with the university in some way."

"UBC?" asked Dog.

"Yeah."

"Well, okay," said Steve. "That makes things a little easier. When was it in?" He leaned forward and reached for his screen.

"They would have left a couple of weeks ago. It might not have been a university ship specifically. The professor there said something about sponsorship. From what I know about their work, I think it could have something to do with Outreach."

Dog shot him a sudden suspicious glance. Jack noted and made the pretense of ignoring it.

Steve merely nodded. He tapped with one finger on the screen surface, then dragged the display down, scanning the lines. He tapped and dragged again, doing another scan. "What were they carrying?" he asked.

"Nothing important, as far as I know," said Jack. "People. Maybe some equipment—archeological equipment, something like that."

"Hmmm," said Steve thoughtfully. He went through the tap-and-drag sequence a couple more times in succession, then stopped. "Okay, this might be what you're looking for. Private freighter. Registered to Symbala."

"Symbala?" said Dog.

"Mmm-hmmmmm," said Steve. "It's an Outreach sub. Not too many people know that."

He leaned forward, peering more closely at the screen. "Hmmm." He tapped a couple of times and the screen changed. "No manifest. Passengers not listed." He tutted. "Can't have that." He closed the display and retuned to the former list, scrolling up and down a couple of times. "It looks like it's your likely candidate in the time period. Everything else is either local or long-haul old freighters around that time."

"When?" said Jack.

Steve looked at him briefly, then returned to the screen. "Thirteen days. No, fourteen now."

Christ, a full two weeks.

"Can you give us anything more?" said Jack.

Steve gave him a round-eyed affronted look. "What do you think I am?" he said. Then he smiled, and there was an element of mischief in it. "Of course I can. Regard!"

He tapped at a couple of points on the screen, then turned to face the wall, gesturing with one open hand for Jack to do likewise. Jack stepped back to look. The blank wall was no longer blank. Loading vehicles hoisted containers through the cargo port of a small dark ship. The picture panned, showing the activity, but also revealing the ship's shape. It too had the telltale bulbous nose indicating jump capability.

"Zoom, center," said Steve, and the picture swept in to focus on what was being loaded. They were not the standard containers, and emblazoned on one end was a logo. The whole sequence was a recorded segment of dock activity. Jack might have guessed that they kept their own private records of everything that went on.

"Can you focus on that?" said Jack, pointing.

"Certainly," said Steve. "Pushy, your friend, isn't he?" This latter was to Dog, who merely grinned.

For a hairy bureaucrat locked in the bowels of a rotating tin can, this Steve had a good slice of attitude.

Steve tapped at his screen, then said, "Focus container." The mark was the UBC crest.

"Okay," said Jack. "That's the ship."

"Good," said Steve. "Hold on a minute." He tapped at his screen a couple of times and the view shifted. A man in pilot's coveralls with an official-looking company logo was entering the hatch. Steve zoomed the picture. "Look familiar?"

Jack shook his head. "No."

Steve skipped the sequence to another. The pilot was back, but with him were two familiar figures. One was the portly, dark-skinned Antille, looking older than the image Jack had of him, and the second was all too familiar.

"Billie," he breathed, catching himself almost leaning toward the wallscreen. She wore jeans and a plain white top. Her blond hair was a little longer, and tied back away from her face. She was in animated conversation with Antille. That was typical. Typical Billie.

The hatch shut, and Billie was locked away.

"Yeah, that's it," said Jack. "That's the one." Inside he felt hollow.

Twelve

"Wait outside for a minute, will you, Jack?" said Dog.

Jack flashed him a quick frown, but slipped outside as requested, tearing his gaze away from Billie's fading image. He shut the door quietly beside him.

It was a full five minutes before Dog appeared, five minutes in which Jack was left with the cold emptiness ringing inside him. Billie had looked fine, but there was nothing to say she was still fine. She could be floating in deep space somewhere, chilly and airless in the outer reaches. He forced the image from his mind. What the hell was Dog doing anyway?

McCreedy closed the door quietly behind him and indicated they should leave.

"What was all that about?" said Jack.

Dog flashed him a quick sign, one he hadn't seen for years, a brief hand signal indicating they were being watched. Jack gave the slightest of nods and strode quickly toward the junction they had come from, Dog closely following at his heels. When they reached the end, Jack stopped.

"So?"

"Just some insurance. I'll tell you about it later."

"Damn," said Jack. Seeing Billie in the replay had thrown him off. "We didn't ask about the destination."

"Covered," said Dog. "Nothing. I checked after you went outside."

Jack sighed. "So what now?"

"I still have to see someone," said Dog. "I can leave you at one of the rec stations while I take care of business; then we can go and check out *Amaranth*."

"I'm not so sure I like all this surveillance." Jack ran his fingers through his hair and shook his head. "Damn well felt like I was being watched in Balance City, and now I *know* I am."

"There are ways of dealing with it," said Dog. "Don't worry."

"Okay," said Jack, but Dog's offhand dismissal didn't fill him with confidence. "Lead the way," he said, resigned to letting the younger man take the initiative.

Dog deposited him in a rec center, just as he'd suggested. It was the normal sort of transit facility. There were game machines, interactive programs, information and communications booths, and Jack was thankful, somewhere where he could sit and have coffee. The staff was pleasant enough, and they left him to his own devices without intruding on his space. The coffee wasn't half-bad either. It wasn't until he was nearing the bottom of his third cup that Dog reappeared.

"Right," he said. "Business done." He slapped his hands together in a dusting-off motion. "Come on, Stein. Let's go and see my baby."

Dog led the way through a series of rotationals similar to those they'd been through before and into the low-gravity region of the loading areas. Jack felt queasy all the way through. He hated low gravity. It was no better when they reached the *Amaranth,* and he had difficulty really paying attention to the things Dog pointed out as he gave him a brief guided tour. As far as Jack was concerned, it was a ship. He grabbed a handhold and stood uncomfortably, waiting for Dog to give him his full attention.

"Okay, McCreedy. I want to know some things. Can we talk here?"

Dog glanced around, frowned, and gave a little shake of his head. "Sure, why not?"

"That look you gave me back at the records place when I mentioned Outreach. What was that about?"

Dog looked like he was going to say something, then stopped. He turned his face away.

"Come on, McCreedy. It's got to be about something."

The young man turned away, then crossed to a seat and sat, pulling a grip into place to keep him in position. "Yeah, all right. How do you think I could get hold of a drive, Jack? Where does a shuttle jockey like me find the resources for something like this? Sure, I run legitimate contracts. Sure, I work hard at it too. I also do a bit of stuff on the side. I've got a rep, and I worked hard to get it. The right people heard. Some of those people work for big companies, and sometimes those big companies want things done and they want them done quickly and quietly."

"And one of those companies is Outreach," said Jack.

Dog nodded slowly. There was a pause before he answered. "It seemed like a fair trade to me."

Jack looked around the small space they now occupied. Everything was pristine. Banks of instruments that meant nothing to Jack covered the walls, and comfortable seats sat at strategic locations. He'd already seen the cargo area and the cabins. All of it, every single part, was slick and new, in total contrast to the small flier they'd come up in.

"Nothing's without a catch, Dog," said Jack. "What's the catch?"

McCreedy sighed. "Bottom line, from time to time I'm at their beck and call." He shrugged. "It doesn't happen very often, but when it does, I'm expected to jump." He gave a short, hard laugh. "Literally. But like I said, it doesn't happen very often."

"What sort of stuff?"

Dog didn't meet Jack's eyes. "I don't ask."

A drawn-out silence filled the small space.

Jack was suddenly torn. There was coincidence and there was coincidence. Running into McCreedy was the type of thing that happened to him regularly, but that McCreedy should have some link to Outreach too . . . that made him distinctly uncomfortable. It didn't look like McCreedy himself was at ease with the relationship, and that was a potential positive. He studied the man as he thought. He could be simply overreacting. The name Outreach Industries was usually enough to raise his hackles, but this time it could be nothing more than that—mere coincidence. Outreach Industries kept coming back like a bad smell that wouldn't leave him alone. Right now, though, he had no other option.

"Talk to me, Jack," said Dog, finally breaking the uncomfortable silence.

"So what's your interest? How come you want to get involved in this?"

"Like I told you, Jack, I need to break things up a bit. I like the idea. Alien worlds, all that. You have to admit, it's kinda captivating. . . ."

Jack looked at Dog dubiously, but he could see the light in the younger man's eyes. Okay—good enough for now.

"So did you get anywhere with that stuff I gave you?"

"Sort of. I'm not a hundred percent certain."

"Well, don't you need to be certain?" asked Jack.

Dog nodded. "Mostly."

Jack simply stared at him. This was interstellar navigation. How could it be mostly?

Dog spread his hands wide. "There's no point going into the finer details, but it's pretty simple. There are paths and there are not paths." He shook his head. "I don't know a better way to explain it. I didn't do a degree in this stuff. I learned it the hard way. You know. I graduated from flying shuttles to flying ships. Then I graduated to jump ships. I know the way it works, and I know how to do it. I can't explain the physics behind it. If you're a little bit out, then there's a correction mechanism built into reality, if you like." He drummed on the arm of his seat, clearly looking for a way to dispel Jack's dubious expression. "Okay, say you want to go in a certain place in Balance City. You don't go straight there. Utrecht, BC, perhaps you ask for directions when you get there. The first part of the process is getting to Balance City, right? No, okay, bad example. Let's try it again." He thought for a moment. "Take the city. There are roads; there are shuttle routes. You can walk, or you can catch the shuttle. The shuttle follows a particular route, and when you're inside the shuttle, you have to follow that route. You have the option to get off at a number of points along the way, but the path remains the same." He nodded. "Yeah. Jump space is like that. The pathways are the roads. The jump ship is a shuttle." He laughed. "Okay, so I'm still a shuttle jockey after all. There go my big dreams." He flicked the hair out of his eyes, giving Jack a wry smile.

Dreams. Big dreams. That was what Jack needed right now—a big dream. One that made sense, and not the sort Dog was talking about.

"Okay," said Jack, deliberately not picking up on McCreedy's self-effacing humor. "I get it. So what else do you need?"

"Some sort of confirmation that what I'm interpreting from those notes is right. I could be way off. And if I'm way off, we're way off, if you see what I mean."

"Hmmmm," said Jack. He repositioned himself, changing the hand that was steadying him. He wasn't sure whether Heering knew enough to be able to give them guidance, but if they went and saw Heering, then it would send a signal to whoever was watching him. He didn't think there was any other choice. Anything to get out of this perpetual feeling that he'd lost the bottom of his stomach. "Like you said, we can try the guy at the university," he said finally.

Dog nodded. "I think that would help."

He swiveled his chair and looked at the console display. "It's late now. No time to do it today. We can go down there, but by the time we got back . . ."

"So you're saying we should stay up here?"

"Sure. We could stay on the *Amaranth*."

Dog was a little too enthusiastic about the idea. "No, thanks," said Jack. "Isn't there somewhere in there? I could do with something more solid around me."

"Sure, there are hotels there, if that's what you want. But you might as well get used to it."

Jack snorted. There was no way he was going to get used to it. Ever.

Dog shrugged. "Okay, if that's really what you want. We can head down first thing in the morning. Meanwhile, I can show you a few highlights of the rat race. Subject you to a bit of real station life."

Anything. Anything to keep him on semisolid "ground" for a while.

Jack woke to stare blearily at an unfamiliar ceiling. His head felt like someone had taken the contents, shaken them, and poured them back in again. His mouth felt furry. He reached up with thumb and forefinger, working at eyes that felt like they'd been glued together, then opened them and closed them a couple of times to try to work some of the blurriness out of his vision. He had no clue where he was. Snatches of the previous evening skittered through his ponderous thoughts. A bar—no, several bars—and some old friends of Dog's, and . . . He groaned. Damn, he was getting too old for this. There was a stirring and snuffling beside him, then mouth sounds, then stillness again. Slowly he turned his head, and more memories came back to him. Curly dark hair, a smooth, rounded back, olive skin, broad hips. That's right. The redhead and the brunette. Apparently Jack had wound up with the brunette. In his half-awake state, Jack looked at the woman lying beside him. Not the usual sort he went for. Images of large breasts bouncing up and down above him and the curve of a rounded belly drifted into his consciousness. Full, dark lips on his dick. Damn, he couldn't even remember her name. Either of their names. He guessed Dog had ended up with the redhead. Nora? Dora? And his companion was . . . Sveta. Yeah, that seemed right.

Jack wrinkled his nose. The room still smelled of sex. And by the way he was feeling, they'd certainly had that. He tried to sit up and groaned again. It had been a while since he'd used those particular muscles. His lower abdomen was sore. Painfully he levered himself upright. Now, where the hell were his clothes?

Sveta—he was sure now that was her name—rolled over, turning to lie on her stomach, her face toward him. She half opened her eyes.

"Hey," she said.

"Hey," said Jack. "Morning."

"Yeah." She reached out a hand and stroked his arm with her fingertips. "How are you feeling?"

Jack gave a wordless groan.

"Yeah," she said.

Jack was still looking for his clothes, feeling slightly awkward with his nakedness. He knew it was irrational, but it was there all the same.

"I had fun last night," said Sveta.

"Mmmm," said Jack. He thought he had. He ran his fingers through his hair, trying to smooth it into place. He didn't want to think what it must look like. He rubbed his chin, rough with stubble. As rough as he felt.

"What are you looking for, hon?" she asked sleepily.

"Clothes."

"Don't worry about that. Grab a robe from over there." She waved vaguely in the direction of a built-in wardrobe. "We can sort that out after breakfast."

Breakfast was the last thing on his mind. There was only one word in his consciousness now, one big word underlined and in bold: coffee.

He staggered over to the wardrobe, slid it open, and reached for a robe hanging there. Dark blue with pink flowers. Lovely. He didn't see that there was much other choice, and he pulled it on. It was way too short, barely covering his modesty.

"Kitchen's out there," mumbled Sveta. "Help yourself. I'll be out in a little while. If you need the bathroom, it's down the hall."

He closed the door quietly, and headed toward the bathroom. There were voices from the kitchen. So Dog and his friend were already up. He glanced down at the robe and grimaced. When he'd finished, he followed the sound of voices back out to the kitchen. Last night's memories were still vague, and he hadn't had much of a chance to check out the apartment.

As he entered, Dog was sitting at a small round table in the center with a mug of something in front of him. He looked up and grinned. The smell of breakfast stuffs filled his nostrils as he walked into the room. The redhead had her back to him, doing something at the counter. Both were already fully dressed.

"Oh, lovely," said Dog. "Suits you, Jack. What do you think, Nora?"

She turned from what she was doing and gave Jack a shy smile. "Good morning," she said. "Can I get you something?"

Jack dropped his gaze, just checking. He was still conscious of the robe's shortness.

"Yeah, coffee would be good. Thanks."

She looked thoughtful for a moment. Pale skin, green eyes. She had a sweet smile. "I think we have some. Wait, let me look."

Oh, great, thought Jack. He could guess what sort of coffee that might be. Anyone who said they *thought* they had coffee usually had some sort of generic crap for the occasional visitor. It would just have to do.

She checked in some cupboards, and finally located what she was looking for. "Ah, here, I thought so."

Jack was right.

"How do you have it?" asked Nora, turning, package in one hand, spoon in the other.

"Strong. Real strong and with nothing, thanks," said Jack. The stronger it was the less likely it was to curl the insides of his mouth, but the way his mouth was feeling, he suspected it wouldn't matter much. He sat, pulling the robe tighter about himself.

Dog was still flashing him a knowing grin, but Jack, first glancing in Nora's direction, waved it away with a slight frown. Dog just shrugged and kept grinning.

"We ought to get moving soon," said Jack.

"Yeah. I'm not the one holding us up, though," said Dog, glancing meaningfully at Jack's borrowed robe.

"Yeah, yeah. Give me a chance to get some coffee into me, and then it shouldn't take me long."

"How's Sveta?" asked Dog.

"Yeah, fine."

"So where is she?"

"Oh," said Nora, bringing Jack's coffee. "I wouldn't expect her to emerge for a while yet. She's on a late roster today."

Jack held the urge to wrinkle his nose. The coffee smelled as bad as he had expected. He took a tentative sip and then a larger one, swallowing while trying to ignore the taste. "Thanks," he said.

He sipped again in the awkward silence. "So what do you two do?" he asked finally. "You probably told me last night, but I can't remember."

"Oh, we're loader drivers. We work shifts loading containers. Not very exciting, but it gets us by."

Jack nodded and sipped at his coffee. Nora reached for Dog's hand and held it, resting lightly on the tabletop.

"So how do you know Dog?" she asked.

He shot a look at McCreedy, but Dog gave a one-shouldered shrug.

"Oh, we go back a ways," said Jack. "Military originally."

She nodded, and then they lapsed into silence again. She turned to watching her fingers playing with Dog's hand. Fortunately, before long the coffee was cool enough to down in a couple of large swallows. He placed the mug on the table and stood. "Well, I'd better get myself together."

He headed back to the bedroom, opening the door quietly. Sveta was asleep again. He located his clothes, strewn casually over a chair, bundled them, and headed for the shower. A short time later he was dressed and halfway presentable. He headed back to the bedroom, draped the robe over the chair, and then crouched down beside the bed. He reached out with one hand and gently stroked her cheek. She groaned and opened her eyes, not all the way.

"Hey," said Jack. "I've got to go now."

"Mmmm," she said. "See you, hon. Drop in if you're through again. It was fun."

"Yeah," said Jack, but her eyes were already closed and he was staring into the emptiness that walked out of the room with him.

Though Dog seemed to have enjoyed being back up there, Jack was just as happy to leave the place. There was just too much that was disorienting, out of true alignment in the orbital—including what he had seen of its inhabitants. He was full of talk about what a great time he'd had when he was one of the "station rats," as he referred to them. Jack couldn't help wondering: If he'd had such a great time, how come he was down on Utrecht?

Jack still felt pretty rough by the time they boarded Dog's small, messy shuttle, and he wasn't really in the mood for conversation. He folded his arms, sat back, and watched the view of the approaching planet. Dog quickly got the hint and seemed content to leave him to it.

Something was teasing at the back of Jack's consciousness, something about last night, but he couldn't quite put his finger on it. He forced his sluggish thought processes to focus. Somewhere there was something he knew he should be remembering. He ran the events over, gradually piecing together images of the bar, the women, the apartment, the strenuous, sweaty activities in the bedroom. They'd been nice enough, a welcome change from the solitude and his own devices that solitude implied. Still, there was something strangely removed and impersonal about it all. Fleeting, shallow. Primal. Yeah, that was the word. The first time had been quick. The second better. But that wasn't it. There was something else. He scanned his memories of the bars they'd been drinking in, and the club, the pounding music, the bodies moving, but there was nothing there he thought he should be remembering.

He grimaced. Something simple. Something he should know.

Then he had it. He'd dreamed. After everything, in that pleasant half-asleep state, he'd drifted. He scrabbled after the images, the fleeting smoke-thought that went with disappearing dreams after the fact. The creatures had been back. He was pretty sure that he'd been in that place with the multilegged silvery beings. They'd been observing him. He had the impression that they'd been watching him, even though they had nothing he could equate to eyes. He had been lying on something, and they had ringed him, observing, simply watching. Dammit, he had enough people watching him as it was, without a bunch of strange aliens getting in on the act as well. . . .

He struggled for something more, but that was it. So what was the significance? He turned it this way and that in his mind, but there was nothing further he could divine.

Thirteen

It was early afternoon, Balance City time, by the time they got in, landed, and debarked. Jack was beginning to wonder how he was ever going to keep up with the time changes. It was playing havoc with his energy levels. As they left the dock area, Dog stopped him.

"So what now?"

Jack thought for a couple of minutes. "I need a proper coffee and a change of clothes. Need to get my brain functioning again. I can do all of that back at the hotel and put in a call to Heering as well. He might be able to help you with the notes." Dog had them tucked inside his jacket again, and he patted them and nodded.

"So," Jack continued, "why don't you meet me at my hotel in about two hours? That will give me time to get back and get myself in order. I'll throw my things together, and then once we've seen Heering I can check out. I'd like to get under way as quickly as we can."

"Isn't that going to cost you extra?"

"What?"

"Checking out in the early evening. Normally they expect you to leave in the morning."

"I don't care about that," Jack said. "If Billie's been on that ship for more than a couple of weeks, time's got to be running out. I can't afford to wait around."

"I'd like to do some things too before taking off on this grand adventure of yours, Jack. Wouldn't it be better to leave first thing in the morning?"

Jack grimaced. "Look, let's see what Heering comes up with. We can decide things from there. I just don't want to waste any more time."

McCreedy chewed at his bottom lip. "So where are you staying?"

Jack told him, and Dog nodded, pursing his lips in a sign of approval. "Nice. Well, I know what I'd do."

"Yeah, I can guess what you would do, Danny Boy . . . sorry . . . Dog. Okay, we're set? Two hours in the lobby."

Dog nodded and slapped him on the shoulder. "It's a date." He spun on his heel and disappeared on up the street, leaving Jack to his own devices. As soon as he'd gotten his bearings, it wasn't hard for Jack to find his way back to the hotel. Once there, he showered again, sniffing at his shirt and crumpling it in a ball before shoving it in the bottom of his bag. Cleaning would have to wait. What he needed was a set of self-cleaners, but they were right out of his price range. He thought better of it, shoved it into a laundry bag, along with the rest of the stuff that he'd been wearing over the last few days, and, after dressing, headed down to the lobby. He didn't know how long they'd be gone, and a ship was a confined space. Two men together in an enclosed ship would start to get a little gamy after a few days, and he didn't know if McCreedy had a self-cleaner on the *Amaranth*. Jack handed the bag over to the desk clerk. Yes, he knew it would be an extra charge for having it ready later that day. Yes, he didn't mind paying the cost. Yes, he would sign for it.

With a sigh, he made his way back up to his room, shaking his head.

Time to put in a call to Heering. With the Sons of

Utrecht showing an interest, and the previous experiences with the artifact, Jack didn't want Heering getting spooked. Someone like Dog turning up out of the blue was unlikely to yield positive results. He made the call . . . and got Heering's assistant. He couldn't remember the young man's name.

"Hi. Jack Stein. You remember me. Is Dr. Heering there?"

The young man looked out from the screen blankly, then seemed to recover himself. "It is terrible," he said seriously.

"What do you mean?" asked Jack. "Is Heering there or not?"

"I do not know what he did," said the assistant.

"Listen, you're not making sense. Can I talk to Dr. Heering, please?"

"Dr. Heering is not here. I don't know if I should be talking to you."

"What do you mean, he's not there?"

The young man chewed at his bottom lip. "Some men came and took him away. They asked him many questions and then they took him away. His office. It is a mess." He shook his head gravely.

Jack leaned in closer to the screen. "What men? What sort of questions?"

"I do not know."

Jack was becoming frustrated. "Look, you told me a second ago that they asked him questions and then took him away."

The assistant pursed his lips and looked down. "I heard them talking in Dr. Heering's office. I was not inside. I did not listen. Their voices were loud, though, and I heard some words, though not very many. I saw them leaving. I watched them through the window. That is all I can tell you." He reached to break the connection.

"No, wait!" said Jack hurriedly. "I'm sorry. Can you tell me anything about these men?"

"They were wearing suits. They were too far away. They were carrying files and a computer."

"And there's nothing else you can think of?"

The assistant shook his head. "No. I don't think I should be talking to you anymore." He looked afraid and glanced back over his shoulder, as if expecting the mysterious suits to reappear at any moment.

"What color were these suits? Can you describe the men?"

"I am not sure. They had very short hair. Big men. The suits . . . maybe blue, or green. I cannot think."

Green suits. Oh, yeah, Jack could think.

"Just one last thing," said Jack. "Do you know what they were asking about? Any idea? Any idea at all?"

"I am sorry," he said, and this time cut the connection.

Damn. Jack sat back, chewing his bottom lip. He could be completely off base, but he didn't think so. Max Aire was becoming a little too interested in the dealings of Jack Stein, and Jack didn't like it a bit. The fact that they'd taken stuff away with them made it even more likely, knowing Heering's connection to the work Antille had been doing on the artifact and the Sons of Utrecht's previous involvement.

Unless there was another player in the game. Jack didn't particularly like that thought either. The thing that was really worrying him was that there was a game at all. He'd come here with the intention of finding out what had happened to Billie, nothing more, and it was quickly turning into something else. Billie still remained his first priority.

He glanced at the time display. Dog was due in about fifteen minutes, and still Jack hadn't managed to get his coffee. With his lips set into a tight line, he headed back down to the lobby.

He ordered a coffee and was three sips in when Mc-Creedy appeared at the lobby's front. He too had cleaned himself up and changed. His long, dark hair was still damp. He nodded to Jack and made his way over, slumped into a seat opposite, and gestured for attention.

"Beer," he said, and waited till the server disappeared before leaning forward, propping his elbows on his knees. "So, any luck with this guy at the university?"

Jack put his cup down carefully. "We have a slight problem."

"Oh? And what's that?"

"Heering's not there. He's suffered a little bout of disappearance."

Dog sat back. "Um."

"Yeah," said Jack.

The server reappeared with Dog's beer, forestalling conversation for the moment. They both waited until he had withdrawn.

"Well, that is a problem," said Dog. "Any idea why?"

"I have a couple of ideas," said Jack. "He was helped. It seems that someone's quite interested in what's going on. Let us just say that it doesn't sound like his disappearance was entirely voluntary."

"Hmmmm." Dog was clearly thinking, and he drained half his glass while he did so. "So is there anyone else?"

Jack looked around the lobby before answering, checking the look of the people, searching for anything suspicious, anything that might indicate they were being watched as well, but the place looked clean. "Not that I know about. My other friend at the university kept things pretty close to his chest. I don't think he was a big one for sharing. I also think I was just lucky that Heering was around."

"Heh, Lucky Stein."

"Or not so lucky, depending on how you look at it."

Dog drained the last of his beer in a couple of quick swallows. "So what do you want to do?"

Jack took a deep breath, then let it out slowly. "I don't think I've got a choice," he said. "I have to follow a hunch, see if I can track down Heering. I don't know how much success I'm going to have, but we need some sort of confirmation before leaping into nothingness. You've convinced me of that much. I need to follow this. It may take me a few hours. Where can I get hold of you if I need to?"

Dog nodded. "You take what you need. I'll be around. You can probably find me at the bar if you need me. Either that or I'll let Rufus know where I am, unless you've got another suggestion."

"No, that works." Jack thought for a moment. He didn't want to let McCreedy know of his intentions just yet. "Oh, and one more thing." He leaned in close. "I might need a little help with what I'm going to do, a little extra insurance. You carrying?"

Dog narrowed his eyes, then glanced around the open space, checking. "Um . . ."

"Come on, McCreedy, give. You know what I mean."

He didn't look happy, but McCreedy leaned forward, his lips set into a tight line. He reached behind him, underneath his jacket, and pulled forth his hand, stretching it forward, palm down, concealing something. "Here," he said. "I don't have to ask if you know what you're doing with it."

Jack slipped his own hand under McCreedy's and took the proffered object, also giving their surrounds a quick glance before he turned his attention to what he now held. It was a small but nasty-looking energy weapon, compact, easily concealed, but clearly sufficient for what he needed.

"Good," he said, slipping it away inside his coat. McCreedy was still looking troubled.

"Don't do anything stupid, Jack," he said. "You're sure you want to do this alone?"

"Yeah," said Jack after a moment's pause. "No sense getting you mixed up in this directly. Not yet."

"Remember, Jack, this is Balance City. You're not home now."

"I've got it, Dog. Don't worry about me."

"Right," said McCreedy. "See you when I see you."

Jack slapped his thighs and stood. "Good. I'll see you in a couple of hours if everything plays out, and hopefully we'll get the answers we need."

Despite his assurances to McCreedy, Jack wasn't feeling completely comfortable with what he was about to do. Dog was right: This wasn't home, not that anywhere particularly was home above any other, but he was on unfamiliar territory.

From Algol, it was only a few short stops to Carlton, hardly giving him enough time to prepare his thoughts. He had a rough sort of plan, but he was going to have to rely on his luck now to pull it off. He toyed with the weapon in his pocket, thinking about how he was going get past the hired muscle. It looked like he would have to bluff it, take things head-on. He pulled it out of the pocket and slid it into his belt at his back, underneath his coat.

A few minutes later he was at the rounded depression in Carlton's streets, the plinth before him. Last time he was here, the green-suited lackey had placed his hand on top of the thing, so that meant it was keyed. The love of surveillance in Balance City led Jack to think that were he to try to operate the entrance, they'd know about it soon enough. Suppressing the urge to check the weapon, he took a deep breath and stepped forward, placing one hand on top of the plinth. A second later a voice came from some hidden device; it was probably part of the plinth itself.

"Yes?"

"Jack Stein to see Mr. Aire," said Jack. If Aire was interested enough to care about what Jack was doing, enough to monitor his movements, he had to be interested enough to find out what Jack wanted.

"One moment," said the voice. "Wait there."

Jack looked around, seeking something that would be monitoring him, but if there was a cam, it was well hidden from view.

It took only moments before the panel slid back, revealing the stairway down. His luck had paid off so far; it looked like Aire was at home.

Jack took the stairs, feeling a vague rush of nervousness as the illuminated panel slid back in place above him, cutting off his retreat. At the bottom of the stairs stood Square Jaw, watching him with a vague frown.

"What are you doing here, Stein?" he said.

"I told you," said Jack as he took each step slowly. "I'm here to see Mr. Aire."

"About . . . ?"

"What's it to you?"

Square Jaw narrowed his eyes. The lackey was sizing him up, his gaze flickering over Jack. Jack descended the last few stairs, his hands out from his sides, his palms spread.

The man stepped back to let him pass. Jack was relying on the fact that the last time he'd been here, he'd come empty-handed. So far it was paying off. The guy took a step forward as Jack passed, and in that moment Jack made his move. He spun on one foot, his outstretched arm crooking, and he drove his elbow backward, straight into the upper abdomen of the guy behind him. In the same movement he slipped his other hand under his coat, whipping out the gun, completing the move by pressing the small ugly weapon up under the man's chin, stopping him from doubling further. The guy's face was screwed up in a grimace, his teeth bared, but his eyes widened as he registered the cold barrel beneath his chin.

Slowly he lifted himself upright, his eyes filling with fury.

"Not smart, Stein," he said. "You'll pay for this."

Jack moved his face closer, looking into the man's gray eyes. "The old lines are the best ones, hey, friend?" he said.

He pulled his face away and stepped around the man's side and beside him, keeping the weapon close against the guy's jaw.

"Okay," said Jack. "Take me to Aire."

There was no sign of the other man who was there last time, though Jack checked around them.

Aire was standing where he'd first seen him, suspended above the vast chasm below. He watched impassively as Jack maneuvered his hired muscle into the room.

"Mr. Aire," said Jack.

"Stein," said Aire, his expression remaining unmoved by the scene in front of him. "You could have just walked in, you know."

"Oh, no," said Jack. "Not this time." He gave a quick glance around the room, checking the couple of doorways that led off, but they seemed truly alone. "We have some things to discuss, and I wanted to give you a little bit of an incentive to help me out, Mr. Aire."

"Hmm," said Aire. The sound was short, dismissive. "What is it you want, Stein?"

"I want to know what's happened to Heering."

Aire tilted his head to one side, then straightened it. "Heering? Who is Heering?"

A flicker of movement to one side and almost behind Jack was mirrored in the barest reaction in Aire's eyes. Jack turned quickly. The other green-suited man was standing in one of the doorways, a gun leveled at Jack's head. Jack pulled his own green suit to block. "I wouldn't do that," he said.

Aire gave a quick wave of his hand, and the man with the weapon slowly lowered it.

Jack, keeping his captive well placed within the line, turned his head to look fully at Aire. "Very smart, Mr. Aire. Now, if you'd like to tell me what I want to know . . ."

"I know no Heering," said Aire. "I'm afraid I cannot help you, Mr. Stein. I apologize, though it should be you who are apologizing to me. You come into my home, threaten my staff. . . ."

"In case you'd forgotten, *Mr.* Aire," said Jack, "last time I was here, I was the subject of the threats."

Aire snorted. "Those were not threats, Stein. Not at all." He looked vaguely amused. Jack narrowed his eyes.

"Heering, Aire. Dr. Heering. University of Balance City. Ring any bells?"

Aire spread his hands.

"All right then," said Jack. He pushed the bodyguard with him forward, crossing the transparent floor to where Aire was standing. "Perhaps this will refresh your memory." He slipped quickly from behind the man he was holding, grabbed Aire's coat, and shoved the gun up beside his head. Square Jaw made to take a step, but Jack pressed the gun harder against Aire's temple. "Back away," he said.

The guy made no move until Aire gave a quick nod.

"So, your memory getting any better?" asked Jack, his mouth close to Aire's ear. The smell of a rich, musky cologne wafted up around his face.

"If I were to know anything," said Aire, his voice calm, "it would be fair to negotiate a trade. You have information I want. I have something you want, apparently." He chuckled.

Jack frowned. What did Jack have? Unless it was . . .

"I think you're mistaken," he said.

"Oh, no," said Aire. "I am very interested in anything you might be able to tell me about the alien homeworld. Perhaps I can help you with your friend. Heering, was it?"

So. The old pattern was emerging. The interest of the Sons of Utrecht hadn't gone away with Christian Landerman after all.

"I've been there before, Aire," said Jack quietly. "I don't particularly want to go back there."

"I don't understand, Jack."

"I mean that I told you guys that I didn't know anything about it then, and I don't know anything about it now. Why don't you just leave me alone to get on with what I'm doing?"

Aire sighed and moved his head sideways, away from contact with the gun. "Please, could you move that thing?"

"Fine," said Jack, and took a step back, keeping everyone clearly in view and the gun still trained on Maximilian Aire's large bulk.

"We know that's not true, Jack," said Aire, sounding disappointed. "You have been in possession of the artifact. You appear at the University of Balance City. Your young companion was there too. We believe that the good Dr. Antille has made a breakthrough, and you know what that breakthrough is. Why else would you be here? It is perfectly clear to us that you are very deeply involved in this matter."

"Dammit, Aire," said Jack. "You can think what you

like. I've got nothing to do with their work. I *know* nothing about it. I'm just here looking for my 'young companion,' as you call her. That's it." If Aire's network was as good as it seemed, then he had to know that much already.

Aire turned slowly, searching Jack's face. "I find that hard to believe. Very hard, Jack. And remember, you are in my city. Help me, Jack, and I'll help you."

This was going nowhere. Jack could see that. The sense of hostility from the other two men in the room was growing. Nothing Aire had said gave him the feeling that he was any closer to Heering. He sighed and shook his head. "I'm going now, Aire. The biggest favor you can do me is to leave me the fuck alone."

Aire narrowed his eyes. "Like you have left me alone," he said quietly. A subtle menace undercut the words and then was gone. "Yes, Jack, you leave now. But if you do think of anything, please be sure to get in touch. I will be waiting for you."

Jack stared at him. He lowered his borrowed weapon and shoved it in his coat. Aire made a gesture to his men, not even turning to look at them.

"Good-bye, Mr. Stein," he said. "We'll talk soon."

The two green suits glared at Jack as he crossed the forbidding gap and made for the hallway leading to the stairs, but they made not a move to follow.

Jack climbed the stairs; the entrance panel was already open as he reached the topmost step, and he stepped out into the harsh artificial light of Carlton. The panel slid shut soundlessly behind him.

Jack stood there for a moment, thinking, reached into his pocket, and turned. He flipped the settings on the gun to high and gave the plinth a quick blast, hopefully enough to cook the programming. It would slow Aire down for a little while, just in case he changed his mind.

What he'd just done had been dumb, but it had filled in a couple of blanks. He knew exactly where he stood with the Sons of Utrecht now. He shoved the gun away and stepped rapidly out on the street, heading for the place where the elevator had descended. Somehow, Jack thought, the only reason he was alive was that the Sons of Utrecht thought he had something they wanted—or at least a way to get at it.

Fourteen

"You think you know what this stuff means. You're the pilot. You tell me."

Dog nodded slowly. "Well, seeing as we're not going out to see Heering . . ." He gestured to the barman, pointing at his empty glass, then returned his attention to Jack's face. "I don't know," he said. "It's your risk. I'm game. Like I said, I would have liked a bit of confirmation. There are some notes at the end that don't make a lot of sense. Lots of question marks. I couldn't understand what it was talking about at all. It didn't seem to relate to the coordinates, though. That part was pretty clear." He shrugged.

"I have to do this," said Jack finally. "I don't have a choice."

"Right, we're doing it then," said Dog. "And by the sounds of your little visit with Aire, we have to do it soon." At that, a fresh beer arrived. Dog waited until the barman withdrew. He lifted the beer and tilted it in Jack's direction. "Here's to the unknown," he said with a grin.

It was the unknown part that was making Jack distinctly uncomfortable. He nodded back, but his lips were set in a tight line. Dog drained the last of his beer, placed his glass down firmly, and slapped his hip. "That's it then. Meet you at the entrance to the docks. I need about three hours or so to make the prep."

"What time then?"

"Make it earlier. We need to get away. Get out of sight for a while, I think. I need to get some supplies in. I'll see you there in two and a half hours. Seven forty-five. Hey, you know, I'm looking forward to this."

Jack leaned forward, beckoning Dog closer. "One thing we didn't sort out was hardware." He reached into his coat, palmed the gun, and held it out surreptitiously to Dog under the level of the bar. "You know, I'm still naked."

Dog laughed. "Not as naked as you were this morning."

"Be serious, McCreedy. You know what I mean."

Dog nodded, the grin slipping from his face. "Don't worry. I've got it covered."

From what he'd seen so far, Jack didn't doubt it at all.

Dog hesitated and pulled his hand back. "In the meantime, hold on to that," he said.

Jack nodded and shoved it back in his coat.

Something was dragging him up through the layers of sleep. He worked his tongue in his mouth, seeking moisture, and levered himself up on one elbow to look at the time. Oh, God. He'd fallen asleep without even trying. And he'd been dreaming. He didn't have time to work through the dream. He had to get ready.

As he stumbled toward the shower, he tried to remember as much as he could. Briefly, he wondered if it had been one of those dreams, and where it would have gone if he'd stayed with it. Something had happened. He didn't know quite what it was, but something had happened.

The splash of hot water brought him closer to consciousness, but it was still way too early. He checked the bathroom, checked the cupboards, the drawers, and the wardrobe, and piled things one by one on the bed as he found them. His laundry was there, neatly folded, but that wasn't going to last long. He decided what he was going to wear and shoved the rest into his bag. He dressed hurriedly, pulled on his coat, made the final adjustments before stowing his toiletries, then gave the room one last check. Something else. No. He could grab a coffee in the lobby.

Satisfied that he'd checked all that he could, he pulled his luggage out into the hall and let the door close. One more pat-down and he verified that his handipad was in place. It was funny, but no matter how many times he checked, he was always convinced that he'd left something behind. Maybe hotels had a built-in unease generator to make people stay longer because they felt nervous every time they were going to leave.

Down in the lobby, he pulled his luggage to a spot where it drifted to rest next to a couch and ordered a coffee — large and strong. At least they got that part right.

He finished the cup and wandered over the desk to announce he was checking out. The desk clerk checked his name and room number before frowning.

"Are you sure you're checking out, Mr. Stein?" he said.

"Yeah, that's what I said."

The desk clerk shook his head. "You are not due to leave yet."

"No, that's right. There's been a change of plans."

"I'm sure," said the clerk, a tone of clear disapproval in his voice, "that you were informed of our advance notification policy if there are to be any variations in your stay."

"Yeah, sure. I'm sorry. I didn't have any advance warning."

"This is most irregular, Mr. Stein." The clerk picked up a phone and called someone.

"Hey," said Jack. "What are you doing?"

The clerk waved a finger at him. Jack had just about had enough. He reached across and grabbed the phone out of the clerk's hand. "Forget your call. Tell me what the damage is, I'll pay, and then I'll leave. I don't care about whether it's irregular or not." In the slow grind from unconsciousness to wakefulness was not exactly the best time to do something like that to Jack Stein, coffee or not. He placed the phone down firmly behind the counter.

The clerk swallowed. "Yes, Mr. Stein. You realize, of course, you will be charged an extra night's penalty."

Jack waved his hand. "Yes, fine. Get on with it." Inside, he was fuming.

"There is your laundry, breakfast, yes? Some calls."

"Just tell me how much."

The clerk's lips were set in a tight line now. He printed out an actual statement. "I would ask you to check this, please."

Jack barely glanced out it, pulled out his handipad, and flipped it open, his teeth gritted. The clerk nodded and performed the transfer. "Thank you, Mr. Stein. I hope you enjoyed your stay and that we will see you again."

Jack's eyes widened in disbelief and he quickly turned away, stalking over to his bag. He didn't care about the cost. If it meant he never had to see this place again, he'd be happy. As he headed for the doorway, his bag trailing behind, Jack glanced back at the front desk. The clerk had picked up his phone again and was talking into it with an animated expression. There was a lot of hand waving going on. Jack had half a mind to stride over and wrench the phone out of his grasp again, but he knew it would have been a pointless exercise. As he stepped out of the front of the hotel and onto the street, he paused to wonder whom the clerk had actually been calling, but he had some fairly good ideas. Million Aire had his fingers everywhere, and the man had more of a reason now to have his palm print firmly on Jack's business.

By the time he got to the place where he was supposed to be meeting Dog, that hint of suspicious discomfort was still with him. Dog turned up a couple of minutes later, arriving from the dock area rather than the city itself. He was all business, and had clearly been at it for some time already.

"Everything's loaded," he said. "All ready. You okay?"

Jack checked the area around them, but they appeared to be alone. He nodded. "Sure. The sooner we get out of here, the better."

"Okay, let's go."

Dog turned and headed back the way he had come, Jack following close behind him.

"Oh, by the way, what was the name of that guy we were going to see at the university again? H-something, wasn't it?"

Jack slowed, a cold chill touching the place between his shoulder blades. "Yeah, Heering, why?"

"Thought so," said Dog. "They found him in the early hours of this evening. It was on the news broadcast."

Jack stopped dead in his tracks. "What do you mean?"

"Bottom of the canyon. Right at the bottom of the spire. It happens now and again. You get the jumpers. So they tend to keep an eye out. It's funny he should turn up so quickly, though."

Jack was still trying to digest this new twist and hadn't moved from where he stood. Dog turned back to him impatiently. "Well, are you coming, or what?"

"Yes, just wait. . . ." Had his visit to Aire prompted Heering's death?

"What is it?" said Dog. "You can't do anything for the guy. He's dead."

"I know," said Jack. "But someone did it to him, and I think it has something to do with me."

Dog shrugged. "Maybe it did; maybe it didn't. You're not going to change it, though. Anyway, we're gone. If you're still worried about it when we get back, then you can do something about it then."

Jack shook his head. "It doesn't work like that. I just can't walk away."

Dog looked distinctly annoyed. "Listen, man, where are your priorities? It's not a damned case. You don't have to solve every little mystery you come across. Do you want to find this girl or don't you?"

This girl? Somehow, he couldn't help feeling offense at that. "Dammit, of course I do."

"Well, move it, Stein."

Dog turned on his heel, not waiting to see if Jack was following. It took only a half second more before he was.

"So what have you done with the notes?" Jack asked as they swept up and out from Balance City.

Dog was concentrating and took a moment to answer. "Hmmm?"

"The notes I gave you . . ."

Dog looked sideways at him, peering through a couple of loose strands of hair uncomprehendingly. A moment later, light broke. "Ah, shit. I knew I forgot something."

"You what?" Jack sat up in his seat.

Dog broke into a big grin. "Ha! Got you." He patted his jacket. "Safe and sound."

Jack settled back into his seat, muttering under his breath.

Dog shook his head, still grinning, and turned his attention back to the panel in front. "Lighten up, Jack. You were always too easy."

Jack crossed his arms and kept his attention on the sky in front of them.

"I was doing some thinking last night," Dog said after a while. "I was remembering stuff from back on those missions, some of the weird stuff that used to happen around you. Me, it's easy to see how I ended up doing what I'm doing. You, it was a different story. Not that we knew each other that well back then. No more than any of the crew did. But remembering those things, it makes a weird kind of sense."

"How so?" said Jack, wondering where this was going.

"Well, you know, running into each other out here. Kinda weird, isn't it? Me being the guy who just happened to have what you needed. But that's the kind of stuff that used to happen around you. You always seemed to be in the right place at the right time. Well, it was more that you weren't in the wrong place. I didn't figure it for anything special, just luck. Some people are naturally lucky, right? It was creepy, though. The other guys felt the same way. Not that we used to talk about it much back in the unit. I guess we didn't want to jinx it."

He glanced over at Jack, then looked back out of the front screen. "So I guess what I'm saying is, I feel kind of lucky to be along for the ride."

Jack turned to look at Dog's pale face, but his companion was looking studiedly at the panel in front of him.

"Hmmmm," said Jack, turning his attention back to the front as well.

The journey up to the orbital seemed longer this time, and the rest of the trip was spent in silence, making it seem longer still. All the while thoughts of Maximilian Aire and Dr. Heering flitted through his mind. The sense of guilt was almost palpable. Jack was relieved when the bristly shape of the orbital appeared and grew ever larger in the front viewscreen. They bumped to a stop, and this time Jack stayed where he was, waiting for the thump and jolt of the connecting tube to match the hatch. He was about to unstrap himself and stand, when Dog waved him down. Dog manipulated something on the front panel, and seconds later there was another jolt and bump.

"Okay," said Dog. He slid from his seat and slid back a panel behind them. He stepped through, waving Jack in after him. In the small cargo area behind, a loading pallet was stacked with packages. Jack ducked into the cramped space.

"Drag the luggage in here," Dog instructed. "Stack it on top."

Jack hefted his bag up on the stacked pallet and waited while Dog opened a broader hatch. Another sealed tube led down and away, but broader and wider than the one they'd entered through on their previous visit. A set of control panels were set close to the sealing lip, just inside, and Dog reached for them. A flat metal shelf swung up, whirred slowly flat, and then clicked into place with a firm thunk.

"Okay, give me a hand with this," said Dog, and together they slid the pallet out onto the platform. On either edge of the shelf there were handrails, one that had a series of touch pads along its front length. Dog stepped to that side, gripping the handrail firmly. Jack followed suit on the other side of the stacked pallet. With his free hand, Dog reached out and pressed his palm against the side of his flier, waiting until the hatch door had slid shut and locked, before pressing the touch pad. The platform shuddered, then pulled back, descending slowly into the station proper.

They were in a different set of conduits, pale green illumination stretching either way. Dog put his foot against the bottom of the pallet and, bracing himself against the railing, pushed. The stacked panel slid out onto a moving travel belt and Dog stepped after it. Jack, quickly following suit, guessed they traveled about a hundred yards before Dog quickly slipped around the side of the pallet and shoved, propelling it down a connecting passage. Three more intersections gave the same process, until they wound up at the end of the moving floor against a sealed dark hatch. More touch pads, Dog's palm applied to a panel, and the hatch irised open, revealing a red-lit circular passage leading to another hatch. How the hell Dog had found his way, Jack had no idea.

"No help for this bit," said Dog, and grunted as he put his weight against the stacked pallet, sliding it carefully down the passage and cursing as it banged up against a side wall. He managed to manhandle it into position, and then stepped past it to key the lock with his palm. The hatch slid open, lights illuminated the compact lock, and Dog pushed the pallet inside.

"Come on," he said, waving Jack forward.

The outer door slid shut a moment after Jack stepped inside, and they waited until the inner door slid open. This time Jack lent a hand helping Dog steer the pallet until it was flush against several others. Jack reached up and retrieved his bags. Pulling a skein of pale green webbing from the floor, Dog draped it over the pallet and secured its other end to hooks on the floor. He pushed himself back, grabbed at a handhold, and then stood, resting against the wall surveying his handiwork. He nodded.

"Okay, that should keep us going. There's enough food and stuff there for a couple of weeks, maybe three. I guess we're not planning to be away longer than that, right?"

Jack nodded his assent. He hoped not.

"So how long do you think it's going to take us to get there?" he asked.

Dog scratched his head. "Hard to say, really. There's not just one jump. There are several interlinked steps. Minijumps, with some conventional travel in between, getting from one point to the other. Let's get up front and settled, anyway. By my calculation, it might be two or three days, so we might as well get comfortable."

"Hmmmm," said Jack. He wasn't exactly looking forward to spending two or three days cooped up in Dog's ship. "You got anything to do while we're getting there?"

Dog palmed an inner door and looked back over his shoulder. "Let's stow that bag of yours; then we can see what's on offer."

Jack pulled his luggage up the passageway, following closely behind. Two-thirds of the way up, Dog stopped at a closed door. He touched a panel and the door slid open. Giving Jack a slight grin, he pulled himself through and called up the lights. "If you can manage it, shove your luggage in there." He pointed at a locker.

Jack hung in the doorway, considering the gymnastic possibilities, and then sighed. Okay, he could manage that.

"This will be yours for the duration," said Dog. "I hope it meets sir's expectations."

"Yeah, it'll be fine."

"We have music, entertainment, books if you want them. They're all available either on the ceiling panel above the bunk or over on the wall. Your choice. Probably enough there, but if you need help finding things to keep yourself amused later, then just ask."

Jack grabbed a handhold and pulled himself into the cabin. After a couple of false starts, he worked out how to get the bag over to the locker and stowed it inside. Dog was watching him with an amused expression.

"It'll get easier once we get under way and the spin kicks in," he said. "Meanwhile, I'll see you up front."

Jack let him leave, checking around the small cabin. It was clean enough. He held himself against the end of the bunk and stood thinking. Did he know what he was getting himself into? He grimaced. It didn't matter whether he did or not. Finding Billie was what mattered. And that was everything that mattered right now. When they got back, he could worry about Heering and what had happened to him. Dog was right: It wasn't a case, and yet . . .

It was funny how feelings of responsibility worked into his consciousness. And yeah, he was feeling responsible for Heering too, though there was really no logical reason why he should. He'd set himself up for that, starting to think of Heering as a client, going down to Aire to find the guy. Another lost cause. For some reason, though, he needed to find out what had happened to the bird-faced academic. Possibly to clear himself of culpability in the man's death? Maybe. Whatever the reason, it wasn't going to be easy. The more time that passed, the colder the trail would get. And frankly, he had no idea how long it would be before he got back, before *they* got back.

With some difficulty, Jack pulled off his coat and placed it inside the locker with his luggage. There was no real need to wear it while on board. Before locking it away, he dug out his handipad and slipped it into his back pocket. There was no reason for him to feel completely naked. He gave the cabin one more scan before heading up to join McCreedy in the front. The blank metallic walls, the uncluttered feeling, gave him a sense of his old working rooms back in the Locality. If he was going to do some real dream work—and he might have to yet before this was out—then this would be the place to do it. His dream aliens were trying to tell him something, and one way or another he had to work out what it was. He just hadn't had time to do it yet.

There was nothing for it, so Jack made his way up the passageway to find Dog occupied, checking figures, cross-referencing against the sheets, adjusting instruments. None of it meant anything to Jack. He cleared his throat, standing in the doorway. McCreedy waved him in without looking up from what he was doing.

"Find yourself a seat, whichever one looks comfortable. I'd suggest one of the front ones. That way you can see what's going on. I'm just about done here, and we can get under way in a couple of minutes."

Jack headed for one of the three seats up near the front viewscreen. He maneuvered himself into place, strapped in, and sat staring at blank screens in front of him. After a minute like that, he cleared his throat again. "Um, any problems?"

"Nah. Everything's fine, Jack. You always were a nervous flier, even back then. Some things never change. This is a jump ship. It's not a jungle carrier."

Jack looked over at McCreedy and narrowed his eyes. "Flying's flying. Doesn't matter where it is. At least back there you could see the ground."

McCreedy grinned and shook his head. "Think of it this way: If you're in a ship, the ship becomes the ground for you. It's as if you're in your own little world. Everything's here, self-contained, all you need."

"Hmmm," said Jack. "Not convinced."

Dog shrugged and went back to his checking. Not wanting to interrupt the process, Jack started fidgeting. After little more than ten seconds of that, Dog sighed. He reached over and touched something on a nearby panel, and the front screens washed into life. "There, occupy yourself for a couple of minutes."

This view was different, and enough to fully occupy Jack's attention. The platform lip swept in a broad arc around the *Amaranth*'s nose, cupping the sleek bulb

where Jack knew the jump drive lay. It made him uncomfortable knowing that here, up front, they were sitting almost on top of the thing, but he had to put it out of
his head. Now, from this perspective, the platform
seemed motionless. It was the central cylinder that rotated. The platform stretched out like some white metallic plain, even lines of humped shiny rivets crisscrossing
in both directions. About halfway in were guide markings, and the occasional small flier, anchored in place by
the connecting tubes sealed to their outer edges. He
watched the cylinder for a while. Blank wall, clear panel.
Blank wall, clear panel. He couldn't see inside from here.
Any view was obscured by silvery-white reflections of
the orbital structure. His attention drifted back to the platform and down to the curved wall against which the
ship's nose was nestled. Clever design. All around the
wall, for as far as the view would permit, he could see
side-by-side hatch doors. So, no matter what the dimensions of the ship, they could accommodate whichever
entry hatch connected to allow ingress. Most of the platform had to be hollow, full of the labyrinth of conduits
and passageways feeding the various docking points. It
didn't explain how they dealt with the long freighter he'd
seen coming in, but he was sure they'd worked out some
method that was immensely practical, designed to do the
job with the minimum of fuss.

"Right," said Dog eventually. "I'm done. You okay?"

Jack nodded slowly. "Yeah, I guess so."

"Well, let's do it." He'd already shoved the papers out
of sight. Dog reached forward and touched a place on the
control panel in front of him. "Orbital Control, this is
Amaranth. Requesting clearance."

The voice that responded was a woman. "One moment, McCreedy. Checking vectors. You're clear. No in-
coming. Have a nice trip."

"Thanks, Raisa," Dog responded. "See you soon."

Damn, did Dog know everyone up here? Well, maybe he did.

McCreedy busied himself with the controls, touching a sequence and then waiting for a second until there was a clear vibration through the ship. He nodded and touched another sequence, then spoke again. "Disengaged. Pushing back."

Jack watched the retreating platform lip as they drifted slowly backward.

"Okay," Dog said. "On our way. We'll clear the platform, and then turn before I fire up. Too much to get caught up in close to the station. We'll have about four hours before I get near the first jump point."

"And then . . . ?"

"And then we jump. We get through the jump, I recalculate, get to the next point; then we jump again. The second leg's going to be longer than the first. Maybe a day. Whatever it is, we'll have some time to catch up, eh, Jack?"

It was probably the last thing on Jack's mind at the moment. He watched the retreating orbital growing smaller as they drifted back to the point where McCreedy would perform their turn. Down below, now revealed, lay Utrecht, mostly obscured by clouds. Not even one last sight of Balance City to send them on their way.

Fifteen

As the drives kicked into life, Jack settled back in his seat. In front of them lay open space, blackness and stars. Jack swallowed, willing himself to relax. It was true: He did have questions he wanted to ask Dog, questions that had been troubling him on and off over the last couple of days. Not all of them were related to Danny Boy McCreedy either. If he was lucky, McCreedy might be able to give him something more on the Sons of Utrecht. And as far as McCreedy himself was concerned, there was time to find out a little about what had happened to the man since their days in the service, how he had ended up on Utrecht in the first place. Sure, McCreedy had given him the thumbnail sketch, but somehow Jack didn't think that was quite enough.

Dog finally settled back in his seat too, finished for the time being with the routines and checks he had to make to get them where they were going. He gave a satisfied sigh.

"All plain sailing from here," he said.

"Well, we hope so," said Jack in response, unable to keep the dubious note from his voice.

"Relax, Stein. Everything's fine."

"So I'm curious, Dog. How did you end up on Utrecht in the first place? Balance City just doesn't seem your sort of thing. Maybe you've changed." Jack doubted it. Looking at the man, the way he carried himself, the attitude, it was all reminiscent of the wild boy he had known back then. Perhaps a little more jaded, but still the same guy, just older.

Dog started playing with a long strand of hair, watching the stars in front of them. "How so?" he said finally.

"Well, I don't know. I would have thought all that order and regimentation would drive you crazy."

"Yeah, it does, from time to time, but if you know the way they work, then you know the way to work them too, if you get what I mean. That whole rigid-attitude thing . . . The problem is, because it's all so bound up in rules and expectations, if there's any loophole whatsoever, they grab it and run. Of course, those at the top are as corrupt as hell. The politicians, the officials, all the same. If you know how to play by their rules, know where those loopholes are, then you can get ahead."

"Hmmmm," said Jack. "And you feel comfortable with that?"

Dog shrugged. "Why shouldn't I?"

"No, I guess you're right." Jack mulled that over for a couple of seconds before speaking again. "So tell me, what brought you here?"

Dog gave a short laugh. "I was doing freighter work, long-haul stuff. The arrangement I had . . . well, it sort of fell apart. The owner and I had a little falling-out. When I popped him one, I found myself on the Utrecht orbital, no ship, no passage out, and no funds. I didn't have a choice really. I worked the hotels and the bars for a while, picking up whatever I could to get by, and then someone heard I was a pilot. I got a couple of short shuttle jobs and then graduated from there. Don't get me wrong; I was doing fine out of the bar work and the other stuff. I just couldn't leave the ships alone. I guess it's in my blood."

"And how'd you pick that up?" asked Jack, indicating the burn scar.

Dog rubbed the mark thoughtfully. "Pirates."

"Huh?"

"Oh, we still have pirates," said Dog. "That's what they are. No other words for them. Long-haul freighter routes can easily fall prey to the occasional bandit. And that far out, there's no one there to help. Every man for himself." Dog lowered his hand from his face thoughtfully. "I gave better than I got, anyway. Half of the crew wasn't so lucky. The other crew, their crew, wasn't lucky at all. They made the wrong choice picking on us. You have to be careful around freighter crews for that reason. They're used to taking care of themselves. And that's also why every long-hauler has an armory. You never know when you need to break out the firepower."

Jack pictured Dog crouched in a passageway, weapon in hand, smoke obscuring the view. He could see it, all right.

"Is it okay if I get up?" asked Jack.

"Sure. It's a while till we get to the jump coordinates. Feel free. You need to stretch your legs? Facilities are back there."

"No, that's okay. I like to walk while I think."

Dog laughed. "There's not much space for walking here."

"There's enough," said Jack quietly.

He paced around the bridge, back and forth between the passageway and his seat, pausing to look at the starscape a couple of times.

"Tell me, McCreedy, precisely how much do you know about the Sons of Utrecht?"

"Them again." Dog snorted. "What do you want to know?"

"I don't know, precisely," said Jack. "I just need to work a couple of things through. After I left you that first time, I had that visit. Or rather, they took me on a visit to

Aire's place down in Carlton. I didn't have much choice in the matter. I don't like that much."

"Okay." Dog had swung his seat around, looking interested, tracking Jack as he walked.

"Rufus told me after that first visit that this guy Maximilian Aire was tied up with them."

Dog nodded. "The rumor is that Aire is SOU. He doesn't come out with it publicly, but everybody suspects. He has front men to do the public stuff. In fact, he's very rarely seen."

Jack gripped the back of his seat. "I've had dealings with them before. I told you that. The whole Landerman thing. I think the SOU are the reason Heering ended up taking a fall. They want to control the information, and Heering wouldn't play."

"Wait, Landerman? Christian Landerman?"

Jack nodded.

"Damn, I didn't make the connection before." Dog's face took on a thoughtful expression. "Yes, it could be. That's not good. Damned SOU are always where you don't want them. But why Heering? And why the SOU rather than Aire himself?"

Jack nodded and sat, steepling his fingers in front of him. "Max Aire checked me out. I had nothing. He knew Antille's connection, also that I'd been to the university and seen Heering. It's exactly the same sort of interest that the SOU had before. It would have been easy to assume that Heering had the stuff that I needed. Heering knew enough about what Aire wanted and—"

"So why would he have him killed?"

"Yeah, I don't get it. Maybe they went too far. Maybe it was an accident. He made it clear, though, that he thought I was more useful to him than Heering."

Dog was looking at him, his jaw set firmly. "And now you've dragged me into it."

"Hey, you're the one who said you wanted a bit of excitement."

"Thanks a lot, buddy."

Jack shook his head. "All of that's just speculation, but it would make sense, wouldn't it?"

Dog narrowed his eyes and swiveled his seat away.

"What's the problem, McCreedy?"

With a glare, Dog swung his seat back to face Jack. "I'll tell you what's wrong, Stein. You're looking at Mr. Anonymity here. You might not think it looking at me, but I make my living by existing below the radar. You've just raised my profile. I don't seem to have been consulted on the matter."

"Come on, McCreedy, it's more than that. Anonymity, you? I don't buy it. What was all that stuff about having a rep? Look at the way you carry yourself. Just about every person we ran into on the orbital knew you. No. I don't believe that for an instant."

McCreedy worked his jaw before answering, and when he did, his eyes were still hard. "There's low-profile and there's low-profile, Jack. You should know that. You of all people. Remember where we both came from. You know what it means." He turned away again, making the pretense of busying himself with the controls in front. Jack sighed and stood.

"Fine. I'm going to lie down for a while. We've a couple of hours, right? Wake me before we jump if I'm not back."

Dog grunted wordlessly without turning around.

As he wandered back to his cabin, Jack thought about their exchange. Something had pressed Dog's buttons, but he couldn't work out why the SOU was such an issue for McCreedy himself. Dog had virtually discounted them, and yet his reactions had clearly said otherwise. Interesting. Sure, Utrecht was Dog's home ground, and also home ground for the SOU, but there was no way, by any stretch of the imagination, that Dog McCreedy was anonymous. Anyway, further exploration could wait. It was about time he started directing his skills instead of letting them do the work for him.

Since he'd arrived on Utrecht, his concern about Billie had kept him almost on autopilot. He had a couple of hours, and that was long enough for a dream session. There were no inducer pads here, no equipment, but with the starkness of the cabin, and his own exercises, it wouldn't be too hard to induce the necessary dreamstate. If he could push away any thoughts of the impending jump, that was.

As soon as he was inside the cabin, with the door securely closed, Jack glanced around, seeking a time display of some sort. Nothing. Maybe there was something in the screen above the bed, or somewhere else. He tried playing around with the system, but drew a blank. He stood in the cabin's center, his hands on his hips, considering. How did you measure time on board a ship in a way that it made any sort of sense, anyway? Dismissing the thought, he started to remove his clothing, placed it to one side, and lay in his accustomed position on the bed, his hands crossed on his chest, his eyes gently closed, letting the sounds and motion around him drift out of his consciousness. Gradually he let an image form in his mind's screen, concentrating. A blond sixteen-year-old, hair messed up, attitude written all over her face. She wore a pale blue sweat top with a hood and jeans. Her jaw was thrust out in the classic pose she got when she was pissed about something. Billie, he thought. Yeah, that was Billie. He left the arms uncrossed. He didn't want the mental image to be one that was blocking him, body language or otherwise. Billie, he thought. Where are you? As he concentrated on the image, all sensation of the cabin, the ship, the space around him started to fade.

Jack's breathing slowed as he drifted deeper into that mental state that was the precursor to the onset of dreams. Images flickered at the edges of his consciousness, but he ignored them, maintaining his attention on Billie's accusatory stare. Come on, Billie, show me where you are. Wilhelmina? Billie? No, not Wilhelmina. He hadn't called her that for years. She was always Billie. Always would be.

Darkness drifted across his mind as his consciousness floated lower, deeper into the receptive state. Billie, where are you?

Light. Light and motion. Metallic star shapes flashing all around. There was noise and yet there wasn't noise. No, there should be noise. Jack was standing at a junction between four large buildings. Shiny surfaces angled up on every side. They were buildings and yet . . . something was strange about them. He turned slowly, trying to get his orientation right. A single shining wall in front swept up at an angle. Up, above, and over behind him. Jack took a step closer, trying to make out the surface. Was it metal? Something else. Another step.

A bright silver shape whipped past up and off to one side, too quickly for him to catch the detail. Then another.

All your senses, Jack. All of them.

The air smelled hard, metallic, like the surfaces of the walls around him. Still there was no sound, and he concentrated, forcing his will into hearing what surrounded him, trying to break through the barrier of complete silence. Nothing. He couldn't hear a thing. Was that significant? Was there a message for him in the silence? He narrowed his eyes and pushed against the deafness, but to no avail.

He stepped even closer to the metallic surface in front and slowly reached out with one hand, touching first his fingers, then the flat of his palm against the smoothness.

It seemed solid enough, but it wasn't smooth, as he'd first imagined. There were tiny ridges in the surface. It was neither hot nor cold, matching the temperature of his skin. He slid his hand up and down, feeling the continuity of the tiny ridgelines.

Why was he here? He turned his head, but behind him was another angled wall, farther away, but looking exactly the same as the one before him. Others stood to the left and the right. Following the path of the opposite wall, he lifted his gaze. The wall angled up and inward, meeting a flat, dark surface some distance above. He suddenly had the impression that he was standing under some giant designer chair, the underside of the seat straight up, and thick arching legs meeting at each corner. He blinked several times in succession, seeing if the image would change, but it stayed. He turned his attention back to the wall, the smoothly ridged surface, and noticed rainbow colors working through the silver sheen, as if multihued patterns shifted deep within the wall's surface. Every time he moved his head, the patterns changed. Nice effect, but it was getting him no closer to working out why he was here. He decided to trace the wall's boundaries and turned to the right.

The wall extended for what looked like about forty yards in front of him and then stopped. Jack walked toward the corner, keeping his senses alert, seeking clues. Below his feet the ground was paved in what looked like broad, square blocks of natural gray stone. He reached the corner and poked his head around. Another wall ran for about a hundred yards and again broke at a corner. Once more, the surface was featureless and smooth. He walked the length of that wall too, reached the next corner, and turned. Again a wall, but this time, about halfway along, he could see a dark square space. A door. He quickened his pace.

Inside the doorway lay darkness, and though he strained, the thick shadow remained impenetrable. Not good. He could feel the spark of unease growing inside. Jack looked back over his shoulder. Behind him was another wall similar to this one, with a dark square breaking the even surface. Something flashed above him, again, too quick for him to see. He had the impression of a small ship, rounded at the front, but couldn't be sure. Whatever it was was long gone. Fast. He turned back to the patch of darkness in front of him and swallowed. It might as well be this one as any other. The silence beat at him, filling his ears with the movement of blood within his own veins. Taking a deep breath, he took a cautious step inside, then another.

The darkness folded around him, almost palpable, heavy like gray cloth, masking all sight. Great, Jack. You can't see, you can't hear. What's next? He took another firm step, reassuring himself that he could still feel his feet, one hand thrust out in front of him, groping in the darkness, scared about what his outstretched fingers might encounter.

"Billie?" he said soundlessly. He could feel himself speak the word, but still there was no sound. "Billie?" he tried again, with more force. Empty silence. Yet he could hear. That slight buzz and whoosh inside his ears was still there, touched by an almost-heard, high-pitched ring. "Billie!"

It was almost as if the darkness swallowed his words before his vocal cords had generated them.

"Welcome, Jack Stein," said a voice. The words came from inside his head, not outside, and they were deep and rich, echoing in the blackness of his perception.

"Welcome to our dream."

"What the fuck does that mean?" said Jack, but his words were swallowed by dark gray fog.

Sixteen

"Jack. Jack Stein!"

Jack groaned.

"Wake up, man. We're coming up to jump."

He forced his eyes open. The dark dream place was still on him, and he groped for reality, taking in the unfamiliar cabin walls and Dog hanging on the edge of the doorway, draped around the corner.

"Yeah, yeah," said Jack. "Coming. Give me a minute."

"And put some damn clothes on," said Dog, grimacing in the direction of those parts of Jack that were plainly on show.

Jack grunted, nodded, and waited until Dog retreated before standing and reaching for his clothes. At least McCreedy kept the ship at a workable temperature. Jack wondered if he had time to throw himself under the shower. Hell, he didn't even know if the *Amaranth* had a shower. He should have paid more attention to his cabin. There were bathroom facilities, but . . . He pulled on his trousers and shirt and slipped into his shoes. No time for that now. Dog's voice had had a touch of urgency.

He walked rapidly toward the bridge, rubbing his eyes with his fists and working his jaw, making sure he was fully awake. Jump. Dammit, he'd forgotten. He wasn't looking forward to it, but at the same time, he wasn't going to miss it for anything.

As he entered the control room and reached for his seat, Dog looked him up and down. "Hrmmm," he said. "That's better. Much better."

"Right," said Jack as he sat and strapped himself into his seat.

"Well, you could have given me some warning. We're all guys here, but . . ."

"How long have we got?" asked Jack.

"About five minutes before I kick it over. I don't get why you're so interested. It's just a jump."

Yeah, just a jump, thought Jack. It was always just a jump. It wasn't *just* anything since the Van der Stegen case, when he'd first seen what it could do to someone if it went wrong. He grimaced. Okay, it had been a few years. Surely the technology was stable by now.

"You never know, Dog," he said to McCreedy. "I don't know when I might pick something up, and because this whole thing's about Billie having jumped somewhere, I just want to be awake to the possibilities."

"Well, you're awake. I don't know about any possibilities." He reached and adjusted something in front of him.

"How many jumps have you done, McCreedy?" asked Jack.

"Plenty enough," said Dog, giving Jack a sidelong look. "What's your point?"

"Nothing. Nothing at all."

"Okay," said Dog, returning his attention to the controls.

Jack looked out in front of them, the spattered stars merging into lines, the blackness illuminated by the glow of starlight. Somewhere far behind them now lay Utrecht. Better the devil you know. He swallowed back the sensation of rising panic, forcing himself to keep his breathing steady. Slow, even breaths, Jack.

"Okay, nearing coordinates. Hold on," said Dog, and reached forward to stab at a single control.

Everything blurred; every cell in his body blurred. His guts wrenched, falling, falling in every direction. He was underwater and in ice. And it was over. A new set of stars took shape in front of them as reality stabilized.

Dog let out a long whoop. "Damn, I love that," he said. "Nothing like it."

Jack struggled for words and cleared his throat. His guts were threatening rebellion, and he forced it back. "You can have it," he said with difficulty.

"Awww, what's wrong, Stein? This is what it's all about."

He took a couple of deep breaths. "I can think of better things."

"Yeah, I'm sure you can," said Dog with a grin. "To each his own." He busied himself checking displays. "Well, it looks like we're in the right place, from what I can see," he said after a couple of seconds more. He peered through the front viewscreen, scanning the starscape. "Hmmm, nothing particularly familiar."

"Well, that's comforting."

"We're not here for comfort," said Dog, swiveling his chair to face Jack's own. "So did you get anything?"

Jack shook his head slowly. "No, nothing. As I said, I never know when I'm going to get something."

"So you can't control this stuff, whatever it is you do?"

Jack thought about that for a moment. "Mmmm . . . I can and I can't. If I have prompts or cues, I can work with them. Other times it just hits me. I touch something or someone and it's like a wave crashing over me, sensation, knowledge, vision; it varies."

Dog sat back. "Okaaaay. That's got to be pretty hard, doesn't it?"

"Yeah," said Jack, unstrapping himself. "Sometimes it is. I just have to wait around until it's there, but normally I have some idea where I might expect to find some sort of cue. I have a piece from the university that I got from Heering. I used that as a dream prompt."

"How?"

Jack thought about that for a minute. "I suppose it has to do with the energies trapped in material objects. I can use proximity to shape the direction of a dream as an initial prompt. From there I take control of the dream, try to steer it in directions that will give me the clues I'm looking for. If I'm holding an object, I'm in touch with those energies. Sometimes, though, I don't need to enter dreamstate to get there. A simple touch is enough to push whatever these senses are, and I get a vision or a picture then and there. It doesn't matter whether it's a dream or a waking vision; I still have to interpret what I see."

"Uh-huh," said Dog, rubbing his chin. "Weird. And you say you never know when it's going to hit you."

"That's right, unless I'm controlling it, and then I can't guarantee it's going to work."

Dog leaned forward, his elbows on his knees, so he was almost peering up at Jack, his long hair falling down around his face. "So is that what you were doing back there?"

"More or less," said Jack. "I went into dreamstate. Let my senses take me wherever they would."

It was Dog's turn to nod slowly. "And . . . ?"

Jack turned back to look into the nearly empty blackness in front of them. "Yeah, I got something, but I don't know what it was yet. Sometimes it takes a while for the images to slot into place and start to make sense. We're all connected. Everything's connected in one way or another. Finding the connections and making sense of them is the trick." He glanced at Dog, who was watching him appraisingly, then turned back to face the front again. "I was in this place. It was dark. Some sort of weird building, and someone was talking to me."

"What did they say?"

"It doesn't make any sense," said Jack slowly, feeling the disappointment of the lingering images. "No sense at all." He sighed. "And thinking about it, it could just have been a dream, just a normal dream."

"That's too bad. How can you tell the difference?" asked Dog.

"Normally, I can," said Jack with a shrug. "If it's really important, I know. There's just a feeling. The waking visions are far easier to be certain of. They're right there."

Dog seemed have run out of questions for the time being. Already unstrapped, he stood. "There's a bit of time to kill. You feel like a drink or something?"

Jack nodded.

"Yeah, me too. Come on, I'll show you the galley."

Fortunately, Dog had some pretty decent coffee on board. Jack hadn't even considered the fact that he might not.

"You want something stronger?" Dog had asked.

"No, thanks. Not the way my stomach is feeling."

Jack's response had brought a short, hard laugh and a shake of the head along with muttering about damned planet-huggers.

Jack sat at the small galley table, cupping his mug between his hands on the table in front of him and staring down into the blackness of the swirling liquid that now half-filled the mug. There were no clues there. "Our dream." What the hell had that meant? He'd tried to steer the dream in Billie's direction, but nothing. The knowledge did little to add any comfort to the way his thoughts were headed. Was she even okay? If she was in trouble, he would have been expected to be led straight to where she was, but there wasn't even the slightest trace of her in the dream, nor in the others he'd had over the last couple of days.

Dog sat opposite, sliding his cup from one hand to the other on the smooth table surface.

The galley was compact, metallic chairs set into slotted grooves that crisscrossed the floor so you could move them into various positions. He guessed you might be able to fit four people in there at a stretch. A row of latched gray cupboards graced one wall above a food preparation bench with a couple of drawers and a disposal unit. A faucet sat above the disposal, and a heater sat close by, affixed to the wall. If you wanted to make coffee, you pulled a mug from its slot in the cupboard, filled it with water and dried coffee from a sealed packet, then shoved it in the heater. Dog had told him that when he was finished, he needed to wash the mug with the minimum of water and slot it back in the rack. Not so with any of the food. It was all in sealed disposable containers that could be heated and then put into the disposal unit when you were finished. No waste, no fuss. It made sense that you'd have to mix convenience and practicality in a utilitarian space like this.

"So what are we going to do when we get there?" said Dog.

Jack looked up from his mug slowly. "I really don't know. Find some clue that will tell us where Billie and Antille have gotten to."

"Well, if they're in a ship, we should be able to pick up their signal if they're in the vicinity. It's not like there are going to be a lot to choose from."

"Hmmmm," said Jack, looking back down into his coffee. Dog was right. And what if there wasn't a signal? What were they going to do then?

Dog cleared his throat. "Okay, Stein, tell me. What's with the whole naked-on-the-bunk bit?"

"Hey, it's just how I work," said Jack, looking up again. "I try to strip away as much as I can that might interfere with the dream direction, and that includes my clothes. I never know what might have accumulated during the day, one way or another. I don't know if it's important or not. It's just what I do."

"I think I get it," said Dog, standing and draining the last from his mug. "But how *would* you know? How did you learn all this stuff?" He gave the mug a quick rinse and slotted it back into the cupboard rack.

"Trial and error," said Jack. "It's not like there's some sort of psychic academy or anything. Some of the intelligence training comes in handy. Some of the tricks from the old days. Bits and pieces along the way."

"Uh-huh," said Dog. Jack seemed to have satisfied his questions for the time being. "I'm going up front just to check the heading. You?" he asked, standing.

Jack stood too, taking his mug over to wash it out, sliding past Dog as he did so. "I think I might try another session and see if I can get anything more meaningful out of it. So remember . . ."

Dog laughed. "Forewarned. I'll call you from up front if anything happens. Otherwise, I'll be in my cabin. We've still got a few hours on this leg."

He slipped out of the galley, leaving Jack to attend to his own mug.

Jack replaced the mug and made his way back to the cabin. It wasn't going to be easy to slip back into dreamstate, having just been there, but there was something about the last session that was worrying him. What he'd told Dog was true enough, but he was sure there was something there, something he had to tease apart to get to the meaning. There was only one way to do that—go back and see if there was anything else.

Back in his cabin, he opened the locker and dragged out his bag. Somewhere in there, he'd remembered to pack the stone shard he'd acquired at the university. His conversation with Dog had reminded him he still had it. With any luck, it could provide the defining prompt he needed. He cursed, unable to find it. He shoved his hand deeper into the back, feeling around beneath hastily bundled clothing. He was on the verge of pulling everything out, convinced that he hadn't packed it after all, when his fingers sent a sudden flash of energy through his arm and chest. Deep in one corner, Jack's fingertips had made contact. He pushed deeper and grasped the stone shard, drawing it forth, his fingers curled tightly around it. That initial flash was enough. The energy was more subdued now, but it was still there, barely pulsing beneath his perception. Jack crossed to the bunk and placed it down in the bed's center. He stood there for a couple of seconds, looking down at it, debating. Would it take him back, or would it lead him somewhere completely different? Finally, he decided it was worth the risk.

Not even bothering to shove his belongings back into the locker, he stripped off his clothes and resumed his position, with the stone shard held beneath his hands at the very center of his chest, but not before he had checked the cabin door to make sure he'd be truly undisturbed.

He felt the energy and tried not to think about it. He needed to fix one thing in his mind, and this time it wasn't Billie. He thought about a voice, a deep, sonorous voice.

"Welcome to our dream."

Gradually, his breathing slowed. Gradually, his thought processes relaxed. Down, he thought. Down, deep, dark. Waves of darkness.

"Welcome to our dream."

Hold it, Jack.

He was back in that darkened doorway.

This time there was something else. He could smell earth. He could hear. Something whooshed past in the air above. A vague buzzing came from all around. He stood in front of the darkness, waiting. He worked his mouth, dry now. This was important, some way; he knew it, and the nerves tingled in his arms and fingertips. The stone shard was there in his right hand. He glanced down at it, stroked his thumb over its surface, but there wasn't anything else he could feel from it. Swallowing, seeking to drive moisture into his dry throat, he took a deep breath and stepped inside.

"Billie?" he said quietly. Now, why had he said that? He pushed the thought away.

"Hello?" Lame, but better.

Silence beat against him. The shadow seemed to muffle any noise that had been outside.

"Hello?" he said again, this time louder.

Nothing.

He took three firm steps into the darkness. Not only was it muffling the sound, but it also wrapped about him, slowing his movements, putting pressure against his chest. It was difficult to breathe. The darkness moved around him, drawing closer, trailing thick, cloying bands across his mouth and nose.

"No," he shouted, trying to force the shadow away with that single word.

He couldn't catch his breath. Tighter still. He was bound in shadow, panic starting to well inside. He bunched his will, pushed, thrusting out with his mind.

"No!"

And it was gone. The space was filled with light. Jack drew a deep, shuddering breath, and another, blinking against the light. As his eyes adjusted, details swam into focus.

He was in a bright, empty room. Dark stone walls marked out a broad, square space, climbing to a dark ceiling. In one corner sat some sort of platform, hovering a mere foot above the stone-paved floor. He noticed for the first time that he was not alone.

One, two, three more of the alien creatures stood around the space, immobile on their four silvery legs, their central trunks stationary.

Jack caught his breath again, waiting. They were still, no movement at all. This time there was no dipping of the central trunk, no unfolding of petals; they could have been identical metallic sculptures spread randomly across the space of the vast room. He took a hesitant step toward one of the creatures, then another. He was standing right in front of it now, though how was he supposed to work out what was the front? He walked slowly around the creature, looking for some sign, something that would give him a clue. His nerves were singing, his breath coming in short gasps, and he could feel the sweat on his body. It was warm here, too warm.

He stopped his circuit and looked up at the central piece, searching for some movement, anything that would tell him the creature knew he was here.

"Hello, Jack."

Jack spun toward the sound of the voice. Talbot stood in the far corner of the room where before there was simply floor and walls, leaning against one wall, his legs crossed.

Talbot pushed himself off the wall and waved at him. Jack almost laughed. The gesture seemed completely out of place.

Jack was almost afraid of speaking. "Talbot, what are you doing here?"

"What are you doing here, Jack Stein?"

And suddenly he was over in the corner, standing in front of the man. Jack was thankful this was the whole Talbot, not the burned one with half a face.

"No, Talbot, why you? What are you doing here?"

"I'm not here," said Talbot.

Jack checked back over his shoulder, but the randomly arrayed creatures had not moved, as far as he could see.

"What do you mean, you're not here? I can see you. I'm talking to you."

"Yes," said Talbot. "But I'm really not here."

"Okay, you're not here," said Jack.

Talbot smiled.

"Am I here?" said Jack.

"Yes, you are here," said Talbot. "And so are they." He waved his arm in a wide, encompassing arc. "All of them."

Jack turned slowly. "So why am I here?" he said, looking from one alien creature to the next.

"I don't know," said Talbot. "We don't know. We have been trying to determine that since the first time you came."

"We?" said Jack without turning around. Talbot didn't answer.

When Jack turned back, Talbot had gone.

Seventeen

Though he tried desperately to stay in the dream, as soon as Talbot disappeared, Jack found himself dragged upward through the layers. The room and the aliens grew foggy, blowing away in wisps and strands that curled around him like the cloying shadow from before. He fought, but soon the cabin lights filtered with dark pink light through his eyelids, and with a grimace he opened his eyes. Back in the blank cabin aboard the *Amaranth*, and if anything, he was more confused than before about what his inner senses were telling him.

With a frustrated mutter, he swung his feet off the bed, reached for his clothes, and slowly pulled on his shirt. He looked at his case, the bundled clothes, and other things protruding from the top, wondering if there was any point in unpacking. One thing he knew for sure: He had to replace the stone shard and keep it out of harm's way. Who knew what would happen if he'd left it lying around and they lost spin again. Standing, pulling on the rest of his clothes, he then bent and pushed everything back into the bag, including the shard, and shoved it back in the locker.

He needed someone with whom to talk through what he had seen. He needed Billie. Ever since she'd come into his life, she'd acted as his sounding board, pointing out flaws in his thinking whether he wanted it or not. Running solo again was different. If he was lucky, Dog might serve the same purpose, though he was a little wary of sharing the insides of his thought patterns with someone like Dog. Not that he didn't trust him. Well, he didn't, completely. Jack had sensed traces of skepticism in McCreedy's reactions, but that was normal. He often sensed skepticism—just about every time he took on a case.

It didn't hurt to try.

He unlocked the cabin door and headed forward.

The control room/bridge, whatever it was, sat empty, along with McCreedy's seat. Jack wandered over to the seat and scanned the controls, but there was nothing there that made any sense to him. Color-coded displays, numbers, symbols; it was all very impressive, but told him nothing. He thought about rousing Dog from whatever he was doing, but decided against it. His fellow passenger would emerge soon enough. Jack wasn't sure how long he'd spent in dreaming, but even if it hadn't been that long, it couldn't be much more time before Dog would have to appear to make the adjustments required before their next jump.

Instead, Jack took his own seat, stretched his legs out so that his feet were resting on the front console, and stared out into the Dopplered stars showing through the viewscreens. Off to one side a weird pinkish cloud shot with orange and trailing off to white tissue at the farthest end dominated the sky. Looking out to the right, he saw a small glowing ball shining with blue light, almost too bright to look at.

He pulled his feet off the console and sat forward, scanning the image in front while he thought. For some reason the aliens had been asking him what he was doing there. Or at least Talbot had been. Were they one and the same? And if so, why would his dream consciousness transpose the two?

One by one, he picked through the images. The tall buildings, the room he had been in—they were the same as the buildings he'd seen on Mandala at the City of Trees, but whole, rather than weathered and damaged by whatever disaster had struck that planet. So it was an alien city, and it had to be on the alien homeworld, where they were headed. What he didn't get was that complete immobility and apparent lack of awareness. Every time he had dreamed the aliens, they had been completely aware of his presence. They had responded; but this time it was Talbot who had been doing the responding. Yet Talbot had said he wasn't there. None of it made sense.

And it was getting him no closer to Billie and Antille.

"Ah, Jack. Any luck?" asked Dog as he wandered in. Jack watched him approach in the slightly distorted reflection in front. Dog was pulling his fingers through his hair in a halfhearted attempt to get it in some semblance of order. By the time he reached the back of Jack's chair, he had given up.

"Not really," said Jack without turning around. "I got some images that I think are the alien homeworld, but apart from that, no clear message. Just some stuff that makes me think I'm not done yet."

"How often can you do this?" asked Dog, leaning on the back of the chair now.

Jack grimaced as he answered. "I really don't know. I've never really pushed the limits, or needed to. When I've tried to go in too many times in a short period, the dreamstate just gets shorter and shorter. I really think I'm done for a couple of days now. I then have to knit the sequences together to anything meaningful, and I can feel that starting to happen now. There's something there, but I'm still not getting what it is."

Dog rocked back and forth on the chair. "Will you look at that?"

Jack looked up at him. Dog wore a rapt expression, staring out at the view in front.

"Damn, I never tire of this stuff, and it just gets better. Better than drugs, you know?"

Jack turned back to look at what Dog was seeing. Yeah, it was impressive, but it clearly didn't stir Jack's emotions in quite the same way.

"The jump drive's made all the difference," said Dog. "Old conventional drives, the same things over and over, day after day, week in, week out. But this . . ." He shook his head, his eyes wide. "Who would have considered the possibilities?" His voice trailed off. "Man," he breathed.

"Yeah, I get it," said Jack. "So how long have we got?"

Dog tore his attention away from the view and glanced over at a display. "Hmmm, about an hour and a half, I'd say."

Jack nodded.

"Sit down, Dog," said Jack.

McCreedy frowned but did as he was asked. "What is it?"

"What's really in this for you, McCreedy?"

Dog lowered his gaze and scratched at the back of his neck. He glanced up at the view again, then back to Jack's face. "That's part of it, out there. Adventure, the undiscovered, something new. I'm serious. I get bored real easy, Jack. You just happened to strike me at the right time. Just lucky, I guess."

"Come on. What gets you, Dog? What do you want?"

Dog was looking down at his feet. "I never owned anything growing up," he said quietly. "I was just shoved from place to place and never had any control. The military was a way to get away from that, but that was a mistake too. In the end, it wound up being just more of the same. I thought I'd escaped." He gave a short, self-deprecating laugh. "But now . . ." He lifted his gaze slowly. "I own the fucking universe, man."

There was a flicker in Dog's eyes, so brief that for a moment Jack thought he had imagined it. But no, there was no doubt. That brief reaction had shown uncertainty. What was Dog McCreedy uncertain about?

"So what do you do when you get back—when we get back?" asked Jack.

Again Dog shrugged. "More of the same, I guess. I don't care now, you know. I own my own ship. I'm more or less my own boss. Sure, I could do with more cash— couldn't we all—but you can't beat the life, Jack. You just can't beat it."

They sat in silence for a while then, Jack wondering if he was that much different from the younger man sitting across from him.

"I need coffee," he said finally.

"You go," said Dog, not looking up. "I've got stuff to do up here."

He didn't know why, but Jack was sure he had to be up front for the jump, or every jump. By the time he got back to the bridge, Dog seemed to have moved beyond his deep, thoughtful mood and was back to his old self.

"After all that coffee, I suggest you make sure you don't need a piss before we jump. It could get ugly," he said. "And you know, Jack, I don't want to have to clean up my nice, clean deck."

"Yeah, yeah, McCreedy. You just worry about getting us to where we need to go," Jack responded.

"Nothing to worry about," said Dog. "You'd better strap yourself in. We're jumping in about two minutes."

Jack felt the coffee stir in his guts with the news. He stepped quickly toward his own seat and did just as Dog suggested. Once he was sure he was secure, he turned his attention back to McCreedy, watching the adjustments, the quick checks, the lightning-fast hand movements across the control panel. There was no hesitation there, and that gave Jack a touch of confidence.

"Ready?" said Dog, his hand hovering above the panel. Jack nodded.

"Go!"

Dog slapped the panel and the wrench flipped through Jack's body. Light. Everything was light. Every particle flipped inside out. He reached out blindly and his hand made contact with something. He turned to look slowly, so slowly. It was Dog's wrist and he was gripping it hard. Dog was turning to look at him, the action drawn out in slow motion. It was Dog, and yet it wasn't Dog. Sitting beside Jack was another McCreedy. He flashed on that transport, Danny Boy's grinning face looking back at him as they thrummed across the jungle canopy. It was Danny Boy. No, it wasn't. The hair was there, but darker, thicker. There was no trace of the burn scar on his cheek. His face was smooth, unlined, except for the traceries of laughter around the edges of his mouth. Then the image faded. A flash of light and they had emerged.

Jack was gripping Dog's wrist. The old Dog McCreedy. The burn scar was back. So was the flash of white at the top of his head. He was looking at Jack strangely.

"What is it, Jack? What's wrong?"

Jack struggled to find words. "It's . . . it's okay," he said haltingly.

"You sure?"

Jack nodded.

"Well, can I have my arm back then?"

Releasing his grip, unfolding his fingers one by one from around McCreedy's wrist, Jack nodded. "Sorry. I guess it's just the jump. I can't seem to get used to it."

Dog nodded, gave one more concerned look, and then turned to gaze out of the front.

"Well, that's different," he said.

Jack's attention was still fixed on McCreedy's face, overlaying memories of the vision on what was in front of him now. What the hell had that been about?

"Look," said McCreedy.

Slowly Jack turned to look at what Dog was showing him.

The sky here was dark. Very few stars were visible. They clustered in small groups at the top and bottom of the field of view. In between, featherlike clouds drifted across the blackness. No, thought Jack, more like the spume whipped from the tops of waves on a stormy day.

"Hmmm, I wonder what's at the back." Dog reached out a hand and hit a spot on the panel. "Shit!" said Dog.

Jack went cold inside; then his heart started racing, the panic sweeping over him.

They were almost on top of a vast, craggy orb, spinning slowly against a dark background, virtually invisible except for the faintest of lights. Suddenly Dog's hands were flying over the controls. "Damn thing's got us," he said. "Shit."

The image in the viewscreen was definitely getting closer. Jack gripped his seat.

"What can we—"

"Shut up, Stein," snapped Dog. "Let me work."

There was a burst of vibration and sound, and the feeling of acceleration.

"Damn it," hissed Dog, his face creased in concentration. "Come on, baby."

Jack couldn't breathe. He couldn't move. And still the vast stone wall grew closer.

Another burst. More push. More concentration. And Dog sat back. "That's it," he said with the slightest touch of triumph, and reached out to stroke the control panel in front of him. He nodded and turned to look at Jack.

"I don't know what made me look. Proximity warning should have gone off, but I guess the jump screwed with it somehow. If I didn't know better, I'd say it was because you were here, Stein. All that old stuff. That sort of shit used to happen to you all the time, didn't it? I remember. Lucky Stein." He narrowed his eyes. "Still working, huh, Jack." He held the look for a couple of seconds, then turned away. "Damn, I'm going to have to recalibrate now, work out the position and look for the next vector."

Jack barely noticed what Dog was saying. He was remembering how to breathe again, his heart still pounding in his ears.

He suddenly had an awful thought that chilled him to his marrow. What if Billie and Antille had done the same thing in their ship? What if what McCreedy said was true and it was just his own presence that had made Dog look? What if that was why he was picking up nothing of Billie? What if . . .

No, dammit. Enough with the what-ifs. He'd know. He was sure he'd know.

"Listen, Jack. This is going to take me about an hour or so," said Dog. "You may as well go back and find something to occupy yourself in the meantime. We have a couple of days to the next point anyway, by my calculations."

Jack rubbed the back of his neck. The vision was still disturbing him. He'd almost forgotten it in the panic, but now it was back. He stared at McCreedy, almost seeing that younger face again.

"What?" said Dog.

"No. Nothing," Jack replied with a quick shake of his head. He undid the straps and stood, taking a couple of deep breaths to steady himself. "You do what you need to do."

He left Dog sitting there poring over the controls. At the doorway he looked back, but all he could see was the large spinning ball that had nearly ended their quest. Despite himself, he scanned the sky, what he could see of the body's surface, searching for wreckage, or something, some sign, hoping that he wouldn't find it. Finally he tore himself away from the doorway and the viewscreen and headed back toward his cabin.

The next two days, relative ship time, were full of long, seemingly endless hours spent either in his cabin or in brief conversations with McCreedy. The confined space, the lack of anything real to do, built tension between them and within them, but there was something else. Jack had noticed it just after the last jump. It was almost as if the air was buzzing around them, barely perceptible, just below the threshold of awareness. He had mentioned it to Dog, but Dog had dismissed it, claiming there was nothing there. It worked in Jack's molars and through his bones. It was there, all right, whether Dog could sense it or not, and it merely added to the already growing tenseness that Jack was feeling. He resigned himself to spending as much time as he could alone in the cabin so he wouldn't get in Mc-Creedy's way. It was also becoming apparent that Mc-Creedy guarded his space jealously — this was his ship, his domain, and Jack's presence was a politely tolerated intrusion.

Jack dreamed twice more in those two days, dreams brought on by the regular patterns of sleep rather than invoked by his own exercises. The first one was back in the alien city, and it was the clearer of the two. When he awoke, the images were fresh and bright in his mind. He had been back in the large room, no darkness, and this time there had been no Talbot. He had walked from one immobile alien to the other, talking to them, trying to establish differences, waiting for motion. Everything was still, and the air had been thick. After a while he had simply stopped trying to invoke any response, and waited in the room's center for something to occur.

For a long time nothing happened, but finally his patience had been rewarded. A wave of sound had appeared in the center of his head, washing forward, then receding, broad, incomprehensible. It grew louder, reached a peak, and then dwindled away into the distance. Five times it had repeated, then stopped. After a pause it started again, but this time he could sense the shape of words. Something, someone, was trying to talk to him. By concentrating, focusing on the wash of sound as words, he was eventually able to distinguish the words themselves. It helped when he had closed his eyes, blocking out the images and light and immersing himself in the dark, auditory sea.

"Jack Stein," the voices had told him. They had been voices, not a single voice, all speaking together.

"Jack Stein," they had said. "You are coming."

He had tried to answer them with words, but that hadn't had any apparent effect. Eventually he just willed his response back at them.

"Yes, I am coming."

"You are coming. It is too soon."

"I don't understand."

"You are not ready," the noise surged against his mind. "Not ready."

"What do you mean?" asked Jack. "Why am I not ready?"

"Your time is not right."

Jack had spent a moment before sending back his response to that one. The construction was weird. If it was the alien voices trying to communicate with him, then that might explain it, but the word choice was peculiar. *Your* time. Not *the* time.

"I don't understand."

"Time will work against you," said the massed voices.

He was still standing confusedly in the room's center when the dream faded, slipping from his grasp like so much smoke.

He had been awake a full two hours before traces of the second dream had come back to him, a tangential flash as he sat sipping at a mug of coffee, alone in the galley. Dog was locked away in his cabin, doing whatever he did in there.

The woman from an earlier dream had been present in the second one, sitting on the edge of a bed, again wearing that shapeless white robe. She had been watching him, and somehow he got the impression that she was waiting for something.

"Hello," he had said to her.

She did not respond. The set of her jaw had become a little harder, as if that had been completely the wrong thing for Jack to say. After a few moments she had stood. The shape of her body was clear beneath the robe's thin material, and Jack had looked on appreciatively. She caught him looking and placed her fists on her hips.

"What are you doing, Jack?" she'd asked accusingly.

"Looking," he'd said.

Her voice was deep, her blond hair slightly mussed. High cheekbones and sharp features served to make her hard look even harder. She wasn't quite his type, but she was pretty attractive all the same. Her flimsy garb made it difficult to keep his mind on what was happening.

"You can stop looking and do what you're supposed to be doing, Jack," she said.

"And what am I supposed to be doing?"

"You're supposed to be here," she said, clear impatience in her tone.

"But I am here," said Jack.

"You are *not!*" she'd said, a hard emphasis on the last word.

With her final accusation ringing in his ears, Jack had awoken.

Eighteen

It was the second dream that stayed with him most, her face lingering in his consciousness with that clear look of accusation. Didn't he have enough blond women in his life giving him orders? Billie was quite enough on her own.

It merely added to the tension he felt buzzing through the ship.

Dog was beside him, making final adjustments to their jump trajectories. Despite their hijacking by the huge rotating mass at their last emergence, he seemed fairly confident that he'd made the proper corrections to get them where they needed to be. Only a couple of minutes remained, but he couldn't help thinking about what might have happened to Billie's ship if they'd gone through the same thing. It was either that, or thinking about the impending jump. Neither was a particularly pleasing prospect.

"You're sure?" he asked Dog yet again.

"Yeah, I'm sure, Jack. Have a little faith, will you?" The response was undisguisedly snappy.

Jack settled back into his seat again, unconvinced. Dammit, this was still relatively new technology. Nobody was an expert. It didn't hurt to be sure, did it?

"Coming up . . . now!" said Dog, and hit the control.

Jack's entire body and mind went through that sucking flip, and again they were through. This time there'd been no vision, just that indescribable sensation.

They had jumped to an area of space that looked normal compared to their last emergence. Dog, just to be sure, flipped the viewscreens through the various options, checking their immediate vicinity, and let out a low exhalation.

"Well, we can be thankful for that."

Jack nodded. There wasn't much else to say.

Slowly he released the straps holding him in his seat and forced himself to try to relax. Damn, but that could become wearing. He didn't envy Dog at all.

He took several deep breaths and reached out with his perception, searching for something, anything. He'd been expecting another episode like the last jump, and strangely, he was almost disappointed that there had been nothing similar.

The weird buzz was still there, even stronger than before. What the hell was it?

"Dog, you're sure you don't feel anything unusual?" he asked.

Dog turned to him and gave him a querying look. "No, nothing. Postjump nausea. Always get a touch of that, but apart from that, nothing else. Why?"

"I don't know," said Jack. "Something. You're sure?"

"Dammit, yes, I'm sure. What is it with you, Stein?"

Jack shook his head.

"Well, if you want to project your own damned insecurity onto my ship and my piloting, you can take it somewhere else."

Jack held up a hand and shook his head again. "No, it's not that. And I'm sorry. I feel stuff, you know. I just want to make sure."

"Well, if you like, I can run a systems check while

we're waiting for the next jump. Not that I think it will do a lot of good. The *Amaranth* is set to notify me if there's anything not as it should be. Anyway, I'd know. I can feel her, feel if there's anything wrong."

"It doesn't have to be the ship, McCreedy. Something, anything. Look what happened with the last jump. I'm feeling something, and I'd prefer just to get it out of the way if I can. Knowing what it is goes a long way toward dealing with it."

Dog sighed. "Okay, if it makes you feel any better, I'll kick in the diagnostics, but we haven't got very long before the next jump. They might not be finished by the time we go through, and who knows what effect the jump might have." He spread his hands wide. "I'm only saying . . ."

"Yeah, I get it, McCreedy," said Jack. Damn, where had that come from? He should have been far more conciliatory than that. "Look, sorry. Whatever this thing is, it's winding me up tight. It's like this constant buzzing in my bones and my teeth. That's the only way to describe it."

"Don't worry about it," said Dog, turning back to the controls. "Anyway, I've initiated the diagnostic sequence. If there's anything to find, she'll find it."

"She?"

"Amaranth."

"Hmmm," said Jack. He'd never quite come to terms with the way people imbued inanimate objects with personae. Okay, the *Amaranth* wasn't quite inanimate, but still . . .

"Two more jumps, plus the next one," said Dog matter-of-factly. "We'll be there before you know it."

Somehow, Jack didn't quite share his optimism.

The next jump was upon them almost before they knew it. It came way too quickly for Jack's liking, and all the while the buzzing sensation persisted unabated. It was almost becoming a routine. Jack would retire to his cabin or to the galley to stoke himself with more coffee, and then he'd wander forward to strap himself in and grit his teeth in anticipation of the jump.

The following transition set his teeth on edge even more, heightening the buzzing sensation deep within his bones and making him disinclined to engage in conversation with Dog. He felt like his veins were strung with taut wire, humming through his system and setting his teeth on edge. When they emerged through the jump and into normal space, his jaw was clamped shut, and he was wincing against the heightened sensation beating through his system.

"What?" said Dog, looking at him a brief few seconds after they had emerged. "What is it?"

Jack shook his head, not saying anything. Not able to say anything. The feeling was coursing through his neural pathways, rendering him unable to speak, making him feel as if every cell in his body were going to explode. There was something happening to him, to both of them. This just wasn't normal. He'd been through jumps before, and it had never been like this.

"Come on, Jack. What's going on?"

"Nothing. It's okay," he forced out between clenched teeth. "How long before our next one?"

"About three hours."

"Fine," he said, the strain evident in his voice. "I'll be in my cabin."

He didn't want to talk to Dog. He didn't want to talk to anyone. It was like that feeling when you'd had too much to drink and were on the verge of throwing up. He swallowed once, twice, then released himself from his harness and stumbled his way back to the cabin, feeling along the corridor walls for support. Christ, he didn't need this. Things were bad enough without the physical symptoms as well.

Jack found his bunk and lay there, the buzzing working through his bones, stringing through his skull. He tried a couple of his relaxation exercises, to no avail. The dull throb in his jaw from pressing his teeth tightly together for too long became his sole focus. Nothing was like this. Nothing.

Dog's voice blurred out from some source in the cabin. Jack was unable even to focus on the direction. It just seemed to come from all around him, barely cutting through the buzz. What the hell was wrong with him?

"You'd better get up here, Jack."

He mouthed words back at Dog's disembodied voice.

"Jack, you coming?"

"Yeah, I'm coming," he said, forcing the syllables through closed teeth.

His vision was blurred. Every one of his joints ached, dull, throbbing pain. He levered himself upright, groaning, and staggered out of the cabin, toward the bridge.

At the corridor's end he leaned in the doorway.

"Dog," he said, barely forcing out the words.

"Shit," said Dog, swiveling his seat to face him. "You look terrible. What's wrong?"

"Appreciate your concern," Jack said, his jaw clenched. "Dunno. You got any patches?"

"Yeah, wait here. Why didn't you say?"

The reason he hadn't said was that using patches hadn't been on his agenda for a while now. He just hadn't thought about it. He could barely think, let alone consider what he might need.

Dog pushed past him and returned a few moments later. Strong analgesic. He waved the patch and Jack snatched for it, peeled the backing, and slapped it on. Anything to help at this stage.

Dog watched him with a concerned expression.

"I'm okay," said Jack. "Do what you have to do."

Dog lingered for a second, but then returned to his seat. After giving Jack one more questioning glance, flicking the hair back from his face, he turned his attention to the controls.

Jack stumbled to his own seat and, supporting himself with one hand, lowered himself carefully into it, and then reached for the restraints. He fumbled with the harness, managing to focus on the task with an effort.

How long before the patch kicked in?

Buzzzzzzzzzzzzzzzz.

It had to be soon, right?

Buzzzzzzzzzzzzzzzz.

He let air escape between his teeth in a low hiss.

"Okay, Jack. You ready? We're coming up. This is it."

Jack's hands gripped the arms of his seat tightly.

Now, he thought. Now.

Dog reached for the controls, flashing Jack a sidelong look, a concerned frown creasing his forehead.

"Now!" said Dog.

Nineteen

That dreadful sucking sensation swept through him, turning his cells inside out and back again. He screwed his eyes tight, pressing his jaw together so tightly that his teeth felt like they might crack. A bright flash lit his eyelids from within, and a rushing sound spilled past his consciousness like a huge wind inside his ears, and then, abruptly, it was gone.

They were through. The jump had been different this time.

Gradually Jack released the pressure in his jaw, unhooked his fingers from the seat, and took a long, deep, shuddering breath.

"Jesus," he whispered.

The sensation was not the only thing that had gone. The buzzing was gone too. It was as if a huge pressure had been released from his body, inside and out, as if he were no longer going to burst from the inside.

Slowly, carefully, he opened his eyes.

In the front viewscreen, he could see a system. Five planets, clustered about a bluish star. This was it. This was what they had come for.

He scanned the system, seeking . . . he didn't quite know what he was seeking. At this distance, was he likely to see a ship, or be able to pick it out from the surrounding starscape?

Three small inner planets, a large giant, and another, smaller body on a wide orbit made up the system, with the star dominating the viewscreen.

Slowly he turned to face Dog. "So this is it?" he asked. "You're sure?"

Dog was staring at him, openmouthed.

Dog was not Dog.

"What the fuck?" said Jack.

In the pilot's seat sat a younger man. It looked like Dog McCreedy, but it wasn't. Gone was the flash of white in the hair, gone was the burn scar and the shadows and lines that gave time and experience to McCreedy's face. This was a much younger man.

"What the . . . ?" he said again, stupidly. This wasn't a dream. It couldn't be. He'd know if it were a dream.

Jack started to fumble with his harness.

"Wait," said McCreedy/Not-McCreedy. "Jack?" He looked puzzled.

"Huh?" Jack blinked.

It was McCreedy. He had McCreedy's voice, though not quite as gravelly.

"What's happened?" said Not-Dog.

"You tell me. Who the . . ."

"Look at yourself, Jack. Just look." He lifted an arm, flexed his fingers, and appeared to be examining his hand. He turned it over, looking at the palm. "Damn," he said. "It's happened to me too, hasn't it?"

Jack managed to release his harness, and stood. He shook his head. This couldn't be happening. It just couldn't be.

"I don't get it," said the young man who was not Dog. "I just don't get it. What the fuck happened?"

Jack left the young man sitting there examining his

hands and left the control room, walking down the corridor rapidly toward the facilities. There was a lightness in his step, an energy that he hadn't felt for years. He reached up and scraped the patch from his neck, balling it in his fist. The patch felt real enough. He reached the shower room, waited impatiently for the door to slide open, and stepped inside, still clutching the wadded patch in one hand. He should be feeling scared, but he wasn't. All he felt was an inexplicable lightness.

"Mirror," he said, and one wall became reflective, showing him standing there, a slightly startled expression on his face, but it wasn't his face, and yet it was.

The man who stared back at him was Jack Stein. He wore Jack's clothes, but it was a Jack Stein he recognized only from memory. It was years since he'd looked like that. The grayness, the slight thinning at the temples, the shadows beneath his eyes, they were gone, all gone. He leaned closer to the mirror, examining, and the figure leaned toward him. Jack raised a tentative hand and prodded at his face. The figure did likewise. He stepped back. What was going on? He shook his head and so did the figure before him. The mirror was a mirror, all right. Just for a second, he had a flash of some of the old comedy vids where two look-alikes mirror each other's actions in an open doorway. One of them is always slightly confused, unsure whether it's a mirror or not, and goes through a series of unusual performances to test the reflection. He had the sudden urge to break into an absurd dance routine, but quelled it. Despite himself, he grinned. The younger image grinned back.

"Shit," said Jack, the grin fading as fast as it had appeared.

He leaned in closer to the mirror again and gently touched his face, seeking changes, differences, assuring himself that it was truly his reflection he was seeing. He flexed his arm, turned and looked back over his shoulder, shook his head again. Any moment he expected to wake, to find himself back on the bunk preparing to ride through the next jump. Leaning in again, he placed the flat of his palm against the mirrored surface and pressed. Mirrors always had strange properties in dreams. The surface was solid, no ripples, no give. He stepped back.

Christ. He could stand here for hours, but it wasn't going to get him any closer to working out what the hell was going on here. He blanked the wall and left the shower room, heading back to the bridge.

As he entered, Dog—and he had reconciled himself to the fact that it was Dog now—was still flexing his hands and turning them one way, then the other, looking at them with a fascinated expression on his face.

"Dog?" he said.

"Yeah," he responded, tearing his attention away from the self-examination.

"Um," said Jack. "I . . . um . . ." He shook his head. "Something happened back there." Understatement of the year, Stein. "I have no idea what's going on."

He stepped to his seat and sat heavily. His mind was racing, trying to think of something to say, but nothing seemed right. He shook his head again.

"Damn, but you look all right," said Dog. "It suits you."

Jack felt a manic urge to laugh rise inside him, but he bit his bottom lip. "Yeah, you don't look so bad yourself."

"Huh," said Dog.

"And once we've finished with this mutual admiration," said Jack, "maybe we ought to work out what we're going to do now." He scanned the viewscreen, looking for options out there where he knew he wasn't going to find any.

Dog nodded slowly. "Man, think of the possibilities."

Jack turned slowly to look at him. "What possibilities,

Dog? We don't even know what the fuck's happened here. How are there possibilities?"

"I dunno," said Dog. "We're younger, aren't we? That's what's happened. Fountain of youth. Water of life. Wow, think about it. . . ."

"I'd say we've got other things to think about first," said Jack.

Dog seemed to stop in midthought. "This is really happening, isn't it?"

"You tell me," said Jack. "Maybe we're stuck in some sort of jump space and all of this is an illusion we've created so we can cope with it. How can we tell?"

Dog swiveled and started playing with the controls, touching panels, looking at readings, scanning from one device to another.

"Everything looks normal," he said. "I'm getting readings on the system. The ship's functioning within normal parameters. I can't see anything unusual."

"Yeah, but that's not going to tell us anything," said Jack. "You might be seeing what you expect to see."

Dog sat back slowly into his seat, his outstretched hand lingering over the controls. "Yeah, but there's too much," he said. "Besides, we're talking to each other. There's more than one of us here."

"We could be constructing that in our heads too," said Jack. "How do I know that I'm just not imagining that we're having this conversation?"

"How do we ever know?" said Dog.

He had a point, and one with which Jack was more than familiar. He drummed his fingers on the seat arm. "I don't know," he said. "I don't know."

It was as if, rather than having traveled through time, time had traveled through them, or trickled out of them, or something.

"We're not going to work it out sitting here talking

about it," said Dog. "We're supposed to find this alien homeworld. Right now I'm not complaining. So let's do what we're here to do. We can worry about it later."

"Uh-huh," said Jack slowly, but his mind was still ticking through the possibilities, and he was not convinced this was really happening at all. Any moment, he simply expected to wake up.

"So what now?" he said.

"I'm going to have to scan these planets, check the system," said Dog. "If this is an alien planet, it might not be something we'd expect. I don't know. It could take me some time. I'd like to be a little closer in so I can be sure of the readings too." He glanced up at the system's image, arrayed on the viewscreen in front of them. He pushed his hair back from his face with one hand, caught himself in midgesture, stared at the hand for half a second, then turned his attention back to the viewscreen, peering at each of the worlds in turn. Apart from that momentary lapse, he was right back to business.

"Okay," said Jack. "If that's the case, I might leave you to it for a while. I've got something I can do in the meantime."

"Uh-huh," said Dog, barely paying attention.

Jack nodded and stood again. He did have something to do. If he could invoke dreamstate one more time, he might get some idea of what was happening to them, or, at the very least, some clue about the system that now lay before them. At least he could feel like he was doing something useful. Though how he was going to be able to concentrate with the change . . . he just didn't know.

Back in his cabin, he went through the ritual, removing his clothing, getting ready to lie on the bunk and assume his standard pose, but there was something he had to do first.

"Mirror," he said.

There was Jack Stein, standing before him, but a Jack Stein that was someone he only half recognized, and then only through the veils of memory. His body was firmer, tighter. The slight softness around the middle was gone. There was chest hair, but dark again, instead of brushed with white. He turned around and looked over his shoulder. His back looked the same, but yeah, he was firmer in other places too. He turned back to face the wall and cast a critical eye over his reflected body. He hadn't really looked like this since he'd left the services. He'd maintained it for a couple of years, the regimen, the exercise, keeping himself taut and fit, but that had faded without the discipline. Self-discipline was the hardest of all. He turned again, checked over his shoulder, and then turned back once more. He held out an arm, inspected it, right from the shoulder to the tips of his fingers and back again. It was his arm, his body.

Was this real?

He felt . . . good.

Now that he was paying attention, other things were becoming apparent. The slight twinge in his shoulder that constantly nagged at him seemed to be gone. He flexed the shoulder, checking.

Yeah, he could live with this.

Was it an illusion?

He closed his eyes, concentrating. Dream within a dream within a dream. That was the risk. When you knew you were dreaming, how did you know when it really stopped?

Slowly he opened his eyes. The image was still in front of him, apparently unchanged. Chewing at his bottom lip, he tried to work out how much younger he looked. Fifteen years or ten, or somewhere in between, he thought, but it was hard to be sure. Your own self-image was colored by the passage of time and the gloss you put on your own perception. Maybe it was more.

Christ. What if it had happened to Billie? What if . . . fifteen years . . . maybe more . . .

She was sixteen. *Was.*

Was that why he had gotten nothing from her?

Jack pushed the thought away with an effort. He couldn't afford to think like that. He didn't want to think like that. First things first. He and Dog had to deal with their current situation and then find Antille and Billie. The alien planet was the first thing, the aliens themselves. If he found them, then everything would start to become clear. His dreams had been telling him that much, if nothing else. First, however, he had to try to find out something more.

With a resolve made solely of the fact that he'd convinced himself it was the only way, he blanked the wall and moved to the bunk to take up his position.

Jack willed himself to relax, closing his eyes and fixing an image of the silvery alien creatures in the center of his mind.

"Dammit, Stein. Concentrate," he muttered to himself, but his thoughts kept skittering away, and try as he might, his breath remained rapid, refusing to slow.

"Dammit."

He stood again and went to retrieve the stone shard. It looked like he really needed a prompt now, and he hoped the tiny rock sliver had not lost the power to guide him. With the piece clutched firmly in his hand, he stepped back to the bunk and lay down again, holding his closed hand to the center of his chest. Eyes closed once more, he forced his breath into an even, deep pattern, breathing through his nose and counting the time of each inhalation and each exhalation, thinking of nothing else. He could feel the stone shard's energy as a warm tingle within his fist. One, two, three, four, five. One, two, three, four, five. His breathing became more regular, deeper. The numbers rolled through his mind, back and forth, and at last taking him lower, deeper into that state of consciousness that would permit him to dream. Gently, gently, he felt himself start to drift.

"Ah, nice," said Talbot, reaching out with two fingers to touch Jack's cheek. "It looks good on you."

"What?" asked Jack.

"The change suits you. And you know what they say about a change."

Jack was puzzled. "No, what do they say?"

Talbot shook his head. He seemed taller. Jack looked up at him. Talbot towered over him.

Jack looked down at his body. He had the body of a skinny kid.

"Hey," he said, and clamped his mouth shut. The voice that came out was high and light, a child's voice.

"Come back, Jack," said Talbot.

Jack squeezed his eyes shut and concentrated. This was his subconscious playing with him. He needed it to stop. Slowly he opened his eyes again, to look directly into Talbot's face. That was better.

"What's going on, Carl?" he asked.

"Good question," said Talbot. "Very good question."

For the first time Jack looked around them. They stood together in a blank space, completely featureless apart from what looked like gray metal walls in every direction. "What is this place?"

"This is nowhere, Jack," said Talbot. "It is wherever you want it to be."

"Oh, you're a great help, Talbot. Next you're going to tell me this is the stuff that dreams are made of."

Talbot laughed. "Oh, but it is."

"Shit," said Jack, and looked away. "No, I don't want to be here."

"No, you don't," said Talbot. "But you have to be here, before you're there."

Jack closed his eyes, willing Talbot away, willing himself back to the room with the aliens. He opened his eyes, but Talbot was still there. Distant gray walls still surrounded them.

"Dammit," he muttered.

"What do you want, Jack?" said Talbot.

Jack ground his teeth. "I want some damned answers. That's what I want. I want some of this to make sense. I want something I can use to find Billie."

Talbot nodded thoughtfully. "Yes, it's a start," he said.

"Okay," said Jack. "Take me back to the aliens."

In an eyeblink, they were back in the broad room with the immobile alien creatures. Talbot stood beside him. A strange metallic bed stood in the room's center. Now where had that come from? He turned to Talbot.

"What's that?"

"What does it look like, Jack?"

"Well, if I didn't know better, I'd say it was an operating table." The realization gave him a sudden chill.

"Not bad," said Talbot. "But only in a way. You can operate on it, but it's not for operations."

"Hmmm," said Jack. More nonsense responses.

He looked around the room, seeking anything else he could probe for meaning. The aliens were still motionless. It didn't look like he was going to get any answers from them. He turned back to Talbot.

"I don't get it," Jack said. "What are you doing here? Why are you always here?"

Talbot frowned, seemingly puzzling out the answer to the question. He gave a slight shake of his head, then looked around the room. He indicated the stationary aliens with a broad gesture of his arm. "Ask them."

"And how am I supposed to ask them?"

"Just ask," Talbot answered.

Jack hesitated, looking from one alien form to the next. "Okay. Why is Talbot always here?"

He was aware of that wash, that swell of sound growing in the back of his consciousness, lapping against his understanding, then ebbing away into his mind's corners. Growing and fading like a tide of meaning.

"It is hard," said the voices. "It. Is. Hard."

There was no sound outside him. It all swelled and grew within his mind before drifting away.

"What is?" he said, almost overwhelmed by the sensation. "What is hard?"

"Talk. Tal-bot."

Jack turned back to face his human companion.

"Why are you here, Talbot?"

Talbot concentrated, lines creasing the space between his brows. He blinked a couple of times, and then the frown relaxed.

"They put me here." He nodded.

"I don't understand."

Again there was a pause before Talbot answered. "They sought something familiar that they could use. Something from your own mind. It was the only way they could reach you."

Twenty

Though he tried desperately to hang onto the dream-state, it slipped from him, resisting Jack's every attempt to hold on to it. Gone. All gone.

He sat up on the bunk, staring at the wall in front of him, into the chasm of what he was remembering. If there was even the slightest shred of reality in what he'd been dreaming, he understood just how important it was. Jack Stein had not been reaching out to the aliens; they had been reaching out to him.

Dreams. It was all about dreams.

Somehow, when he was in dreamstate, they knew he was there. They were aware of him.

Jesus. Why him?

For a moment he doubted himself.

Who knew? Perhaps he wasn't the only one. It was all happening too fast. He flexed his shoulders, feeling the fluidity of the motion, the lack of stiffness. And then he remembered the change as well.

He jumped from the bunk and stepped into the bathroom to check. No, he hadn't been dreaming that as well. Young Jack Stein still stared disbelievingly at him out of the mirror. He ran his fingers back through his hair. He could get used to it, he guessed. Still, he rather missed the old weather-beaten Jack looking back at him. He leaned in closer to the reflective wall, pulled down his eyelids, looked at his eyes, made a face at himself, and then stepped back. Maybe it was an illusion brought about by whatever happened to you in jump space. Maybe it would just go away.

He shook his head. He had more important things to worry about right now. He need to get up front and see how Dog was going with the search. There was no question in Jack's mind now; there was an alien world out there in front of the *Amaranth*.

First things first: He needed clothes. As much as he was in favor of his new look, he wasn't quite prepared to go parading it in front of Dog McCreedy yet, and he was sure Dog wouldn't really appreciate it either.

When he reached the bridge, Jack couldn't help the automatic double take on seeing Dog's new form. He pushed the reaction aside and stepped up to Dog's seat.

"Any luck?"

The worlds in the viewscreen were larger now. They'd moved in closer while he'd been under.

Dog glanced up, grinned, then turned back to his displays. "A couple that might be candidates, but I'm flying blind here. Do you know what I'm looking for?"

Jack scratched the back of his neck. "Mmmm. I'm going to guess that it's human-friendly. The City of Trees was on Mandala, and that was a resort world. They're not going to build an open city on an inhospitable planet."

"No shit," said Dog.

"Well, you asked. . . ."

"Yeah, I did, didn't I? Still doesn't narrow it down much. There are two that read as being habitable. Anything else?"

Jack thought for a moment. "Have you looked for transmissions of any sort?"

Dog sighed. "You think I haven't done a scan? If there was anything out there I'd have seen it by now."

Jack thought about the dream. Perhaps they didn't communicate by conventional means at all. There was no reason to presume that they would. Or they might use some form of technology that was completely unknown. Dog was looking at him expectantly.

"I don't know," said Jack, a touch of exasperation creeping into his voice. "We take a chance. Can you get closer to one of them and check it out? Maybe we can see something from orbit."

Dog nodded and reached for the controls.

Jack had a sudden thought. "Have you scanned for other ships?" he asked.

"What?"

"Or have you forgotten why we're here? This is the destination from Antille's notes, isn't it? Shouldn't we be seeing their ship?"

Dog frowned. "Yeah, you're right. Sorry. Not surprisingly, my mind's been on other things."

He touched a couple of panels, watched the readings, made some adjustments, and scanned again. After a few seconds he shook his head.

"Nothing."

Jack stared out at the approaching system, a hard constriction in his throat, not wanting to draw the conclusion that lay staring him in the face. Something had happened to Billie and Antille. Either here or on the way here. He kept his gaze focused on the screen, not wanting to look at Dog.

"We'll try the nearest one first."

Jack nodded.

If there was no sign of Billie's ship, then what might have happened to them? The possibilities tumbled through his head. Who was to say that these aliens weren't hostile? He'd seen the damage to the City of Trees on Mandala. It was as if the entire upper section of the city had sheared away as the result of some vast force.

He had no indication that they were hostile. None whatsoever. He had to hold on to that thought.

"Thirty minutes," said Dog, "and we'll be close enough to do a decent scan. You know, this is weird, Stein. We're in the unknown in more ways than one. Look at you. Look at me. Look at the system." He gave a short laugh. "It's weird, but it's great. I might have known when I ran into you that some strange stuff was going to start happening."

Jack looked at him sidelong, and then turned back to the screen. "Listen, Dog," he said. "I'm going to see if I can get anything from the planet. I need to concentrate."

"Right," said Dog, the grin slipping from his face. He turned his attention back to the controls.

Jack didn't want to think about the weird things that were happening. He tried to clear his mind instead, reaching out with his senses to the world slowly growing in the screens in front of them. The bridge, the controls, Dog, everything faded as he stilled his thoughts and reached focus.

The planet they were headed toward was blank. It sparked nothing in his guts or his chest. There was nothing. He took a deep breath.

"Not that one," he said. "Head for the other."

Dog frowned at him but complied, trusting him at least that much.

Their heading changed, and the image in the viewscreen slid across. The second planet was smaller, but greener at this distance. It centered in the screen, and again Jack reached out. This time there was something. The barest twinge, but something.

"Yes," said Jack. "That's the one."

"How can you tell?" asked Dog.

"I can feel it." He closed his fist in the center of his chest. "Here."

"Uh-huh." Dog was watching him curiously, as if expecting to see some sort of alterative. Jack didn't know what other change he expected. Personally, he thought they'd both changed enough for his liking.

Jack tried sending his thoughts out, questing for some sign that would indicate Billie's presence, or at least alert her to the fact that he was looking. He didn't know if it would do any good. He'd never even attempted anything like it before. He and Billie had a bond, but he had never thought to experiment with using that bond to try to communicate. There hadn't ever been the need. He sent the thoughts out and didn't know where they went, because there was no sign of a response. Jack sighed, turning back to focus on the approaching world.

"If their ship's down there, would we know it?" he asked.

"I don't know," said Dog. "But if it is, that's not a good thing."

Jack frowned. "What do you mean?"

"These ships aren't built for planetary landing. Why do you think I had *Amaranth* berthed at the orbital? That's what we have the shuttles for. If their ship is down on the surface, it means something bad's happened to it. Something very bad. If they've crashed on the surface and there's no signal, I wouldn't like the chances of survival."

Jack swallowed.

"Oh," he said.

They performed three full orbits while Dog checked readings and displays, monitoring for anything that looked like traces of civilization. All the while Jack kept his senses on alert, seeking anything more than the subtle pull resting faintly in the base of his chest.

"I wasn't sure on the last pass," said Dog, waving Jack over. "But it looks like there's something down there."

The reading meant nothing to Jack, but he knew there was something down there already. He didn't need any display to tell him.

"So what is it?"

"Can't tell from here, but it's big."

"Big enough to be a city?"

"Oh, yeah."

Jack peered down at the planet, trying to see marks of what Dog was pointing to, but nothing was distinguishable at this distance. A wide continent lay below, shaped something like a five-pointed star. Light clouds swirled in spiral patterns above it, obscuring much of the green-brown surface. A deep steel gray ocean bordered the landmass, darker, more monohued than Jack might have expected. Dog had matched the *Amaranth*'s orbit to what lay below them, and Jack reached up a hand to touch the screen.

"Hey," said Dog. "No finger marks. They're hell to get off."

"Sorry," mumbled Jack, still caught by the vision of the unknown world below them.

"Is it safe?" he asked finally.

"As far as I can tell," answered Dog, still checking his displays. "Atmosphere's fine. Looks hospitable enough. Somehow I don't think there's going into be any bars down there, but damn, I could do with a drink."

"Yeah, me too," said Jack. "Me too."

"So, what next?"

Jack took a few moments before answering. "I guess we go down."

The small ship that they used to get down to the surface was in much better condition than the one Dog had ferried them to Utrecht in. Like the rest of the *Amaranth*, Dog seemed to take pride in its upkeep. Perhaps the other shuttle, the one sitting back at the orbital, was merely a front. There were things about Dog that worried Jack still. How much more was a front?

On the way back to the shuttle, Dog had opened a locker, revealing a healthy array of primed and clearly well-maintained weaponry.

"I think we should take precautions," said Dog as he hefted a large rifle. "Take your pick."

Jack chose another, the same, and almost reached for a small hand weapon, but somehow he didn't think he was going to need it. Feeling the weight of the rifle in his grip brought back memories of a long time ago, when he was much—He cut the thought off almost as soon as it formed. Memories of a time when he was as young as he was now. He rested the weapon in the crook of his arm and automatically checked the charge pack. It was primed and ready to go. Some patterns you never forgot. They could almost be back, heading out on a mission together. He glanced at Dog, but the long hair, the leathers, quickly dispelled the image. They were here for something completely different.

Stowing the weapons in racks behind them, they took their seats and strapped in. Dog hit the controls, and the doors swung open. The craft had detached from a section toward the rear of the ship, and until Dog had pointed out the bay on the way down, Jack wouldn't have even known it was there. Seamless. He'd tucked that thought away for later too.

After consultation, they had agreed to land some way off from the cluster of structures that was their destination. Both of them knew that if you were heading into the complete unknown, caution was the way to go. Get the lay of the land first and then you could work out what your next steps would be. Sometimes there wasn't enough advance intelligence, or that which you did have couldn't be relied upon. This time they had nothing.

The shuttle swept in to land on an open, grassed field.
It was grass, or at least it looked like grass. They were
still in bright daylight. The light had a blue cast to it, and
felt very bright. Jack squinted out of the front viewscreen,
screwing up his eyes against the glare until Dog touched
a control and the screen tinted. Even through the shading,
Jack could see the greenish tint to the sky.

Dog let the craft settle, and then sat there, simply scanning the field. Jack did the same, looking for movement
or any other sign of life. They'd seen trees on the way in,
or what looked like trees, but from their position now,
there was nothing but slowly undulating fields. Dog
could have chosen a spot with a better vantage point.
Slowly Jack released his harness. A couple of moments
later Dog did the same. He reached forward and opened
a previously concealed compartment, scrabbled about inside, and flipped Jack a pair of shades.

"You might want these," he said with a grin, slipping
another pair onto his face. "You know the Dog. Always
ready."

Jack turned them over in his hands. Nice. Ex-military.
Image intensifiers, light enhancers, or filters, depending
on the prevailing conditions. Jack frowned. They were
top of the range, and Dog had just flipped them out casually, as if they were nothing. He kept the thought to
himself as he slipped them on. He reached around behind his seat and pulled out the rifle. Now that Jack
thought about it, the hardware was pretty good, and
looked relatively new too. It wasn't the sort of kit you'd
expect your average shuttle jockey to be sporting. He
rubbed his hand up and down the weapon's barrel as he
thought about that.

"So, are we doing it, Jack?"

He thought Dog might have caught the moment of
speculation and he tried to cover. He slapped the rifle.

"Ready or not, here we come." It was what they used to say in the unit.

Dog grinned.

He punched the release and the doors swung open. Jack jumped to the ground, absorbing the spring with his knees, and quickly looked around, checking that there was nothing they had missed. He kept close to the craft's body, presenting less of a visible target. The old routines were kicking in automatically. The planet's gravity was a touch heavier than they'd had on board the *Amaranth*, but the way he was feeling now, it barely made a difference. Senses alert, he stepped to the front of their craft and scanned the fields. A moment later, Dog joined him.

Jack smelled the air. Damn, that was familiar. A slight tang like old sweat.

"You smell that?" he asked Dog.

Dog wrinkled his nose. "Yeah." He was still slightly crouched, his rifle held at the ready.

Okay, that was good, thought Jack. He could have been imagining the scent, overlaying old dream images over what he was experiencing, because this was all too familiar—the sky, the smell in the air, the slightly rolling grassed fields. He looked around, almost expecting to see Talbot stroll over the crest line. He took a deep breath of the tainted air, trying to steady himself, trying to convince himself that this was not just another dream.

"What now?" asked Dog.

"We walk, I guess."

"Okay, wait a minute," said Dog. He disappeared around the shuttle's side and retuned a moment later with a pair of small packs. He tossed one to Jack. "Water, some rations. We might need them."

"Yeah, good idea," said Jack, shouldering his pack.

"Which way?"

Jack didn't need prompting. He knew the way. He

indicated with his chin. "Over the hill and down. We should be able to see it before long."

Dog gave him a strange look, but said nothing.

Jack took the lead, striding up the hillside, not waiting for Dog to follow. It was like treading familiar ground that he'd been over countless times before. The top of the hill revealed nothing more than he'd expected to see. He stopped there at the very top, looking down over the gentle slope. Off to one side sat a grove of cathedral trees, silvery and catching the light. Four uneven trunks met in the middle, joining at a knotted central shaft, arched hollows between the legs. Something lumbered through the grove, something large, and Jack watched it with interest. Dog had joined him, and he saw the movement too.

"What the . . ."

Jack caught him lifting the rifle and slapped it down.

"It's nothing. It's harmless. Besides, it's too far away."

Dog tutted at him. "I was only trying to get a better look at it."

"Shit, sorry," said Jack. "I'm just a little jumpy, I guess."

"Yeah, you too, huh?" said Dog.

Farther in the distance lay the city Jack had been expecting. It looked exactly as it had appeared to him in the dreams. Unlike the City of Trees, these constructions were complete. Four buttressed legs rose in thick, even supports to a central spire, the place below the legs hollow. Just like the trees. Just like the aliens themselves. The city—for it was clearly a city—shone in the distance. Something metallic and semireflective coated the building surface. There was movement up between the spires. Glinting lights spoke of motion, rapid and, from this distance, silent to them. Jack stood watching, staring down into the distant cluster and feeling nervousness growing inside him.

"What are we doing, Jack?" asked Dog.

Jack looked at him, but couldn't see his eyes through the dark lenses. He wondered if Dog was feeling as unsettled as he was.

"There," said Jack. "That's where we're going."

"Yeah, of course. But how do you want to handle it? Are we just going to walk right up there?"

Jack considered. They should temper the approach with caution, but if he was right, the aliens already knew they were here. Would they have a reception? he wondered.

Twenty-one

Jack and Dog walked for what seemed like hours, but Jack knew it was far less than that. All the time he kept glancing nervously around, checking for some apparition, for one of the aliens, for Talbot, for what he didn't quite know. He wasn't worried about the lumbering spiny beast they had seen in the cathedral trees. He guessed it was some sort of forest dweller and it would keep to its natural environment. The real thing that worried him was that he might still be dreaming. A couple of times he experimented, trying to will himself into the air, or to another place, but with no results. The place seemed real, as corporeal as Dog trudging beside him, swinging his rifle slowly from side to side as they walked.

As they neared the city, the true size of the buildings became apparent. They swept up into the sky, towering above them. The motion amongst the spire was far, far above, far enough that they couldn't make out the true detail of whatever it was that moved up there.

Even though the quick movements were distracting, there was something more important that caught Jack's attention now. A shape was moving toward them from the city's edges.

A long, low platform was skimming across the ground toward them, and on it rode a familiar shape.

The four silvery legs held it steady. The central trunk was upright.

"What the . . . ?" said Dog, dropping into a crouch, his rifle ready.

"Stay," said Jack, waving at him with one hand.

Dog slowly eased upright, but there was nothing relaxed about his stance.

Jack lowered his rifle so that it was pointing at the ground and gestured to Dog to do the same.

The vehicle drew closer, and still there was no reaction from the creature riding it.

Jack's heart was beating loudly, his mouth dry. He swallowed, trying to work the moisture back. He could hear a slight hum now as the vehicle neared.

The aliens were real.

Closer still, and the creature had still not reacted.

The aliens were real.

The thought kept on going around and around in his head.

The vehicle was almost upon them when it suddenly veered away and headed in another direction, off and behind them. The creature riding it ignored them completely.

It was as if they didn't exist.

Jack turned to track its progress into the distance, his mouth open. He turned back to Dog, finally remembering to close it.

"Well, that was interesting," said Dog. He looked back behind them, but the vehicle had already gone. He shook his head. "Not quite what I expected."

"Um, no," said Jack. For a second he was convinced he really was dreaming again.

"Come on, Stein, what are we doing?"

Jack lifted his weapon again. "Onward."

They reached the edges of the city, with no further

encounters. They stood together in the building's shadow, and the lenses automatically adjusted to compensate for the change in light. Jack felt slightly ridiculous, two lone humans bearing weapons and standing in front of an alien city. It was more than a little surreal. He beckoned Dog forward and walked quickly to the empty paved area between the building's legs. At least that way they'd be out of direct view and he could feel somewhat less exposed.

Together they stood beneath the huge structure above them, necks tilted back, straining to take in the true enormity. Just like in his dream, the paneled walls surrounded them, vaguely reflective, rainbow colors working through the surfaces in shimmering uneven lines. Just one of this building's legs was the size of an office building back home.

"Jack?"

"Wait," he said, holding up a hand. "Give me a moment." He closed his eyes and concentrated, seeking the pull, the tug that would show him which way he should go. It was there, but now it was nondirectional. The sensation seemed to be coming from all around him. He opened his eyes to see Dog watching him.

"I don't know," said Jack. "We're just going to have to hope we get lucky."

He picked one of the directions at random. "If I'm right, the entrance is on the opposite side."

He was right. They worked their way around the edge and onto a flat expanse of paneled wall. Just like in his dream, the broad doorway halfway along led into darkness. Jack took a deep breath and headed toward it. A shape whisked overhead, giving him a start, and he had to struggle to bring his breathing back under control and to still the beating of his heart in his ears.

"You okay?" he asked Dog.

"Sure. Lead on."

As they reached the doorway's edge, Jack slowed, senses prickling, listening for noises. Another vehicle zipped overhead with a whoosh and Jack tracked its passage, turning to follow until it disappeared from view between the building spires.

"Well, the place seems alive enough. I wonder why they haven't done anything. It's as if we aren't even here."

"Perhaps they can't see us," said Dog. "It didn't look like that thing had eyes."

"But they have to perceive what's around them some way, don't they? Somehow, I don't think that's it. Maybe we're just beneath their notice."

Inside the doorway lay only shadows. The empty space gaped at them forbiddingly. Jack ducked his head around the corner, but saw nothing but veiled darkness. He quickly pulled back.

"It looks like it's open in there. I couldn't see much. Not enough time for the shades to work."

"Well, there's nothing for it then," said Dog, hefting his rifle and stepping forward. Jack held out one arm, blocking his path.

"No. Me first," he said. Steadying himself, he took two strides into the darkness with Dog close on his heels.

Within two seconds, though it seemed like an eternity, the light intensifiers kicked in, revealing a broad, empty space. At least it looked empty, until Jack noticed the pair of alien figures standing off to one side. They seemed unaware of him. Dog cleared his throat and indicated the occupants with a quick gesture of his hand. Jack nodded. He hadn't finished scanning the room yet, if a room it could be called. It was more like an arena, a covered sports ground. Dog was repositioning his rifle. Jack shook his head and Dog lowered it, but not before licking his lips and biting the lower one in a clear indication of doubt.

Just like the building in his dreams, there was some sort of platform hovering about a foot off the floor in one corner. Looking up, Jack noticed a wide square hole above it. That was how they got from level to level. Seeing nothing else of note, Jack took another couple of steps into the open space. The floor was hard, paved with some type of interlocking gray-brown stones, just as the floors had been in the City of Trees. In the darkness it was difficult to tell the exact color, despite the light intensifiers in his shades. He let his gaze rove over the walls, the ceiling, the floor, but the room was unremarkable apart from its size.

Diagonally across from them, one of the aliens moved. Dog's rifle whipped to his shoulder and he started tracking it. Jack thrust out one hand, pushing the barrel down.

He was intrigued. In the dreams he hadn't really seen the creatures walk. He could understand Dog's jumpiness, but for Jack, it was all strangely familiar. One of the four silvery legs swung forward, then the one on the opposite side. Next, it swung the one behind the first forward and then the one opposite that. It lifted the central trunk and then repositioned the two front legs, drawing up the rear ones behind. In this manner it slowly approached, looking almost as if it were tottering across the floor toward them. Jack suppressed a grin.

"What?" hissed Dog.

Jack waved his hand again. Wait.

The alien stopped mere feet away from them. Close up, Jack could see the snakeskin mottling in the epidermis, if it was skin. The central trunk was about as thick as a man's thigh, except where it bulged outward at the place where Jack knew lay the mobile petals and the slightly recessed chambers. Here, now, he could smell the creature. It gave off the barest hint of burned wiring.

He wondered if the creature could smell them too—some sort of musky animal scent. He swallowed, wondering what to expect next.

The creature stood where it was, towering above them, not moving. Jack could see Dog's fingers flexing and unflexing on his weapon. Jack chewed at the inside of his bottom lip, waiting. Another eternity passed while they stood there nervously. Jack had visions of the old vids. Hail, we come in peace. Palm outstretched. We mean you no harm. Dog was starting to fidget.

"Hello," said Jack.

Nothing.

They stood where they were as the seconds ticked by.

Without any warning, the upper part of the alien's central trunk tilted forward, then straightened. A moment later it started moving away from them in that strange tottering gait, merely reversing the motions it had made before. It reached the spot where the other creature was standing and stopped. Again it was motionless.

Jack waited where he was.

"Um," he said finally.

"That was it?" whispered Dog.

"Yeah, looks like it."

"So much for first contact," said Dog, sounding disgusted.

"I guess this isn't where we're supposed to be," said Jack. "And anyway, who's to say it *is* first contact?"

Dog just grunted.

Giving the vast room and the motionless aliens one more look, he turned and headed for the door. A moment later Dog was behind him.

As they stepped out into the light, the shades adjusted rapidly, recognizing the conditions immediately.

"So if that's not where we're supposed to be, where are we going?" asked Dog.

"I don't know."

Dog stared at him. Jack guessed he was staring, though it was hard to tell through the dark lenses.

"Okay, listen, Mr. Psychic Investigator," said Dog. "I suggest you work out what we're doing. I don't like standing around like a bug, because that's what I feel like right now. If there's a reason we are here, let's find it; then let's get the hell away."

Jack laughed. "Can't take it, Dog man?"

Dog's grip tightened on his weapon and his jaw clenched.

Jack shook his head. "Relax. I don't know. We're supposed to be here, but I'm not sure quite where. I wasn't getting at you. But you have to admit, this is not quite what we might have imagined."

Dog made a noise in his throat and looked away. "Okay, which way?"

Jack looked at the buildings towering around them and realized that he had no idea. The broad street they stood on stretched into the distance, where the details merged into a monotone backdrop. He closed his eyes and concentrated, turning slowly around on the spot, seeking a direction. The city was not only big, but the buildings themselves were virtually indistinguishable from one another. If they started randomly wandering down the streets between them, they could get lost in no time, not knowing which ones they had visited and which ones were new. Jack opened his eyes and rubbed the back of his neck.

Five doorways later they were no closer to finding what they sought. Jack thought he knew what they were looking for, but now he was becoming uncertain. Each of the stops had revealed vast shadowed rooms, some with alien inhabitants, and nothing to tell one of them from another.

"Wait," said Jack, when it was clear that Dog's patience was wearing thin. "I have an idea."

"Well, it'd better be a good one," said Dog. "I'm getting a bit tired of silver coatracks."

"Let's cut over this way."

Jack led off, shouldering his rifle. He no longer cared if Dog was following or not. He walked down a side street until he reached an intersection, stopped and looked carefully each way down the cross-street. It was the same as the last. He moved on to the next junction. After four more blocks he found what he was looking for. There was something different about the street that ran from right to left. It was broader than the previous cross-streets, and a recognizable pattern was worked into the stones that bordered each side.

"Ah," he said.

"What?" Dog was still with him, even though Jack had been virtually ignoring him.

"This street is different. If the City of Trees is any clue, I'm guessing this should lead down to a plaza. With any luck, what we're looking for will be there."

"What makes you so sure?"

Jack lowered his rifle and sighed. "I'm not sure, but you have to follow the clues."

"Okay, Mr. Detective Man, lead on. Let's hope you're right."

They turned onto the wide avenue and started walking toward the city's center. Six blocks farther in the buildings still rose around them, indistinguishable from one another. Jack stopped, pulled the small pack from his shoulder, and reached inside for a water bottle. Despite the deep shadows cast between the buildings it was warm, and a sheen of sweat had broken out on Jack's brow. He took a healthy swallow, moistened his lips, and replaced the bottle. Dog did likewise.

"Have you wondered where they all are?" asked Jack.

"What do you mean?"

"Well, look at the size of this place. It looks like it could hold millions of them. Where are they all?"

Dog frowned. "I hadn't thought of that." He looked around at the buildings and the empty streets. "Maybe they're hiding."

"Did it look like they were hiding?"

"No. Guess not." Dog shrugged.

Jack shouldered his pack again and lifted the rifle.

A few blocks later they found what Jack was looking for. The building that occupied this block was larger than the others were, and intricately patterned stones paved the flat expanse beneath it. Plinths stood dotting the edges, and set into their tops were metallic tablets, designs and figures worked into the surfaces. He'd seen a tablet like these before; the artifact that had led them here in the first place. Jack walked carefully into the ringed center, looking down at the patterns in the paved floor. From the central point beneath the building, lines radiated out to each plinth. At random, Jack chose one of them and followed it out to the stone and its tablet while Dog stood at the edge, watching him, seemingly more interested in what Jack was doing than what they had found.

Jack stood in front of the tablet, just staring at it. It could easily have been the artifact that Antille had been so careful about guarding. It was identical in shape, but the raised patterns on its surface were different. He lifted a hand and carefully traced the surface with his fingers. The tablet was warm to the touch, and he could sense a slight vibration. He withdrew his hand and stepped back. He thought for a moment, then walked over to the next plinth. Another tablet stood fixed to its top, with figures and symbols covering its surface, just like the last one.

He turned and glanced around at the other plinths and the tablets they bore. This had to be the place.

"What is it, Jack?"

He walked over to Dog. "I've seen places like this before, both in the City of Trees and elsewhere. Those things at the top are like the artifact Antille used to derive his notes."

Dog whistled. "Yeah?" He crossed rapidly to one of the plinths, placed his rifle on the ground, and then reached up, gripped one side of the tablet, and tried to move it. When it didn't budge he used both hands, applying pressure back and forth and straining.

"What the fuck are you doing, Dog?" said Jack.

Dog stopped with his hands still gripping the tablet's edges. "These have got to be worth a fortune, right?"

Jack shook his head with disbelief. "Are you crazy?"

"What?" Dog lowered his arms. "What?"

Jack just shook his head. Dog shrugged, stooped to pick up his weapon, then crossed back to join Jack. He shot the tablet one last lingering look and sighed. "It was worth a try," he muttered.

"Yeah, but getting killed isn't."

One more time, Jack closed his eyes and concentrated. There. He was right. The pull had been with him constantly ever since they'd arrived, but had faded to something barely below his awareness, just like the smell. Now it was back, and stronger. He focused on the direction, then opened his eyes.

"It's here." He pointed to one of the building's legs. "Over here."

"I hope you're right," said Dog. " 'Cause if you're not, we're getting out."

Jack held back his response and started walking toward the building leg he had indicated, his pace slightly faster than before. Dog had to jog to catch up.

On the walls on the other side lay another doorway, almost an arch but angular in construction, revealing nothing more than shadow inside. Jack nodded. The sensation growing in his chest was stronger now. This was the place. He took a couple of steadying breaths and walked quickly toward the door.

Twenty-two

Jack stepped into shadow, shadow that disappeared as soon as it enfolded him and the light intensifiers kicked into action. This vast room was too, too familiar. All around the space stood immobile aliens, alone and in groups of two and three. Jack stood in the doorway, hesitating. Did he really want to enter? The smell of shorted wires came to his nostrils, and he felt his sinuses reacting. He grimaced and sniffed, not wanting his eyes to start watering. To one side lay the apparatus he'd seen in his dreams. It was like a bare metal table, but in sections, giving it a slope and cant that would match the shape of his body. A central column and four angled legs supported it. It was funny the way the aliens seemed to reflect themselves in everything they built.

He knew this was where he was supposed to be, but he wasn't sure what he was supposed to do. If the aliens were aware of his presence, they'd made no sign.

"What now?" said Dog behind him.

"Here, hold this." Jack turned and handed him the rifle. Somehow he didn't think he was going to need it. He walked slowly across to the bed, table, whatever it was, acutely aware of the multiple alien presences around the broad enclosed space. The sound of his footsteps was loud in his ears. As he walked, he became aware of something else. There was an energy in the place, a barely sensible buzz working through the air and below the threshold of conscious awareness. He could *feel* it, though, and it prickled his skin like the buildup of energy before a storm.

He looked around at the nearest aliens as he approached the apparatus that he knew waited for him and him alone. He had decided he was going to call it a table. He stopped beside it, reached out, and ran his hands over the surface. It was warm, metallic, like the tablets outside. How the hell had they made this? He looked about himself, at the aliens and up at the ceiling. Still, they hadn't moved.

"What are you doing, Stein?" said Dog. There was a trace of unease in his voice.

"What I have to, McCreedy. I suggest you turn away unless you want your tender sensibilities offended again."

Jack reached up and dropped the pack from his shoulder onto the floor. Very slowly he pulled one arm free from his coat, and then the other, and dropped it, resisting the temptation to make use of Dog's comparison to coatracks from before.

"Oh, shit," said Dog. "Not this again."

"Wait outside," said Jack. "I need to be able to concentrate."

"No, it's okay. I'm going to . . . um . . . watch your back." He coughed.

Jack stripped off his shirt and trousers and everything else, letting it all drop to the ground in a pile.

As he stood there, naked, exposed, he gave one last look around the crowded but strangely empty room. The hairs on his arms were standing up, though the air was warm.

"This is what you want, right?" he said.

There was no response.

He swallowed and clambered up on the table. He swung his legs up and lay back, resting his head on the curved platform toward the top. Three breaths passed before he lifted his hands to cross them on the center of his chest.

"Are you sure you know what you're doing, Jack?"

"Shut up, Dog," he said.

The warm metallic surface beneath him felt as if it were humming, but it could have been his imagination. With difficulty, he closed his eyes. The waves ran through his skull immediately, damping his perception and filling his mind with a pleasing numbness. It was as if the table had built-in inducer pads. He was drifting. Awareness trickled away from him, and within moments he was awash in a sea of dreamstate.

Jack opened his eyes. Nothing had changed. He sat up on the table and looked around. The aliens still stood there, immobile. Dog still stood near the doorway, one rifle by his feet, the other moving back and forth, as if he didn't know where to aim.

"Shit," said Jack.

Then he realized: There was nothing on his face. He reached up, feeling for the shades, but they were gone, and yet he could see clearly. Gone was the slight colored hue that accompanied light-enhanced vision. An alien nearby adjusted its position, and another. The motion took him by surprise.

Gradually growing in the back of his mind, washing forth like waves beating against a beach, came the noise, swelling and receding again, swelling and receding.

"Jack . . . Stein . . ."

He was dreaming. He had to be dreaming.

"Jack . . . Stein . . . welcome . . ."

The last word drifted away, echoing.

"Too . . . hard . . ."

"It's too difficult for them," said Talbot from behind him. Jack recognized the now-familiar voice immediately.

Jack whirled to face him. "What are you doing here?"

Talbot smiled. "I am a product of your own mind, Jack."

"I don't understand."

Talbot crossed his hands in front of himself. "It's simple, Jack. Trying to communicate mind-to-mind is difficult for them. The structure of your thoughts is too different. Too alien. They looked for an image that you would recognize and could identify with."

Jack stood. "If that's the case, why you, Talbot?"

He shrugged. "I was fresh in your mind, walking the dreamscape. I was there the first time you saw them. I was accessible."

"Well, they could have made a better choice," said Jack. "That whole burned-away face thing is not a good look."

"You would prefer someone else?" Talbot asked. He grew and stretched, his body and face elongating. The dark hair paled and thinned. His skin became mottled and pale. His teeth grew suddenly, filling his mouth.

"Jack, dear boooooooy."

Pinpin Dan!

"No!" said Jack. "No way."

Pinpin Dan was dead, like Talbot, but there were too many memories attached to the particular repugnance that was Heironymous Dan.

Pinpin looked disappointed.

In a rapid succession of transformations, figure after figure from Jack's life appeared before him and melted away.

"Stop!" said Jack.

The figure in front of him stopped in midtransformation, halfway between Van der Stegen and Alice the librarian from the Locality.

"One," said Jack. "Only one."

The figure in front of him shrank, and its hair grew longer. Jack grinned.

"Billie."

"Is that okay, Jack?" she asked.

"Yeah, that's fine." He glanced down quickly and saw with relief that he was clothed. He wouldn't have felt comfortable standing naked in front of Billie. It was funny. This was the younger Billie, from when they had first met about four years earlier. He wondered why she should be foremost in his mind.

"Hey," he said.

She crossed her arms. "What are you waiting for, Jack?" She frowned. "Hey. Something's happened to you." She tilted her head to one side and frowned. "Hasn't it?"

"Don't you like it?" he asked. Dumb question, Stein.

She shook her head. "Nuh-uh."

"So," he said. "Where are you?"

"I'm not here, Jack. You're supposed to be finding me."

"I know that," he said. "How am I supposed to do that?"

Billie shook her head.

Jack propped himself on the table edge and stroked his chin, thinking. He had to ask the right questions. If you didn't ask the right questions, you didn't get the right answers. And all the time this whole thing, he knew, was being colored by his own dream expectations. He glanced across at Dog, but he was immobile, frozen. No help there, then. This was Billie, but it wasn't Billie. He knew that his own consciousness, his understanding and knowledge of her, was shaping the way she reacted, as Billie *would* react, as he'd expect her to react. The right questions, Jack.

"What's happened to us?" he asked.

Billie looked at him approvingly. "Temporal energy, Jack." She climbed up on the table and hugged her knees in front of her, just as she would if she were starting to explain something to him, something that he might have trouble getting at first.

"What's temporal energy?" He hitched himself up on the table to sit beside her.

"It's what's happened to you. When you jump, it's not only space, but it's time as well. When you pass through the portal there's a buildup of temporal energy. It accumulates within living cells, accumulating at a subatomic level. It doesn't matter if the life-form is carbon or silicon or something else. It always works the same."

Jack shook his head. "I don't get it. What do you mean, subatomic level? What's temporal energy?"

Billie sighed, giving him that gee-you're-stupid-Jack look. "Okay. Time is energy. You don't know it because you're in it all the time. Wormholes disrupt that steady state. They change space and time. That change has to go somewhere. Living beings fill with time. They live in the timestream like they are swimming in it. We learned that centuries ago when we first started traveling through space."

Jack held up one hand. "Do me a favor? Don't use the 'we' for a moment. It's easier if I'm just talking to Billie."

Billie released the grip around her knees and crossed her legs. "Uh-huh," she said.

"So," said Jack. "Time is like energy."

She nodded.

"And every time we jump, that energy builds up inside us."

Again she nodded.

"So what happened?" he asked.

Once more, the look. "Unless it's dissipated, it has to be released. The cells can't hold it forever. If there are a number of jumps in succession, there is no time for it to dissipate. That's the paradox."

"So this"—Jack waved his hand down the length of his body—"is what happens."

Billie pursed her lips. "Sometimes."

"Sometimes?"

She shrugged. "Depends if it's negative or positive. There's something else, Jack."

"Hmmm?"

She leaned forward. "A living thing can take only so much. The energy buildup disrupts the cellular pattern. Dissipation is limited."

"What do you mean?"

"If it happens more than one time, *you* can dissipate."

"What?"

"Matter and energy are linked. You are playing with the bonds that make stuff what it is."

Jack was starting to understand where she was going with this. "You mean, if we jump again, it could make us dissipate too."

She nodded.

"Shit."

Something was happening. Billie was growing pale and insubstantial. He could see the outline of the table beneath and through her.

"Billie?"

"Stay calm, Jack," she said, but he could barely hear the words.

The wash of voices was back. "Too . . . hard . . ."

Jack was awake again.

*   *   *

He swung his legs from the table and sat up, hand going automatically to cover his crotch.

"Dog?"

McCreedy was looking distinctly uncomfortable. "What have you been doing?" he said. "They've been moving."

"Come here," said Jack.

Dog stooped and scooped up the other rifle, then walked quickly up to where Jack was sitting. He kept looking back over his shoulder as if eager to be outside the door.

"What is it? Can we go now? And can you put your damn clothes back on?"

Dog was glancing around at the aliens nervously.

"Sorry, not yet," said Jack, lifting one hand to still him. "I'm not done."

"You're going to tell me something happened while you were sleeping, aren't you? I've been standing out here with these things for at least half an hour."

"Yes, something happened. I've been talking to them."

Jack couldn't see Dog's eyes, but he could read the expression of disbelief.

"You can believe me, or you can doubt me. Frankly, I don't give a damn. But I suggest you listen to what I have to say."

Dog slapped Jack's rifle down on the table beside him. "Take it," he said. "You're going to need it."

He spun on his heel and started stalking toward the door.

"McCreedy!" yelled Jack. "Stay where you are. You can't leave."

Dog stopped in midstep but didn't turn around. "And why the hell not?"

"Because if you leave, you'll die."

"I'm tired of your stupid fancies, Stein. You always were weird. I've got what I need."

Jack almost let that one pass. He reached for the rifle. "What was that, McCreedy? I suggest you turn around, *slowly.*"

Dog turned. Very slowly he placed his own rifle down on the floor and lifted his hands.

Jack was suddenly struck by the ludicrous nature of the situation. There they were stuck in an arena full of aliens, and he was stark naked and pointing a heavy-beam rifle at his pilot. He laughed.

"What, Stein! What? What's so damned funny?" Dog's words were full of fury.

"Look at us, McCreedy. Look at us. Look around you."

An alien shifted position and he glanced in its direction, but quickly returned to watching Dog.

"Leave the weapon where it is. Come over here. Slowly."

With his hands still raised, Dog did as he was told, walking carefully across the intervening space.

"And put your damned hands down," said Jack. "That's far enough."

Dog's jaw was set, and though Jack couldn't see them, he knew his eyes would be full of anger.

"What?" Dog spat the word.

"Look at you, McCreedy. Look at me. Is that some weird fancy? It's real and there's a reason for it. *They* told me what it was."

Dog glanced around at the aliens.

"Yeah, them," said Jack. Without lowering the weapon, Jack recounted what the alien Billie had told him. Though he didn't completely understand it yet, he thought he had the details right enough.

As he finished, he could sense the tension going out of Dog's stance, and he carefully lowered the weapon and laid it across his lap.

"Are you ready to listen yet?" he asked.

"Damn," said Dog. "Damn."

"Yeah."

McCreedy turned, linking his fingers behind his neck, and looked up at the ceiling. "Damn," he breathed again. "What are we going to do?"

"Your choice, Dog," said Jack. "You can go and take your chances, or you can let me finish what I'm here to do."

Dog let his hands drop to his sides and turned back slowly to face him. "I'm sorry, Jack. This is all too weird. I'm not used to this shit."

Jack considered for a moment. "Yeah, all right."

He didn't know if he could trust him now, but he couldn't afford not to. Without McCreedy he was stuck here anyway. He rubbed his cheek with one hand and sighed. "Okay. I have to try to go back under. I've got to find out what we need to do. Can I trust you, Dog?"

Dog bowed his head. "Yeah," he said quietly.

"Good." Jack lifted the rifle and proffered it, stock first. "Take this. It's only in the way. You might want to go and have a scout around outside while you're waiting. I don't know how long I'm going to be."

He had a momentary second thought, a quick rush as Dog reached for the weapon, but he needn't have worried. Dog took the gun and held it, barrel down. He stood there for a couple of seconds looking at Jack.

"You'll be okay here . . . alone?"

"Yeah," said Jack. "I'm fine."

Dog nodded. He turned without another word, his head still slightly bowed, and crossed to the door, then disappeared outside. He'd left the other rifle on the floor.

Jack watched him go, then swung his legs back onto the table and lay back. It was strange how calming an adrenaline rush could be. Crossing his hands on his chest, he closed his eyes.

Twenty-three

Billie was back beside him and Jack felt a wash of relief. It was far better talking to Billie than Talbot. It felt . . . natural.

"That was nice, Jack," she said.

"What?"

"The way you handled the other one. Nice."

"Thanks, I think," said Jack. So they were aware of him and what he was doing. That was confirmation enough.

"What do you want to know, Jack?" asked Billie.

"I want to know where you are."

She shook her head. "We cannot tell you that."

Jack sighed. " 'We' again."

Billie pouted. "Sorry."

"It's okay."

She narrowed her eyes at him, then rubbed her already messy hair.

"Okay, then," said Jack. "Why can't you tell me?"

Billie frowned, concentrating. "She could be anywhere. There are many pathways. Where the portals lie, often many paths come together and lots of doorways. It's like a hall. If you go too far, you can take the wrong door. If you do not know the door, you don't know where it leads."

Jack thought about that for a moment. "But what about all those charts outside? They're directions, aren't they? Maps, right?"

She nodded. "Sort of."

If this were the real Billie, she'd be showing signs of boredom by now. Instead she uncrossed her legs and let them dangle over the edge of the table, still looking at him intently.

"So if I want to find you, I need to find the right door."

"Uh-huh."

She looked sideways at him.

"But to do that, I have to be able to travel. You just got through telling me that there was too much risk."

Billie sighed. "You think they haven't thought of that? How do you think they travel, Jack?"

"How?"

"They've been making jumps for centuries."

Jack frowned. Of course they had. "But how?"

"Temporal dispersers. It's a small piece of technology that sucks up the temporal energy and scatters it. It stops it building up. If you have one of those, you can jump."

A silvery shape suddenly appeared in the air between them, slowly spinning. It was star-shaped, four points and a thickened center. The surface shimmered with strange patterns. Jack watched it as it turned.

"And that's all I need?"

She nodded enthusiastically.

This was weird for a dream. It was as if he were back home just chatting away with her, working through the details of a case. Billie had done the research and was giving him the answers he needed. He shook his head. He'd lost count of the number of times he'd used Billie as a sounding board. He missed it.

Jack leaned back. "And these guys will give me one?"

"Nuh-uh."

"What do you mean?"

Her face grew serious. "The device is configured for them. It could be reconfigured, but it would take time. They are not sure how it would work on your form, if it would work at all. There would have to be study."

Time was something he didn't have. "Shit," he said. "So what am I supposed to do?"

She looked thoughtful. "Wait." There was a long pause. "You could risk the jump, or you could spend time enough between the jumps for the temporal energy to disperse."

He shook his head. "I can't do that. Can't you just give me one of these things?"

"No. It is impossible. We haven't traveled for centuries."

Jesus.

He thought about what he wanted to ask for a moment, something to fill the space while his head processed what he'd learned. "This is a pretty big city," he said. "There don't seem to be many of you about for something this size."

"The city has been here for a long time," she said. "A long, long time. Before there were lots more, but many became tired or bored. They left, or stopped living. Here, some would stay. For thousands of years we thought we were alone, or too far away. There were others like you, others that we could dream."

"Dream? I don't understand."

"As you dream us, we dream you. Like now. You join us in the place of our dreaming."

Jack blinked a couple of times as he processed that. "You said there were others."

Billie nodded. "Uh-huh."

"But then?"

"They were either too primitive, or too far away. We

are an old race. We have long given up the urge to travel.
We still wish to dream with others. To dream alone is limited, but there is the challenge."

He stared at the young girl sitting next to him, watching her feet as they swung back and forth. She turned to
look at him and grinned.

"Hi, Jack," she said.

"Is this a normal dream? It doesn't feel like it's
normal."

Billie's grin slipped away and she became serious
again. "I don't know. Maybe."

Well, of course it wasn't normal. He was damned well
communicating with aliens. What was normal about that?

"Wait," he said. "What happened to the City of Trees?
What happened on Mandala?"

Billie was concentrating again. She was working her
mouth as she thought. "Oh," she said after a while.
"That's a very old place. There was another race. There
was a war. We lost many. That time has passed long ago."

He nodded. It made sense. He suddenly realized he
didn't know what else to ask. He was the wrong person
to be having this conversation. What did he know about
talking to an alien civilization? Let someone else do this.
He had other things to take care of.

"It's all right, Jack," said Billie. "They understand."

They knew what he was thinking? Even in the dream?
Damn.

"And Jack," she said with a quick frown. "You need to
be careful now."

"Huh? Careful of what?"

"There are still other races out there. They will know
about you. If not now, soon. Remember what we said
about a war. You have announced your presence now."

An image of the City of Trees flashed through his
head. Damn.

"Careful of those around you. Bye, Jack," said Billie, and then she was gone, and waking consciousness filled his senses with awareness.

Jack jumped from the bed and started gathering his clothes together, shaking them out and laying them on the table before getting dressed. There was faint motion all around him, but he was still distracted from the dream-state and didn't pay much attention. His eyewear was starting to cause him discomfort too, and he removed it, massaging his temple and rubbing at the bridge of his nose where the constant pressure had begun to pinch. Without the light enhancement, darkness immediately obscured his vision.

He stood there in shadow, taking stock. First, he had to find Dog and get away from this place, work out a way to deal with their problem. He was tempted to go back into dreamstate, but he knew, deep in his gut, that he wasn't going to find the solution there. Now all that mattered was tracking down Billie and Antille. Her dream image had only spurred him more.

Still thinking, he replaced the shades, and was immediately startled by an alien looming above him close by. It dipped the upper part of its central trunk toward him and then straightened. Dog was right: They could be coatracks. Coatracks for giants, if it were not for the missing hooks at the top. How they built anything or did anything with those strange limbless cylindrical bodies, he had no clue. A weird thought came to him then. They seemed to spend most of their time stationary, and the movements, the stubby petal-like limbs, made him wonder if they'd actually evolved from trees. Sentient trees? No, it didn't make sense. Why would a tree want to build a city? The City of Trees. Yeah, right. He shook his head.

"So now what?" he said to the room.

Jack had no idea if the aliens could hear him in the
normal sense. He still hadn't worked out how they perceived things, even though it was fairly clear that they
were aware of what went on around them. He looked
around seeking some clue, and noticed the pack and
weapon where Dog had left them, so he crossed and retrieved both. He stood on the spot, the weight of the rifle
in his left hand, the pack hitched on his shoulder, and
looked around the room, waiting for some further response. An alien across the other side stirred into action,
swinging its legs around and tottering toward the room's
center. Just for a moment it reminded Jack of an absurd
giant silvery spider, or no, a praying mantis.

He waited, presuming the alien was going to move to
where he was, but it stopped about sixty paces away and
was suddenly still again.

"Hey," he said.

Nothing.

How long was he supposed to wait? He had no idea
how these creatures perceived time. What if it didn't
mean anything to them? He chewed at the inside of his
bottom lip, wondering what he was going to do next.

Jack crossed the room, walking around a cluster of
three aliens, and avoiding another, all of which seemed
completely oblivious to him.

The noises were coming from the square place in the
corner above him, and he stood, his head tilted back,
watching. The buzz became a hum, and a couple of seconds later the platform slowly lowered from the ceiling
back down to the floor. This time it bore another alien.
Jack tracked it, watching as it settled with a slight bounce
about two feet above the floor. The alien swung its legs
forward, extending one of them down, and then the other,
until both were placed firmly on the paved surface. For a
moment Jack thought it was going to topple forward, but

as it moved its rear limbs forward, the central body
canted backward until the other legs had also met the
floor. The central body then straightened.

Jack waited.

It took several minutes before the alien was spurred
into motion again. It tottered toward Jack until it stood
right in front of him, towering above his head. The central trunk bent toward him, but this time it stayed in that
position, looking as if it was peering down at him.

"Um, hi," said Jack.

The central part straightened again.

What now?

Just as in his dreams, around the circular bulge three
petals folded down. Behind them lay dark spaces, but
there was nothing there. When he'd dreamed the aliens
on past occasions, the petals had unfolded to reveal the
tablet he'd been seeking, the tablet just like the ones set
into their own stone platforms outside. Jack craned forward to get a better look, but there was nothing there. He
rubbed his mouth with the palm of one hand.

The three petals that had detached first, elongated and
split at the ends, the tips separating into four flat digits.
So that was how they manipulated things. In unison, the
limbs—he couldn't quite think of them as hands—
curved into the center. The limbs stretched forward, pushing outward, toward him. Jack stood there. Again the
alien made the gesture. He didn't need any prompting.
The creature was telling him to go.

One by one, the petals folded back into place, leaving
that seamless bulge around the middle of the alien's central trunk, and then it went still.

"That's it, huh?" he said.

The alien did nothing. Although previously there had
been slight movement around the room, now everything
was still.

"Okay," said Jack. "That's it."

He looked over at the table thoughtfully, wondering if there was anything else he should ask, but Billie's goodbye had had an air of finality about it. No, he was done here. He had gotten as much as he was going to get.

Outside the building Jack called for Dog, but got no response. All he was worried about now was getting back to the ship and finding Billie, then getting her back to Utrecht. Funny, it almost seemed as if Utrecht were the alien place now. Context framed so much of what you thought. He looked up at the surrounding buildings, his hand shoved into his pocket.

The air out here was almost fresh, making a relief from the burned electrical smell pervading the atmosphere inside. The shadows were darker and the temperature a few degrees cooler. He guessed night would be drawing in soon, and he'd rather not have to make the journey back to the shuttle in the darkness. He called for Dog again. He had no idea how long he'd been in there; Dog could be anywhere by now. He just hoped he hadn't managed to get himself into mischief, though realistically, he found the prospect unlikely. Standing here like this, you could almost believe the city was deserted.

"McCreedy," he yelled at the top of his lungs.

"Yah!" came an answering shout, faint and distorted by the city's walls.

"Dog, get your ass back here!"

"What?"

Jack sighed and leaned back against the wall to wait for Dog to emerge.

A few minutes later Dog's face peeked around the far corner. "Ah, there you are."

"Find anything you liked?" asked Jack.

McCreedy sighed, then made as if he hadn't understood the comment. "The place is dead. Just building after building, all the same. A few coatracks here and there, but most of them don't seem to be doing anything. I may as well not have been there."

Jack pushed himself from the wall. "Well, you should feel pretty much at home then."

"What?"

"All that sameness, nothing much going on. Just like Balance City."

"Yeah, very funny, Jack."

Jack shrugged.

"It almost made me want to carve something in the walls." Dog reached out with one hand and, remembering, Jack handed him the rifle reluctantly, wondering if he was going to use it to burn his name into the side of the building. Instead he tucked it into the crook of his arm.

"What now?" said Dog.

"We go back to the ship and retrace our steps. I think I know what happened, but we're going to have to try it out."

"And the temporal-energy thing?"

Jack took a moment to answer, framing his words carefully. "They told me how to deal with it."

"So can you tell me?"

Jack grimaced. "It's kind of complicated. I'm not sure I can."

It was Dog's turn to sigh. "Okay, if that's the way you want to play it. But you'd better be right."

The light was fading noticeably, and Jack pulled off the eyewear to let it dangle around his neck. He'd had enough of it impressing lines into his face. He'd just gotten rid of the lines; he didn't need them back again. He glanced at Dog, but McCreedy's face remained unreadable, so he turned his attention back to the trek in front of them. The planet's sun was behind them, and the city cast long shadows in front.

As they walked, saying nothing, Jack toyed with what he'd learned. He hadn't exactly lied to McCreedy. He wondered how long before he told Dog about it, and what he would say when he did. He'd have to tell him, sooner or later, and he could imagine what the reaction would be.

Heading back toward the rise, Jack was once again struck with the sensation of having done this before, of having done this many times before. It wasn't often that the dream reality became so real, plucked from his unconscious thoughts and given substance. Why him? Why Jack Stein? He failed to see why he should be singled out to have this alien adventure. Why didn't they pick on someone who was . . . engaged . . . in this stuff?

He played with that thought for a while, then turned to Dog. "Hey, Dog. Have you ever wondered why you end up in certain places?"

"I'm not sure I . . ."

Jack pressed his lips together, and then started again. "Everyone ends up in certain places, in certain situations, right? Sometimes it's like there's a reason it happens, as if the world pushes you into doing certain things or being in particular places at particular times."

"Uh-huh." Dog was scanning the fields to the side and the distant stands of trees as they walked.

"Well, do you think there *is* a reason?"

"Hmmm." Dog shrugged. "I've never really thought about it."

"Well, I've thought about it a lot," said Jack. "Shit happens to me all the time."

"Yeah, I'd kinda noticed that. . . ."

"The problem is, I can't control it. I might be aware of it, because of what I do, you know, but it seems to happen regardless of whether I'm aware of it or not."

They lapsed into silence for a while, and then Dog finally answered. "So you're trying to tell me that something makes this stuff happen."

"I don't know," said Jack.

"You're not going all religious on me, are you, Stein?"

Jack gave a short laugh. "Hardly that. I just can't help wondering sometimes if there are forces at work that we're not fully aware of."

"If you ask me, there's a hell of a lot we're not fully aware of, and it doesn't have to be some mysterious force. Think about where we've just come from, Jack. Think about that."

Twenty-four

As they reached the shuttle, Jack was still debating how much he should tell him. Billie's admonition — well, really the aliens' admonition — to be careful was nagging at him. He strapped himself in after stowing his weapon and handing the pack to Dog, who put it somewhere out of sight. What else did he have neatly stowed away on this little craft? Jack finally decided he'd be better off not knowing.

The last light was disappearing by the time the craft left the ground, and the sky was tinged with purples and greens. Interesting sort of sunset. Did you even call it a sunset? Somehow, starset just didn't sound right. The shuttle swept above the top of the reaching spires, and from their vantage the whole thing looked like nothing more than a hairbrush fixed to the ground. Cities didn't look like that. The regularity, the sameness was wrong. Cities were about chaos and disorder, random growth — Balance City aside. It was those things that attracted him to the urban existence, and in that respect the Locality, despite its sins, had been ideal. As he thought about that, Jack glanced at Dog, who was presently concentrating on the controls. What was a guy like him doing in Balance City anyway? He had heard the explanation, but he couldn't help feeling that there was something else, something more to it.

Dog caught him looking, made one or two adjustments to the controls, and then settled back.

"Hey, about that stuff down there——" he started, but Jack cut him off.

"Don't worry about it."

"Are we okay?"

"Yeah, we're fine, Dog. It's all a bit relative, though, isn't it? I mean, look at us."

Dog grinned. "Hey, I'm not complaining. I think the old Dog's going to have a bit of a party when he gets back into town. This new body could do with a tryout. What do you think, Jack?"

"Hmmm," said Jack noncommittally. Actually, the thought couldn't have been farther from his mind.

They broke the atmosphere and Jack looked down, watching the receding continent, now swathed in darkness. There were no lights, nothing to indicate there might be a trace of civilization below. Everything about them was different. When you came into a populated world, you expected the traceries of cities sparking illuminated spiderwebs across the landscape, the chatter of communication, the flash of transport arriving and departing, but here there was nothing. In some ways it amused him to think that Landerman and his crowd had held out such hopes, now that he'd seen the reality. Sure, the aliens had technology, but Jack wasn't sure anymore that it was truly so advanced. It was different. The aliens had traveled across the reaches. He'd seen the evidence, but it didn't look like they had much interest in it anymore. They were confined to their world and they wanted it that way.

Technology. Almost unconsciously his fingers strayed to his pocket, seeking something, and as if on cue, Dog turned to him once more.

"What are you thinking about, Jack?"

"Oh, nothing. Nothing important, anyway." That wasn't true. Were they going to survive the next jump? The one after that?

"So when are you going to let me in on this big secret?"

Jack looked away. "And what secret would that be?"

"I dunno. You must have gotten something interesting from them. You were in there for a hell of a long time."

Jack turned back. Dog was looking at him expectantly.

"I only asked them what we needed to know," said Jack with a shrug.

Dog's jaw dropped then. "You're telling me that you had an opportunity like that and you missed it? Damn. There were so many things you could have asked. Imagine what they know. I can't believe you, Stein."

Jack shrugged again. "What should I ask? I don't know."

"You might never get a chance like that again."

"You forget one thing, McCreedy," said Jack, narrowing his eyes slightly. "I can talk to them just about anytime I want. I don't actually have to be here to do it. And I'm starting to think that there are others just the same, like me."

Dog clamped his jaw shut and simply stared at him. Jack gave him a slight smile, nodded slowly, and looked away, out at the approaching ship.

"Shit," breathed Dog.

"Yeah," said Jack quietly.

Dog was very quiet after that, saying barely a word until their shuttle had docked in its bay on the *Amaranth* and the outer doors had slid firmly into place.

Once he'd dumped his coat, joined McCreedy on the bridge, and strapped himself firmly into place, he considered the options. Dog was looking at him expectantly. When Jack took his time to react, Dog spoke.

"What is it you're supposed to do? I can get us back, but unless I know what you're planning to make sure we don't go through this again, we're going nowhere."

Jack returned his gaze, holding it for a few seconds. "Okay," he said finally. "They told me how to deal with it, how to counter the effects. There's a particular technique to dealing with the buildup." That much was true.

"And I'm supposed to trust that?" Dog asked.

"You worry about getting us where we need to go. I'll worry about the rest." And damned if he wasn't going to worry about it.

"Uh-huh," said Dog, sitting back. "And we're supposed to trust that too? How's it work?"

"I have no idea."

Dog stared at him. "And you didn't ask?"

"I didn't need to."

Dog gave a hefty sigh. "Well, I don't know." He looked out of the front screen for a few moments, and then turned back. "Maybe you need to go into one of your dream things and work out how we're supposed to use it."

Jack slowly shook his head. "Nope. That's not going to do any good."

"Fine," said Dog, settling back and crossing his arms. He sighed in turn. "Jesus, McCreedy. You have to trust me. I'm the one who can talk to them. They're the ones who know. Do you think we've got any more time to waste sitting here arguing like kids?"

Jack sat back. Dog was looking at him half with disbelief, half with suspicion on his face.

"Dammit, Stein, if you kill us . . ."

"We'll both be dead and it won't matter," Jack finished for him.

Dog nodded, his lips set into a tight line. "Yeah, okay." He turned and hit the sequence to take them away

from the planet and back to the final jump point that had
brought them here.

Much of the voyage to the jump point they spent in silence. What had occurred between Jack and Dog on the
planet surface had left tension working between them.
Jack spent some time thinking about it. He hadn't really
known McCreedy back in the services, not really. He
didn't really know him now. As much as you thought you
knew people, anyway, Jack understood the reality. The
things he dreamed had just as much truth as the things he
remembered, in the scheme of things. Sometimes he wondered if that was what dreams were—merely memories
of things future and past, all mixed up together. The alien
encounter made him question that even more. The thought
that the aliens were dreaming him at the same time that he
was dreaming them worried him. As much as he spent
time in the dreamstate, in the borderlands between what
was real and what was unreal, when it came down to it, he
liked the solid and the tangible, that which he could hold
on to with a firm mental grip. It was one of the reasons it
had taken him so long to come to terms with his abilities
and accept them for what they were. Sometimes he wasn't
really sure that, even now, he truly had. The alien encounter had sealed it once and for all. He could no longer
simply play along with the reality of it.

In the absence of concrete verifiable reality, he had to
have something to hold on to. You couldn't find that existing on the fringes alone. Perhaps that was why the
bond with Billie had become so strong. She provided the
hard-nosed practicality that anchored him in the real
world. Without her, he would probably have ended up
drifting, aimlessly going nowhere. Looking at Dog, he
wondered if he was so different. Were any of them? He'd
lost touch with most of those he'd served with. The brief

contacts he had managed over the years since he'd left had shown an assortment of similar lives, different in their own ways, but still the same types, existing on the fringes or buried in the underbelly of legitimate society.

He had been following that train of thought when he sat back and gave himself a wry laugh. Pretty deep for someone who didn't know whether he was going to make it through the next jump, or the one after that. Was that what he was doing—coming to terms with the state of his own existence?

Shit, Stein, you're becoming morose. There was no time for that. The jump was almost upon them again.

Dog's hands hovered over the controls, hesitating. He glanced at Jack, and Jack looked back at him, closed his eyes, and then opened them before nodding.

Dog hit the controls.

Existence flip-flopped inside him, and Jack gripped the seat arms, willing it to be past.

The next moment they were through, and Jack heard Dog breathe a sigh of relief.

"Well, we're still here," he said. He reached forward and patted the control panel. "Looks like your alien friends have done the job."

Jack reached out with his senses, seeking the buzzing sensation, the almost-static he had noticed before their transformation. For now, there was nothing, but he didn't know how many jumps they had to make for it to appear. How long did it take for this temporal energy to build up—no, that was wrong . . . how many jumps did it take? It wasn't a matter of time, and yet it was. He shook his head. No, it was just too confusing.

"What is it?" asked Dog.

"No, nothing. I'm just trying to get to grips with all this stuff."

Dog narrowed his eyes, but let it pass. He had to be just as nervous as Jack was feeling himself.

The next couple of jumps followed the same way, the tension, the buildup, and then the release. In the between times, waiting to get to the jump point, they kept pretty much to themselves. Still Jack hadn't told him anything. It just wouldn't help them get to where they were going. Jack watched a few vids on the ship entertainment system and stayed away from dreaming as much as he could. That was one of the things that had never attracted him about space travel—the time. Those long, interminable spaces between points had to be filled with something to counterbalance the emptiness. At least when he was in a city, Jack could pretend he wasn't alone. Even if he walked around in his own constructed bubble, there were people there, things with which he could interact. Here there were blank walls and a meaningless starscape and Dog McCreedy. Sure, there were pretty stellar clouds and distant nebulae and passing stars, but for Jack it was like sitting in an art gallery. You could stare at an individual painting for only so long.

He did have one conversation with Dog in which he had explained to him the pathways as the aliens had explained them to him. Doors in a hall. Dog had seemed taken with the concept and ran with it. When Jack had described what he wanted them to do, Dog's enthusiasm had carried over. Although Jack wasn't entirely sure, he thought it was the only real possibility they had to find Billie and Antille.

"But how will we know when to jump?" Dog asked.

"For that, I'm afraid you're going to have to rely on me," answered Jack. "You're just going to have to trust me."

"What's there to trust?"

"Okay, maybe not trust me, but trust my senses. I'm going to let them tell us. It's worked in the past. We just have to be lucky."

"Or hope we're lucky," said Dog. "But if what you told me is right, then we don't have too many choices, unless there are a limitless number of doorways. From what they told you, it doesn't sound like there are."

"That's what I'm hoping. And if there are only a limited number of possibilities within any given area of space, then we'll have better odds of hitting the right one. If I'm right about what happened, then the chances are going to be better still."

"So we get to that dead star or planet or whatever it was, and then . . ."

"Then we let my senses take over and we jump."

Dog rubbed at his scalp rapidly with his fingertips, then shook his hair. "I hope you're right. Damn, but I hope you're right," was all that he said.

Twenty-five

They emerged in the area of space where they had nearly met disaster the last time, Jack's senses alert for any further buildup. He could deal with temporal energy if and when it happened, and if it killed them . . . at least he had made the effort. He tried to rationalize the guilt about McCreedy. Dog had known the risks, known what he was signing up for. Inside, he knew they were just words, but Billie was the important part of the equation. Her safety outweighed any moral dilemma he might be feeling.

He settled back for the ride, running the possibilities through his head. If, as he thought, the gravitational pull of the lightless body had screwed with Antille's navigational calculations, then what they needed to do was try to simulate what the university ship's pilot would have done. Jack needed to place himself inside Antille's head and try to re-create what had happened, and for that he had to rely on Dog and his piloting skills. He knew McCreedy was a good pilot; he always had been, one of the real hotshots attached to the service.

Dog finally called him to the bridge. Barely discernible in the forward viewscreens lay the large body that had almost spelled disaster for them.

"Proximity alerts are working this time, so it seems,"

said Dog, indicating the view out of the front screens with a tilt of his head. "And it's not that I don't trust you, Jack, but I really do hope you know what you're doing."

Jack nodded. He wasn't about to enter into an argument, but the truth was that it was only his gut that was guiding him now. He looked out at the approaching sphere, little more than a rotating ball of gray rock, and struggled to suppress the nervous edge growing in his gut.

Before long they had moved into range, and the body's pull started to touch the ship.

"Okay," said Dog. "It's got us. It's not going to be long before I'm going to have to start fighting it. What do you want to do?"

Jack could feel the pull. "How far are we from where we emerged initially?" he asked.

Dog glanced at his readings, hunched over the controls, looking rapidly from display to display. "I can't be sure," he said. "But I'd say about five minutes. Last time the controls weren't exactly accurate. I'm guessing from the calculations as much as not."

Jack bit his lip and nodded. Okay, he had to have a bit of faith here. This time there weren't any benevolent aliens to guide him. He closed his eyes and reached out, concentrating his senses into a hard ball deep in his abdomen. "Tell me when you think we're there," he said without opening his eyes.

The seconds ticked past, feeling like minutes, and still Jack didn't open his eyes.

"Coming up . . . now!" said Dog. "Shit, okay, it's got us properly now. What am I going to do?"

"Let it run," said Jack, pushing everything he had into trying to feel for what they were looking for.

"Come on, Jack," said Dog. "Come on. Soon, man. Soon, dammit!"

And Jack felt the spark.

"Do it!" he said, through clenched teeth, his fingers gripping the edge of the seat.

He didn't have to open his eyes to see Dog hitting the control. He felt it through every particle of his being, crashing through him like a wave of altered existence. He caught his breath, sucked air into his lungs, and then they were through.

Jack slowly opened his eyes.

Dog was already busy with the controls, checking readings and positions. Jack watched him for a couple of seconds, and then turned his attention to the image on the viewscreens. They appeared to be in a virtually black area of space. The starfield was thinly populated, and there appeared to be no nearby bodies to focus on at all.

"Do you know where we are?" he asked Dog.

Dog shook his head. "Not a clue." His hands flew over the controls, stopping only to push strands of hair out of his face. "But then, I wouldn't expect to," he said.

Jack looked out at the black emptiness, waiting.

"Okay, I've got a relative position, though that doesn't make much sense on its own," said Dog. "What now?"

Jack thought about what he was ready to propose. It felt right. "All right. Put yourself in Antille's shoes. You've just emerged from a jump. You know something's not right, but you have your calculations and you have faith in them. You're pretty sure you can't risk jumping straight back. You also have to assume that you've probably jumped through the right point. What do you do?"

"Take the calculations and project the next point from your current relative position," answered Dog.

"Yeah," said Jack. "That's what I think he'd do, anyway."

Dog nodded. "It makes sense. Okay, that'll take me a little while."

Jack unstrapped himself and stood. "Before you do

that, I want you to scan the surrounding area, see if there's anything out there just in case."

Dog watched Jack as he crossed behind his seat and rested his hands on the back, rubbing his palms back and forth on the top edge. "Just in case?"

Jack stared back out at the surrounding space, looking for any sign of a ship. "I don't think they're out there. I think I'd feel it. Just in case."

He felt like sighing; he felt like . . . he didn't know what he felt like. He had to rely on his senses. They could be in the middle of nowhere, driven by nothing more than half-baked supposition, and it would all be his fault. He wasn't going to let Dog see that, though.

"I'm going to leave you to it for a while," he said. "I need to think."

Really, he just needed to be alone.

When Dog called him back up to the bridge, Jack returned with a sense of trepidation. He lingered in the doorway, hesitating until Dog beckoned him fully inside.

"You were right," said Dog finally. "Nothing."

Jack nodded. He hadn't expected anything else, but there had still been a faint glimmer of hope. Was this going to be the pattern after every jump they made? He didn't even know how many jumps they would have to make. It had to be the same number as they themselves had taken to get to the alien system, but then, if there was no sign of Billie and Antille, he had no idea what they would do next, and still there was the problem of the temporal buildup.

"Okay," he said after a few moments, the sense of doubt weighing heavily inside him. "Next."

It was nearly two days, relative ship time, before they reached the next calculated jump point, and Jack was despondent. The more time they spent, the less likely they were to be to find the ship, with Billie and Antille alive in one piece. Every hour they spent, the odds against them grew.

Back on the bridge, Dog tried to lighten his mood with encouraging words, but they did little good. Jack simply looked out into the blackness, feeling nothing inside. He wasn't even nervous about the approaching jump anymore. He cinched his straps tighter with a sigh and waited for Dog to hit the controls.

The familiar sensation swept through him, and it had barely passed before he was fumbling with the straps, ready to return to his cabin, overwhelmed with a sense of wry irony. It wasn't much of a trade-off—to make it through the jump without any trauma and to lose Billie in return.

He had barely stood before Dog lifted a hand, waving him down. "Wait," he said. "There's something out there."

Somewhere within him, a small spark grew. Slowly, very slowly, he lowered himself back into his seat, barely daring to ask what it might be.

"Yeah," said Dog. "There's a signal." He pointed to the upper right of the viewscreen. "See that system up there? Coming from there, somewhere." He leaned over the controls, focusing on what he was reading.

"A signal? What sort of signal?" asked Jack.

"I think we've found what we're looking for," said Dog. "We need to get in closer. Something's interfering with it."

Jack leaned forward, hoping, resisting the urge to reach out with his hand to the image of the system on the screen in front of them.

"How long?" he said.

"I don't know. Bear with me."

Dog did something with the controls and the image in

the viewscreen changed. "It'll take us about twenty minutes to clear whatever it is."

Twenty minutes. It might as well have been an eternity. Jack closed his eyes and bit his lip, reaching out, feeling, trying to sense what was out there.

"That's it," said Dog after a short while. "This is the *Amaranth*, hailing unnamed ship," he said, leaning forward. "Can you hear me?"

Nothing.

"This is the *Amaranth*, hailing unnamed ship," Dog said again. "Can you hear me? Captain Dog McCreedy hailing unnamed ship."

"Hello?" said a voice. "Hello?"

"I say again, this is the *Amaranth*. Who is this?"

"Hello? Yes, yes. We can hear you. We need help."

Jack recognized the intonation, if not the voice. It was Antille. Where was their pilot?

"Antille, is that you?" said Jack. "Hervé Antille. Can you hear me? This is Jack Stein."

Dog waved him down. "What is your situation?" said Dog.

"We have lost our pilot," said Antille's voice. "I don't know how much longer we can last. We don't know how to operate these controls."

"Jack?" another voice.

"Billie? Are you okay?" Her voice sounded strange.

"Where have you been, Jack? You were supposed to be here."

He could feel the annoyance, the accusation in her voice, though there was definitely something else about it. What did she mean, he was supposed to be there? They weren't done yet, but he could feel the sense of relief growing.

Dog pushed him back. "What do you mean, you've lost your pilot?" he asked.

Antille's voice came back on. "Our pilot did not survive the last jump."

Jack leaned forward again urgently. "Are you okay? Is Billie okay? Tell me. . . ."

"We are . . . okay," said Antille.

"Just get here, Jack," said Billie. "It stinks in here."

Jack settled back in his seat. Yeah, that was Billie. He gave Dog a questioning look.

"About an hour," said Dog, reading the query without prompting. "But then we'll have to work out how to get in there. We should be able to dock with them, and then maybe I can talk them through the procedures."

Jack gave a short laugh. "Billie's probably worked them out already."

Leave her long enough on the ship, and she would have worked out how to fly the damn thing. The relief within him was palpable.

"Very funny, Jack," came Billie's voice from around them.

"Damn, is that still on?" he asked.

Dog nodded with a grin. "Ending communication for now," he said, reaching forward to flip something on the controls.

"Crap," said Jack. "I think I'm in enough trouble as it is."

As the *Amaranth* matched orbit with the university ship, Jack scanned the vessel, looking for damage or anything that would indicate what they'd been through. Below them a world turned, but he had no interest in it or the system they were in now at all. All he cared about now was seeing that Billie was all right.

Dog talked them through the docking procedure, and Jack sat back, drumming on the arms of the seat with his fingers, impatiently waiting for the signal that he could move.

"Okay, go," said Dog, and Jack was out of his seat and heading down the corridor, toward the lock, before McCreedy had even moved. He waited, one hand resting beside the door, ready to step through. A couple of moments later Dog was with him and cycling the controls. The inner door opened, and Jack stepped through, giving Dog a hurry-up look while the door closed and Dog turned to operate the outer door.

It slid open to reveal a semiopaque umbilicus, attaching them to the outer door of the other ship, slightly tinged with blue, and with pale rings giving it both stability and flexibility. Jack was first to the other door. Dog reached for a panel beside it, waited as the cover slid back, then tapped out a sequence. The door in front of them slid open to reveal a darkened lock. Stale air tinged with the scent of something unwholesome washed over them, and Jack wrinkled his nose. Billie was right: The place did stink. Dog stepped through first, Jack a mere step behind him, taking air through his mouth.

"Come on, McCreedy," he breathed.

"Yeah, yeah, I'm getting to it," said Dog. He manipulated the inner controls, waiting while the outer door sealed, then for more seconds as the mechanisms cycled and the inner door swung open.

The door opened into a corridor, facing a blank metal wall, and with the flow of air from inside the ship, the smell intensified. So where were they?

Jack stepped into the corridor, looking up and down its length. They were probably waiting for them on the bridge. The corridor lighting was low, washed-out and yellow. He stepped rapidly toward the ship's front, his heart beating in his chest. He could feel Dog close behind him, but the only thing that mattered at the moment was getting up there, seeing that Billie was okay.

He reached the control room door, ducked slightly, and stepped through.

"Oh . . ." he said.

Two people sat on the bridge, looking expectantly at him. There was Antille, but the portly, dark-skinned archeologist had aged by about a decade since Jack had last seen him. His face still held the smoothness of those with too much flesh on their bones, but a grizzled ring of white hair encircled his shiny scalp. That wasn't what held his attention, though. Perched on the edge of one of the seats, dressed in an off-white robe, was the young woman from his dreams.

"Jack?" she said.

He closed his eyes tightly and opened them again. He recognized he voice, yet he didn't.

"Jack?" she said again. "Is that you?"

"Billie . . . ?"

She smiled, launched herself from the seat, and was across the room in an instant. The next thing he knew she had her arms around him, squeezing him tightly. Jack stood there helpless, still struggling with his confusion. Rationally he knew this *was* Billie, and yet . . .

The next moment she stood back, planted her fists on her hips, looked him up and down critically, and then spoke.

"Why did you take so long?"

"What do you mean?" asked Jack.

"You were supposed to be here."

Jack shook his head, and she turned and crossed back to her seat.

"Billie?" he said again.

Antille was watching them both with an expression of mild interest, but then, he remembered Antille watching just about anything with an expression of mild interest.

Billie had resumed her seat, crossing her arms across her chest, and was staring at him with an accusatory look.

Of course, Jack knew what had happened. It was the temporal energy, the same sort of buildup that had affected him and Dog. The dream Billie had spoken about positive and negative. Somehow the route Antille and Billie had taken must have resulted in the reverse effect.

"How did you know we were coming?" asked Jack.

Before Billie could answer, Dog was in the doorway behind Jack, looking over Jack's shoulder.

"Well, hello," said Dog.

Jack stepped out of the way, half turning to look at his companion. Dog's attention was clearly focused on Billie, having already dismissed Antille as being of only marginal interest. And focused he was.

"And who is this?" he asked Jack.

"This is Billie and Dr. Antille," said Jack. "The people we were supposed to find."

Dog scratched his head. "Huh? Billie? But you said . . ."

Jack closed his eyes, composing himself. He didn't like the way McCreedy was looking at her.

"The temporal effect," he said.

"Oh, yeah," said Dog, not really paying attention.

Jack pressed his lips into a tight line and then looked back to Billie and Antille. "What happened to your pilot?" he asked.

"Unfortunately," said Antille, "he did not survive the . . . um, change."

"Oh," said Jack. "Oh."

Antille bowed his head and nodded.

"Where is he?" Jack asked.

"We had to place him in one of the cabins," said Antille. "I do not like to think what state he might be in now. We have not ventured into the cabin since."

Dog was still staring at Billie with a slight grin on his face. Billie was looking back at him, her eyes narrowed, her arms still crossed.

"Hey, McCreedy!" said Jack,

"Yeah?" he answered, tearing his gaze away.

"What are we going to do?"

Dog ran his fingers through his hair, pushing it out of his face. "Get back to the *Amaranth,*" he said. "We can work it out from there. We're going to be a bit pushed for space, though." He grinned again.

"Enough, Dog," Jack said quietly, narrowing his eyes as McCreedy gave him an innocent shrug.

"What shall we do about the pilot?" asked Antille, getting to his feet. Jack had almost forgotten how round the archeologist was.

"We can't do anything for him," said Dog. He had stepped fully into the control room now and was glancing at Billie even while he addressed Antille. "We leave him, just like we leave the ship. I'm guessing that neither of you can pilot this thing, and anyway, it's not equipped to deal with the temporal buildup. No choice."

Billie pushed herself to her feet. Jack still couldn't come to terms with the change, with the way she looked, but in that robe and nothing else, he could see why Dog was a little distracted. Damn, but she looked good. Her hair was messy, her face was drawn, and she still looked good.

"Billie, what the hell are you wearing?" he said.

She looked down at her clothes, then back up. "It's one of Hervé's things," she said. "I didn't have anything else to wear. Nothing fits anymore."

"But—"

"Jack," she said, a tone of exasperation creeping into her voice.

"Yeah, sorry," he said. "Let's get out of here and into some clean air. This place is a bit—"

"Are you sure?" asked Antille. "We can't just leave it."

"We just don't have a choice," said Jack. "Come on."

"Wait," said Billie.

She pushed past Jack and Dog. Dog turned to follow her with his gaze as she disappeared up the corridor.

"McCreedy, cut it out," said Jack in a low whisper. "Billie, what are you doing?" he said in a normal voice.

"Getting stuff."

"I too must collect my things," said Antille, lumbering across the control room and maneuvering his bulk past both of them. As he passed Jack, he stopped and turned briefly. "Thank you for coming," he said. "I will not be long."

Jack watched him as he too disappeared up the corridor.

Jack turned to Dog, giving him a narrow-eyed look.

"What?" said McCreedy. *"What?"*

Twenty-six

They left the other ship floating there in an unknown system around an unknown world as a silent memorial to the pilot who hadn't made it. Who knew if it would ever be seen again? Jack watched it dwindle into the distance in the viewscreens, unable to avoid thoughts about what his memorial would eventually be, if anything, ever. It wasn't a good feeling.

They were together on the *Amaranth*'s bridge, Billie now decked out in some of Dog's clothes that surprisingly—to Jack, at least—seemed to just about fit. In the dark clothes and pilot's jacket, her blond hair and pale features contrasting, Jack couldn't help looking either. There was a tough confidence about her, and that combined with the way she now looked, he kept catching himself giving her speculative glances, assessing, catching himself again, and admonishing himself all in turn. The inner conflict was hard enough, but the real concern was the lingering fascination Dog kept showing in his interactions with Billie. Billie, no fool, was clearly aware of them, and though Jack expected her to rip his head off at any moment, it wasn't happening. Maybe she was just relieved to be heading back, now out of immediate danger of joining their dead pilot.

Dog was deep in conversation with Antille. The archeologist was questioning him in detail about the jumps, about the alien homeworld, about the temporal buildup, about the aliens themselves. Jack had had just about enough of the aliens for the time being.

"Billie," he said quietly.

"Hmmmm?" she responded, half listening to Dog and Antille's conversation.

"We got cut off before, on the ship. What did you mean, we were supposed to be there?"

She turned to face him, drawing her knees up on the seat in front of her in an old familiar posture. She linked her fingers in front of them.

"You were there."

"I don't understand," he said.

"I saw you, Jack. You were there on the ship."

"Huh?"

She nodded. "Uh-huh. Right there in my cabin. I thought you were really there for a minute, but then you were gone."

Jack's mind was racing. Billie had never shown any real psychic ability. This was something new and different. If they had that sort of connection . . .

She shrugged. "It was weird."

Maybe it had been some sort of projection, some as-yet-undiscovered ability he had inside himself.

He shook his head. "What, I just appeared there?"

"Uh-huh. I looked up and you were standing there looking at me. I said something to you, and it looked like you were saying something. Then you were gone again. I knew it meant you were coming. That's all." She swiveled her seat to face the front viewscreens. "I'm glad you came," she said.

"So am I," he said, watching her, looking for signs that she really was okay.

She looked back over her shoulder at him, and there

was something in the look that he couldn't interpret. Then
it was gone and she was looking back at the viewscreens.

"You really got to see them," she said. "The aliens, I
mean."

"Yeah," he said. "More than see them. I talked to them.
Sort of talked to them. It was weird. I had to dream them to
communicate with them, and they had to do the same
thing." He gave a short laugh. "Dog calls them coatracks."

She pursed her lips. "I wish I had been there," she said.

"Really, you weren't missing much," said Jack.

She set her jaw and took a deep breath, but surprisingly said nothing. He knew he'd said the wrong thing as
soon as the words were out of his mouth, but it looked
like she was going to let it pass.

He watched her for a while before speaking again, and
when he did, he framed what he was going to say as carefully as he could.

"Have you had enough of it yet, Billie? Are you
satisfied?"

He could see the muscles working at the side of her
jaw before she responded. "Nuh-uh. I'm going to go too.
We're going to go. Hervé and I."

"You're serious, aren't you?"

"Uh-huh."

"Dammit, Billie. You just nearly had one disaster, and
we're not out of it yet. You can't really . . . Come back to
Yorkstone with me. Leave all this alone. We're good together, you and me. I want you to come back." The words
had come out in a rush, and he hadn't expected any of
them. He caught his lip between his teeth.

She was a long time answering, and the silence was
killing him.

"I can't, Jack," she said.

Dog took that moment to interrupt. "Hervé and I have
been talking," he said. "We've got a problem."

Jack had to drag his gaze away from Billie with an effort.

"What?" he said, not really caring right now about what McCreedy had to say.

"The jump. The next jump after this one."

"What about it?"

Both Dog's and Antille's eyes were fixed on him, their faces deadly serious.

"If we jump back to where we were," said Dog slowly, "we're liable to end up in the middle of that ball or rock. What are we going to do about that?"

It took Jack a moment to process what Dog was saying. "I don't see what—"

"Listen, Jack. I'm a damn good pilot, but I don't know if I'm that good. The *Amaranth* is a good ship, but she's not made for that kind of stuff. I don't know if we can jump and then get out again. If that thing gets hold of us . . ."

Billie turned to look at Jack too. What made them think he'd have any sort of answer?

He got up from his seat, looked at each of them, then walked off the bridge and back to his cabin. He could feel them staring at him as he left them.

Billie came back and found him. She entered the cabin unannounced and stood in the doorway just looking at him. Jack, lying flat on his back and staring at the ceiling, turned his head to return her look. He still couldn't get used to the way she looked, and inside he knew she was still a sixteen-year-old girl with an unusually mature view of the world. He recognized the look, though—partially concerned, partially pissed off with him.

"What is it, Billie?" he said finally.

She pursed her lips and, after giving a little shake of her head, came into the room properly and perched on the end of his bunk.

He hitched himself up so that his back was against the wall. "So?" he said.

She sighed. "What's wrong, Jack?"

"I don't know. I guess it's expectation. It's all a bit too much, I guess. Look at you, Billie. Look at me. And then everyone seems to think that I've got the answers all of a sudden. Dammit, Billie. We were lucky. We had help. That's all. I don't have the answers."

She looked down at her hands. "No one thinks that you do," she said quietly. "But you got us here. You found us." She looked back up to meet his eyes. "You cared enough to come get us. It's not the first time." She reached out and placed one hand on his leg.

"You're important to me, Billie. What am I going to do . . . leave you there?"

"Yeah, but nobody else was going to come for us. I knew you would."

Jack drew his legs up, away from her touch. Reluctantly she withdrew her hand and crossed it with her other one in her lap. She chewed her bottom lip and looked back at her hands again.

"You're special, Jack."

She sat there for a couple of seconds, and then, as if suddenly making her mind up about something, she quickly stood, took two steps, and, leaning over, kissed him firmly on the cheek.

The next moment she was gone from the cabin, leaving him sitting there to think about what had just happened, leaving him to think about the extra burden of risk he now faced taking them through the jumps. Every single one could be their last. He had to tell them.

"Jack, get up here." Dog's voice came from around him. "We're coming up to the jump point."

Jack nodded to himself, swung his legs from the bunk,

and headed back up the corridor to the bridge. Whatever happened, they were in this together.

"Hey," said Billie as he entered.

"Hey," Jack said in return. Antille looked back and nodded at him. Dog appeared focused on his controls. It was as if nothing had just happened. He wondered, briefly, if they'd been talking about him in his absence. It didn't matter.

"I suggest you get strapped in," said Dog, without turning. "We're coming up on the point pretty fast."

Jack's mouth was dry. It wasn't just the jump; it was as much the knowledge that if something was going to go wrong, then it was as likely to happen now. He took his seat, also knowing that the thought wasn't rational, and that there was nothing in his gut telling him that something was wrong.

He glanced at Billie, and she gave him a little smile.

Dog's hand was hovering over the controls, waiting. "You set?" he said.

"Uh-huh," said Jack.

"Coming up . . . now!"

As they flipped, Jack watched Billie's face, her new face. He watched her swallow, grimace, and then relax, reacting purely to the physical sensation. Then there was no time to watch. They were back in normal space again, the huge ball of uneven rock spinning in front of them, covering the viewscreens and bearing down on them fast, rushing toward them. Jack held his breath.

"Shit," said Dog, hands flying over the controls. "Adjust, adjust, adjust. Come on, baby. Shit. Too damned close! Shit!"

He paused for half a second. "Christ, if you've got any of that luck, we need it now, Jack," said Dog.

His face was screwed up in concentration, his teeth bared, and yet his hands didn't stop.

"Adjust! Close, close . . ."

Antille was pushed back into his seat, his eyes wide, his face pale.

Billie was just staring out the front, immobile, her mouth partway open.

And still the giant ball of rock was rushing toward them.

Jack looked from one to another of them, watching them, watching the reactions, and inside he was blank; everything outside of him appeared to be moving in slow motion.

"If I can just . . ." Dog's voice was strained. "Dammit. Here." His hands moved, tapped, touched. Still no one else had moved.

"Arghh! . . . Yesssss!" he said.

Jack felt the change, and it was evident on the viewscreens. The vast rock wall was moving, but it was moving sideways, not closer.

"Come on, baby," said Dog. "Come on." He was hunched forward, his hands spread, their frantic movement having slowed. He bounced slightly up and down, as if urging the *Amaranth* faster. "We're not out of it yet."

The gray rock whipped past, faster and faster. Blackness broke the edge of the screens, and then their captor was gone. They were shooting out and away.

Dog leaned back, a long, low exhalation coming from his mouth. He turned to Jack and grinned.

Just then Jack remembered to breathe, pulling in a deep lungful of air. He nodded slowly at Dog, his lips pressed together. Good job, McCreedy.

Billie seemed to remember too, and closed her mouth. "Wow," she said.

Dog gave a short laugh. "You can rely on the Dog," he said, leaning across to pat Billie on the thigh. "Always have faith."

Jack narrowed his eyes, but Dog seemed not to notice. Surprisingly Billie hadn't drawn back from Dog's touch. Jack spent a moment processing that, and then decided it wasn't worth reacting to for now.

Dog turned back to the controls. "We're not done yet," he said. "We need to find the other point, which means we have to get back in range of that thing. This one's going to be easy though, in comparison."

He let out a low whistle and rubbed his palm across the front of the panel. "Yeah," he breathed. He turned back to look at Jack. "It's going to take me a little while to recalibrate. Feel free to stretch in the meantime."

Jack undid the straps. He could do with a drink, but somehow, just at that moment, he didn't think that was an option. He looked at Billie, but she was watching Dog. Jack cleared his throat.

"You coming?" he said.

"Nuh-uh," she said without looking at him. "I want to watch."

Jack narrowed his eyes but said nothing.

"I will join you," said Antille. Hervé struggled with the straps restraining his large bulk and pushed himself from the seat, using one arm to lever his body awkwardly into an upright position.

Jack followed Antille as he waddled down the corridor toward the galley. Antille had one hand pressed to the small of his back.

"I am getting too old for this," he said. "Now . . ."

As soon as they reached the galley, Antille found a seat and lowered himself carefully to sit. His bulk seemed to occupy much of the space in the small room. Jack too pulled out a chair and sat, leaning his elbows on the table and cupping his hands in front of his face.

"So . . ." said Jack.

Antille looked at him and blinked a few times.

"You wanted to talk about something?"

"Yes, I suppose you are right. I fail to understand how you could have found us. The calculations, my work, they are . . . um . . . esoteric. I wouldn't expect you—"

"To be able to work it out," Jack finished for him.

"Yes. Precisely," said Antille.

"It's not as if I didn't have help," said Jack. "Heering at the university—"

"He gave you my papers?" Antille sat forward, leaning on the table, his eyes wide.

"Would you rather he hadn't?"

"No, no. Of course you are right."

"I've got some bad news, though," said Jack. "Heering's dead."

Antille's face went through a range of expressions, and then he reached up with his hand to massage his temples with one thumb and his forefinger spread across his face. "No. This is not possible. How?"

"I have my own theories about that," Jack answered. "The official story is likely to be suicide. He was found at the bottom of the spire. That doesn't make sense, though. I saw him at the university and he was fine. His assistant—I can't remember the guy's name—said that he saw Heering being taken away by a couple of men, and they took equipment and papers with them too."

Antille gave a heavy sigh, removed his hand, and then shook his head and sat back. "Will it not end?" he said.

"Not as long as you've got something people want," said Jack. "You must know that. Look what happened before with the artifact. You knew about it then and you were prepared for it. It doesn't matter if it's politics or business; they don't care."

Antille nodded slowly. "Of course, you are right again. You have your theories?"

"Yeah," said Jack, sitting back as well. "I had a brief

encounter with a guy called Max Aire. He seemed to be pretty interested in what I was doing. Heering's disappearance came not long after, and then he wound up dead."

"Aire?" Antille sat up. "Maximilian Aire? So it is the Sons of Utrecht again."

"It would make sense, wouldn't it?"

Antille's shoulders slumped. "Yes, it would. If they took my notes, if they got access to my work, that is not a good thing. We have no idea what use they might put it to if they get exclusive access ahead of anyone else. Once I have published, and everything is in public domain, I can avoid the risk of exploitation without fair competition or checks and balances. The free interaction of competing forces in the world at large tends to balance things out. But now . . ." He let out a deep sigh. "I thought we could avoid this."

"And now that we're coming back," said Jack, leaning farther forward, "the attention isn't going to go away, is it? We've already seen the lengths that the SOU is prepared to go to, and they're not alone in that. I don't know what you can do to divert their interest, but I have to tell you, I'm concerned. Before, when Billie was a kid, a real kid, she sort of had her own defenses built in, if you know what I mean. She taught me that. People don't pay much attention to kids. They don't think they're a threat. But now, looking like she does, she's got to be at risk, right? More of a risk, anyway. People are going to start paying attention to her . . . a whole lot more than before."

Antille looked at him for a couple of seconds, clearly thinking about what he had just said. "And this is your major concern? Nothing more?"

Jack sat back, resting his palms flat on the edge of the table, his arms straight out. "Yeah. What else is it going to be?" He looked back up to meet Antille's gaze.

"Listen, people like the SOU will get involved in plenty of things we can't do anything about. But the things I can do something about, they matter. I've already talked to Billie. She didn't want to hear what I had to say. I think you might be able to convince her. Until all this business is sorted out, I don't think it's safe for her to stay at the university, to stay on Utrecht. I want to take her away from the place. You're a smart guy, Hervé. You've got to be able to see what I'm telling you."

Again Antille nodded. "Yes, I suppose you are right."

"Damned right, I'm right," said Jack. "So talk to her, Hervé, will you? We have a couple of days before we get back, and then maybe some time after we do, but not too much. I've done my bit. Now it's up to you. And quite frankly, I think you owe me that much."

Antille said nothing.

"Right," said Jack, slapping his palms down on the table. "We should get back up there." Now was as good a time as any. "But before we do, there's something else I need to tell you. We can't make this next jump."

Antille frowned. "Why not? I thought they had given you some way to deal with the temporal effect."

Jack slowly shook his head. "They explained it to me. That's it. They said they had no idea whether whatever this thing was would work for us. They wouldn't give it to me."

Antille's eyes widened. "And yet you jumped anyway?"

Jack said nothing.

He rose without seeing whether Antille was going to follow and stepped out of the galley before wandering up toward the bridge.

He reached the door and stepped inside to see Dog busy over the controls. Billie was standing next to him, watching what he was doing and asking a question here and there. Dog was explaining as he went. The thing that gave Jack pause was that Billie's hand was on Dog's shoulder as she leaned over to observe.

Jack cleared his throat in the doorway. Billie looked around, gave him a little half smile, and then turned back to what Dog was doing. Jack wasn't sure whether she'd caught his brief, questioning frown or not.

"Ah, good," said Dog. "We're coming up to the point. I was just about to call you two. Where's . . . um . . ."

"Antille," said Jack. "He'll probably be back up in a minute."

Jack moved to his own seat. He couldn't help glancing in Billie's direction and tasting the thoughts that were running through his head. He wasn't really sure that he liked where they were going.

"Dog, we need to talk."

"What is it? You'd better hurry. We haven't got long."

Billie was frowning at him, perhaps sensing something.

Antille appeared in the doorway. "Tell them, Jack."

Jack bit his lip, and then let the words tumble out.

"What the hell?" said Dog, half rising from his seat. It was Billie's hand that held him back.

"The longer we stay," said Jack, "the more we lessen the risk. It lets the energy fade or something. That's the only way without one of these temporal dispersers. We've been lucky up to now."

Dog was staring at him, breathing shallowly. "The longer we stay," he said, "the greater the chance that we're all going to die anyway. There are four people on this ship now, Stein. We're consuming resources at double the rate. Have you thought about that? Sometimes you can rely on luck a bit too much."

"Jesus, Jack," said Billie, glaring at him.

Dog seemed to be about to say something else, then clamped his jaw shut, his eyes widening. "Shit," he breathed.

"Um . . ." he said after a pause.

"What?" said Jack.

"Um . . . you don't happen to know what these temporal-disperser things look like, do you?"

"Yeah, I think so. . . ."

Dog bit his lip and nodded. "Wait here." He jumped from his chair and disappeared rapidly down the passageway. Moments later he burst into the room carrying his pack. Flipping it open, he shook it out, strewing the contents across the control room floor. Several pieces of alien artifacts slipped out, chips of stone, other unrecognizable things, but there, off to one side, lay a silvery star shape, thicker in the middle, with a surface shifting with colors and a definition hard to focus on.

"Shit," said Jack. "There." He pointed.

Dog bent down and carefully lifted the item. He squatted there, hefting it in one hand.

He looked across at Jack and grinned. "While you were busy in there, I went on a little shopping trip. The coatracks just didn't seem to notice." He shook his head.

"Lucky, Jack. Damn lucky."

Twenty-seven

The next jump passed without incident, and Jack could almost deal with the sensation, it was becoming so familiar. There was a long interval, a couple of days before they reached the next jump point. He had decided that he would give Antille enough time to work on Billie—not that she was talking to him at the moment—so he tried to stay out of her way, but she was spending more and more time with Dog up on the bridge. He even caught Dog letting her take a turn in the pilot's seat, touching the controls and making changes under his direction. It was just like Billie. She could pick up just about anything and had an insatiable appetite for learning new things. Somehow he couldn't believe that Dog's accommodation of her interest was purely innocent. He had to keep reminding himself that Billie could look after herself. She generally knew exactly what she was doing and the potential repercussions of what she did. She'd spent enough time in the Old end of the Locality and with Pinpin Dan to know all about the interactions between men and women. It didn't make him any more comfortable, though.

The thing that was unsettling Jack even more was the strange half glances she kept giving him, always with the hint of a smile. It was most unlike her.

About halfway to the next point, Antille ambushed him in the corridor and drew him into the galley.

"Jack, I am sorry. I have not had a chance to speak to her yet, but I have been thinking over what you said."

Jack perched on the table edge, waiting.

"Related to our previous conversation," Antille continued. "You have provided the evidence I need to verify my findings, even though I have not yet been able to go there myself. I will, of course, as soon as the opportunity arises. I may have some difficulty explaining the loss of a ship and a pilot to my sponsors, but I am confident that I will be able to overcome that eventually. All that being said . . ."

Jack held up a hand. "Get to the point, Hervé."

Antille became flustered. "Yes, well." He took a deep breath before continuing. "I have so many questions to ask you. I need the information, descriptions, evidence, anything you can give me to support the publication."

"And the point is . . . ?"

"I need you to stay for a while on Utrecht so I can finish the work."

Jack looked at him blankly. "I don't need to be there for you to ask me questions," he said. "Do I?"

"No, I suppose not."

"No, of course not. And if you've been holding off talking to Billie because of that . . ."

"No, no, no," he said, waving his hands, but his face had flushed, despite his protestation.

"Okay," said Jack, pushing himself off the table edge and moving to edge past Antille and out to his own cabin again.

"But there is one other thing, Jack," said Antille, grabbing his sleeve, quickly recovering his self-composure.

"What?"

"This Dog person, can you trust him?"

Now where had that come from? "Yeah, I think so. Why?"

"Well, it's just that he's had access to all the research notes. He's been with you to the planet. His ship is now fitted with the technology. That is a lot of information."

Jack stared at Antille. He hadn't thought of it in those terms before. "I can't see any reason not to trust him, Hervé. We served together a long time ago. He's given me no real reason to doubt him, and he came along to help me. His ship rescued you, after all." He thought for a moment. "Yeah, I'm sure."

"Oh," Jack said after a pause. "There's one more thing I think you need to know. They said something that could be important. They said that there were other races out there and that we had announced our presence. You may want to consider that in what you do."

This time Jack did extricate himself from Antille's grasp and walked slowly back to his cabin.

Despite what he'd said, though, Antille's words had reawakened the seed of doubt. He'd questioned Dog's motivations in his head before, but then dismissed the thoughts, taking everything he'd seen as mere evidence of the way McCreedy was and how he functioned. In all of it, there was one thing that didn't add up: Why would someone like Dog McCreedy risk his ship and his livelihood on some half-baked quest for a missing person? Sure, Jack was damned grateful that he had, but on the other hand, what was the payoff? What was really in it for McCreedy?

He was chewing on that right up until the time that he drifted off to sleep.

The kid pushed himself from the pillar and strolled across the intervening floor, his hands clasped behind his back.

"A friend, eh?" he said as he neared, looking Jack up and down. He did a circuit, walking right around the spot where Jack stood, all the time subjecting him to scrutiny.

Finally he stopped in front and stood, hands still clasped behind his back like an old man.

"And what sort of friend are you looking for?" he said quietly. "A boyfriend or a girlfriend? Hmmm, New Man? What is your fancy? A boyfriend or a girlfriend?"

"Neither. Just a friend. A *particular* friend. Maybe you know her."

The kid stopped his circuit and peered up into Jack's face.

"She said she had some friends in Old."

The voice came from behind him this time. "Maybe we could arrange something. It depends."

Jack had had enough. He spun and grabbed the kid by his jacket and drew him close so they were face-to-face. "It depends on what?"

"Nuh-uh," said the kid, pulling his jacket free with a wrench and smoothing it down with his hands. He looked up and gave a shake of his head and a knowing smile. "You won't get anything that way."

Too much familiarity there, and the familiarity hurt. How ever old this kid was, he'd seen too much for his years. It immediately put him in mind of Billie.

"Dammit," spat Jack from between closed teeth, feeling slightly ashamed for trying to monster the kid. "I'm looking for a friend, that's all. Either you can help me or you can't. Perhaps I can persuade you." He reached into a pocket to retrieve his handipad and the kid took a hasty step backward, glancing warily from side to side, making sure of his escape route.

"I wouldn't do that if I were you, New Man," he said quietly, and followed it with a long, low whistle through his teeth.

"But I was just . . ."

There were other noises from beyond the shadowed gloom. Then Jack could see figures clustered in the archway, and others back behind the kid.

"Daman, you okay?" said a voice from the doorway— young, like the kid's, but somehow hard. There was the sound of metal scraping along a wall or floor; he couldn't tell.

"It's okay," Jack said, holding his hands out, and slowly, carefully he reached in and withdrew the handipad from his pocket. "I was just going to see if I could make it worth your while to help me out." He thumbed the handipad on, looking for the kid's reaction.

The kid lifted a hand, palm toward the vast doorway. "We like numbers, New Man. Now you're talking our language," he said. His face was still hard. "Who's your friend? Perhaps we can work something out after all . . . or, even better, find someone who might be even more to your taste. Sometimes you make discoveries down here in Old—discoveries that might surprise you."

"No, listen, kid—Daman, if that's what you call yourself—you've got it wrong. This really is about a friend. Her name's Billie." Jack stopped for a moment, right there in the middle of the dream. Was Billie a friend? Or was she something else? The thought dissipated and he was back to the dream.

Daman looked thoughtful and then suspicious. "Billie, eh? And what's she to you? You a relative or something? We sometimes get relatives down here, or people who *say* they're relatives."

"No, not a relative. Nothing like that. Do you know her?"

Daman was silent for a long time. Finally he seemed to make up his mind. He gestured for Jack to follow, turned his back without a care, and headed toward the vast doorway. "No," he said over his shoulder. "But there's someone here who might."

Jack set his mouth in a grim line and followed. He didn't like the implications of what he was seeing at all. The connection Billie had to this place was painfully obvious, and he didn't need his gut feeling to tell him it was something uncomfortable. He watched Daman as he led the way. The kid's step was confident, relaxed, as if he owned the building. There was still something about him, though, that *felt* out of place. The kid just didn't *belong*. Sometimes there were people like that, but Jack had come across them only rarely.

As he moved beyond the doorway, the lurking shadows resolved themselves into shapes. About a dozen more kids stood eyeing him warily. He couldn't tell how old they were—after Billie, Jack couldn't be sure—but they were young, all of them. Most were boys, and a couple of the older ones held lengths of metal either hefted in two hands or dangling from one hand, resting casually against the floor. That had been the scraping sound. All the kids had one thing in common—a haunted, pinched look and eyes that seemed to go on forever. It was the look Billie had worn the first time that he'd seen her. Jack suddenly felt very exposed. But that was stupid; they were only kids. Sometimes, though, kids were more than kids. He should have learned that much.

Daman gestured, and the shadowy figures slipped away with barely a sound, melting back into the darkness.

"This way," said the kid, motioning Jack to follow.

Across the broad expanse of floor, a large staircase swept up to the levels above, and Daman headed toward it.

"Be very sure you know why you're here," he dropped casually over his shoulder with no further explanation. Biting back a response, Jack followed.

The staircase didn't look like it belonged in the original building design, but it was hard to tell in the dim light. Jack couldn't imagine that it would be functional in an office block. Perhaps in its earlier incarnation in New, it would have made more sense. It was grand, but somehow wrong. There was a lot about this place that was wrong.

The stairs wound on and up, and he mounted them one after the other, trailing Daman's steps. After what seemed like three floors, but with no breaks in between, no landings or entranceways, they came to a stop. Daman stood above him, waiting. Another vast doorway, and within, a pale glow.

"Are you sure, New Man?" said Daman quietly as Jack reached the landing and stood beside him, waiting for the next move. When Jack said nothing, Daman nodded briefly and motioned him to follow.

An archway gaped in front of him, leading off into darkness. A faint light emanated from beyond the pillared entrance. Daman stepped through and said, "Lights," then gestured for Jack to follow. "It's kind of like that," he said, "when you first step through. All new places are full of wonder, New Man, and there are wonders to be found here if you make the right choices."

Daman was gone, leaving his last words echoing in Jack's head, and in the next instant the dream was gone.

He struggled back to consciousness full of a realization that he couldn't possibly have had back then, in the time period that he'd just dreamed. The dream, the flashback back to the time when he'd first met Billie and when he'd gone to Old to try to find her, had shown him something. That strange young/old kid called Diamantis or Daman had been old beyond his apparent years, and there was a reason for that. The kid had been through the jumps. His words, his gestures, the way he had carried himself, had all been the signs of a much older person trapped in a kid's body. He must have been a subject in Outreach's early experiments.

That meant only one thing—Outreach knew about the accumulation of temporal energy.

That was why they had been so interested in locating the alien homeworld. They had been looking for a solution to their problem. They had known about the temporal accumulation, and they weren't stupid. They'd rightly reasoned that the aliens have to have a means of dealing with it. How else could the creatures have traveled the great distances from their world to Mandala?

Even now, years later, Billie had been the key.

Just like Billie often turned out to be the key.

He tucked the information away and left his cabin, rubbing the sleep out of his eyes with his knuckles, wanting to process what he'd just learned, but eager to join the others on the bridge for the moment so that he could be occupied with something else while his mind went through and worked out the connections.

It took nearly two days and one more jump before Jack tried to broach the subject of his dream with Billie. By the time he'd rejoined the others, it was clear that Antille had managed to have his little chat with her, and she was clearly pissed with him. Gone were the vague half smiles. Instead he was back to narrowed eyes and set jaw. He decided to let her cool off before he tried again.

When he finally did, she lifted one hand and pushed past him to stalk down the corridor, saying just one thing back over her shoulder.

"You talk to *me,* Jack. Not Hervé. You talk to *me.* Haven't you screwed things up enough?"

"I am talking to you, Billie. I need to talk to you. *Now.*"

She stopped in the corridor, planted her fists on her hips, and waited.

He started telling her about Daman then, about his revelation and the connection, but before he'd even gotten to mentioning Outreach, she lifted her hand again.

"Boring, Jack," she'd said, then spun on her heel and disappeared down the corridor.

From that point on, she made a point of staying close by Dog, hanging on his every word, and shooting meaningful looks in Jack's direction. By the time the orbital and the jeweled curve of Utrecht started to grow in the front viewscreens, his sense of relief was almost palpable.

It was almost over. They could get back and get out of there.

As they drew in to dock, Jack realized that he hadn't made any plans. He had nowhere to stay and nothing apart from what he carried in his luggage. He didn't know how long it would take Billie and Antille to sort things out, and now, with the current mood, he had to rely on the archeologist to work on her and try to convince her of the wisdom of what he'd suggested. He was even tempted to talk to Dog and try to get him to convince her, but he knew exactly what Billie's reaction to that would be. Maybe later. Right now it wasn't worth the risk.

It still left him with the problem.

He drew Dog to one side in a quiet moment.

"Dog, I need somewhere to hole up while Billie and Antille sort things out."

Dog grinned. "I was going to suggest it, Jack. You can stay at my place until you're ready to leave. You are planning to leave, aren't you?"

"Oh, yeah," said Jack. "There's no doubt about that. Not even a hint of doubt."

Dog clapped him on the shoulder. "That's settled then. Good."

Dog looked genuinely pleased with his decision.

They rode down to the surface in Dog's other transport, amongst the rubbish and the detritus and the stained seats. Neither Billie nor Antille seemed to notice, and as they broke through the clouds and Balance City swung into view, all other thoughts were swept away. It didn't matter whether Jack had begun to hate the place; the city was magnificent, and the approach made it more so. Once again, Jack was swept away by the majesty, craning in his seat to get a better view of the spire and the clustered buildings spread across the upper plateau and crawling, supported, down the sides. Even the color was unimportant; whether it affected his sensibilities or not, the sight was still something to inspire simple awe.

Even Billie and Antille seemed captivated.

As they docked, Billie turned to Dog.

"We should go out to the dormitories at the university and get some stuff organized."

Antille nodded his agreement.

"Then we can meet back here or somewhere to talk about what we're going to do."

"Billie . . ." said Jack.

She turned to look at him. "I have to do some stuff, Jack. I need to get some clothes and other things. I need to get cleaned up. We can talk later."

He understood the sense of what she was saying, but he still wasn't very happy about it.

"It might be better if we met in the morning," she said.

"Yeah, that makes sense," said Dog.

Thanks a lot, McCreedy, thought Jack. A big help. Jack looked at Antille, and Antille gave him the barest of nods, signaling that he knew what Jack wanted of him.

Dog suggested they meet at the bar around midday. He gave Antille directions and they agreed it was a plan.

In the open spaces of the docks, the ordered lines of ships all around him, Jack stood and watched as Billie headed off with Antille to the entranceway that would take them to the surface. He'd just found her, and now she was leaving again. He watched the doorway they'd disappeared through for a few seconds, his hand holding his luggage lead loosely in his grasp.

"You coming, Jack?" said Dog.

"Yeah," he replied after a moment, letting out a sigh as he turned to follow.

Twenty-eight

Dog's apartment was deep in Algol, and McCreedy led him unerringly through the narrow streets, barely looking to check that he was following. Jack was still uneasy at the prospect of letting Billie go off alone with Hervé back to the dorm rooms at the university, but right now he had to accept that it was the best course of action. They'd meet up as soon as Billie and Antille had gotten their stuff in order. He guessed Billie had some other things to think about too . . . and hopefully Antille would have the opportunity to talk some sense into her.

Despite the encapsulated nature of Balance City's levels, the apartment building was much the same as any other in any city Jack had known. Of course, they were different from anything back in the Locality, but these were fixed buildings, not programmed. Dog's place was on the third floor, and they took stairs, rather than an elevator, and then went down a dimly lit hallway to a plain unmarked door. There was a number on the door—thirty-six—but nothing else. Dog palmed the outside lock and stepped back to allow Jack to pass.

The apartment was small but functional, and Dog led him through the rooms. There was a lounge, a kitchen/dining area combined, bedroom, bathroom, and a spare room. Dog indicated that Jack should drop his bags in there, and then led him back to the living room.

"Take a seat," he said, indicating the plain, square sofa. It was beige, just like most of the other fittings and fixtures in the apartment. There was nothing about the place that spoke of Dog, no personalization, none of the little things that people accumulated. It was anonymous. If Jack didn't know better, he would have thought the place was completely unlived in. Still, if you were a pilot, hopping from place to place, maybe an apartment would have that feel—just a simple practical utility, somewhere to sleep when you were in town. He'd seen Dog with that woman, though, on their first meeting. This didn't look like the sort of place Dog would be bringing someone like that back to either.

"Can I get you a drink?" Dog asked.

"Yeah, bourbon if you've got it."

Dog opened a cupboard off to one side and clattered around in it, finally turning back waving a bottle in one hand. "Scotch okay? It'll have to be. I haven't got anything else right now."

Jack nodded and Dog poured the drinks. He spoke to Jack without turning around as he busied himself with the glasses.

"There's someone I want you to meet, Jack. He should be here soon."

"Here?" Jack took the proffered glass and settled back on the couch, swirling the warm golden liquid. "How's that?"

Dog settled in a chair opposite and cupped his own glass between both hands, staring down into the contents before peering up at Jack through his hair. "I put a call in from the ship."

"Okaaay," said Jack. "Why would you do that? What's this all about, McCreedy?"

Dog settled back in his own chair, brushing his hair out of his face. "You've been very useful, Jack, and hopefully you'll continue to be useful. Now with the navigational material and the location, we'll be able to expand the contact with the aliens. The temporal disperser was an unexpected bonus, and once we work out how it operates, we should be in a position to exploit the technology properly. Who knows what else they've got."

Jack narrowed his eyes. "We?" he said.

Dog waved his hand. "Not important for now. Of course, we're still going to need your services until we work out some other way of communicating with the coatracks. I can't see why they won't look after you properly in the meantime."

"Okay, McCreedy, what are you telling me? I'm not doing anything with anyone. I'm getting the hell off this planet, and if I can convince Billie to come with me, then that's that."

Dog leaned forward again. "Wait and see, Jack. You don't have much of a choice."

"Oh, I get it. . . . You're hooked up with the damned Sons of Utrecht. Is that it? I don't know why I didn't see it sooner. Antille suggested something, but I dismissed it. I told him I could trust you." Jack slowly placed his glass down. "I can't believe it, after what we've been through. What, was it a setup all along?" He got to his feet.

"Sit down, Jack. Drink your drink. It's nothing to do with those idiots."

Jack narrowed his eyes, but did as instructed. He was interested now despite his growing anger.

"So what's your angle, Dog?"

McCreedy lifted his hand, rubbed his thumb and finger together in the universal gesture, and grinned. "What do you think? You know me, Jack. A job's a job. Follow the cash. You should understand that."

Jack made a sound low in his throat. "I'm not interested, McCreedy. As soon as I can I'm out of here."

Dog shook his head. "It's not that easy, Jack. I wish I could tell you it was, but it's not." His voice was deadly serious, and there was the vaguest note of resignation in it.

The door announced an arrival, forestalling any further discussion, and Dog placed his glass down and went to answer it. Jack contemplated trying to leave, but right now there was too much remaining unanswered. He wanted to see where this led for the moment, and whom the mysterious visitor would turn out to be.

He didn't have long to wait; Dog returned a few moments later, followed by two men. The one in the rear was clearly hired muscle, making Jack's mind up for him immediately about what he was going to do. The other one looked strangely familiar.

"Ah, Jack Stein. Hello," said the newcomer. His companion moved to take up position on one side of the door, his hands clasped behind his back. The man who had spoken was graying, a plain, unremarkable face, a dark suit, the latter marking him out as an offworlder. Jack knew the face, but he couldn't remember from where.

The man paused, frowned, and then moved to take up a seat. He gave Dog a curious look as well. He leaned forward, crossing his hands in front of him.

"You don't remember me, Mr. Stein, do you?"

The way he spoke was familiar too. Jack looked from him, to Dog, to the two standing by the doorway, and then back again.

"No. Should I?"

"Probably not. The name's Thorpe, Mr. Stein. Andrew Thorpe. The last time we spoke was a couple of years ago. It was only very brief, but I remember it quite well. You seem to have changed somewhat since then."

Jack suppressed a wry grin. Yeah, he'd changed all right. "No," said Jack. "Refresh my memory."

Thorpe nodded. Meanwhile, Dog had taken one of the other vacant seats. The other man remained by the door, watching impassively.

"Around the time you had located the artifact, when you became involved with Christian Landerman and the others, we expressed interest in retrieving the item, and I spoke to you then."

Again the *we*.

"Enough of the mystery," said Jack. "I've had enough games for the moment. Who are you and what do you want?"

Thorpe sat back. "I represent the interests of Outreach Industries. Mr. McCreedy here is one of our freelance agents."

Suddenly it all clicked into place. The ship, some of McCreedy's comments. Jack turned and looked at Dog accusingly. Dog merely shrugged. And Jack did remember this guy Thorpe. He'd called back at the Yorkstone apartment, but Jack had told him what he and Outreach could do.

Thorpe continued speaking. "Ever since then, we've been keeping a fairly close eye on you, Mr. Stein. When you ended up on Utrecht, we became interested, very interested. It seemed wise to make use of what we knew about you, and we know quite a lot about you, Mr. Stein."

"I don't see what—" Jack started, but Thorpe cut him off with one hand.

"We know even more now," he said. "McCreedy sent in his reports as soon as he was within communication range. And very interesting they were too. We had no idea how valuable his past associations with you would turn out to be."

Jack's mind was racing now. The big man by the door was severely limiting his options. There was Billie to think of too. He knew the way Outreach operated, and not a lot stood in the way of their quest for what they wanted. Already they owned the technology around the jump drive. They knew all about Antille as well. The best thing he could do for the moment was pretend to play along until he found out exactly what they wanted, but he could guess. His revelation about that kid down in Old put it firmly into place.

"Tell me what you want."

Thorpe gave a little smile. "I'm pleased you see things our way, Mr. Stein. Of course, assisting us will have its rewards. We need you to help us communicate with the alien beings, establish contact—introduce us, if you like, until we establish our own mechanisms. We need to study how that all works. Unfortunately, or fortunately, depending on how you look at it, you are our sole means of doing that at the moment. For that reason, you have become a very valuable resource."

Jack felt anger growing within him anew. He wasn't quite sure if it was anger with Outreach, or anger with Dog. He clenched his teeth together, trying to keep it under control. He couldn't help saying one thing though.

"You get well paid for this, McCreedy?"

Dog looked down at his hands, but didn't answer.

Jack sniffed and turned his attention back to Thorpe. "And what if I just leave? What then?"

"I'm sure you've seen the way things work in Balance City," said Thorpe. "I think you would find it difficult to leave. Besides, I believe there are certain things that are important to you here. We wouldn't want anything to happen. . . ."

Jack started to stand, the anger boiling up inside him—Thorpe could only be referring to Billie—but as he moved, the hulking man by the doorway took a step forward. Jack gritted his teeth and sat back down.

"Dammit," he said. "This goddamned place. I've had enough of it."

Thorpe smiled fully this time. "Oh, I'm glad you feel that way actually, Mr. Stein. I'm sure you remember the Locality. We have a nice little place arranged for you there. It will be just like coming home, won't it?"

"The Locality? But Billie . . ." said Jack.

"Will be taken care of. We are far more interested in you, Mr. Stein. Your niece is unimportant."

Jack glared at Dog, who was unable to meet his gaze.

"We are very excited about the work we are about to do together, Jack," Thorpe continued.

Jack simply stared at him, the anger bleeding away, leaving him sitting, half-empty glass in his hand, and a hollowness nestled deep inside.

Somewhere out there, there was an alien race, and it looked as if Jack had become the key.

Read on for a sneak peek at the exciting
conclusion of the Jack Stein,
Psychic Investigator, series:

Wall of Mirrors

Coming from Roc in December 2006.

B illie stood in the doorway to Dog McCreedy's sparse living room. Her fists planted on her hips, she stared at him incredulously.

"What do you mean, he's gone?" she said.

"I don't know," said Dog, shrugging his shoulders helplessly.

"Gone where?"

"I told you I don't know."

"Well, what happened?" Billie stepped into the room, her fists still on her hips, her expression turning hostile. "What happened, Dog?"

"Some suits came and took him. What can I tell you?" Dog McCreedy flicked a stray strand of dark hair out of his eyes and moved to the couch. "Jesus, Billie. There was nothing I could do. I suppose you wanted me to get shot. And yes, they had guns, all right. I think I look better without gaping holes in me."

Sneeringly, she let her gaze wander from head to toe and back again, leaving him in no doubt about what she thought of his last statement. He sighed and sat heavily.

"Nuh-uh. Not good enough, Dog."

She'd only been gone from Jack and Dog for a few hours, having left them to pick up a few things at the university. It didn't make sense. She glanced around. There was no sign of any sort of struggle. The empty order of the apartment looked like just that—empty order. Thinking, she chewed at the side of one finger as Dog watched her. What would Jack do in her place?

Dog reached down and lifted a glass with a few sips of what looked like scotch in it. He took a swallow, grimacing as the burn hit his palate. Another glass sat on a side table next to one of the armchairs. Jack's glass, Billie presumed. That much tied in with Dog's story, not that she had any reason to doubt him. She was just naturally suspicious, she guessed. Her life up to now had taught her that much.

"So tell me again what happened."

Dog leaned forward, cradling his glass between his hands and staring down into what remained of the contents.

"Jack and I were sitting here having a drink, talking. Someone came to the door. I answered. They forced their way in. Three of them. One suit, two others. Somehow they knew Jack was here. One of the guys pulled a gun when I made a move. The one in the suit said that Jack was going with them. He said something about the Locality or something like that, about knowing him from there." He lifted his face to look at her. "And that's it."

She crossed to the vacant chair and sat, pulling her legs up in front of her, keeping her gaze fixed on Dog's face. "That's it?"

"Yeah."

"Uh-huh." *Think, Billie. What did they want? What could they want with Jack? And the Locality.* Despite herself, a chill went through her. There were too many things about the Locality that she just didn't want to remember. She had spent too long with the Family in Old, in shadows between crumbling walls, servicing the clients who came to find them with one sole purpose in mind. That was, until Pinpin Dan had found her and taken her to a better life. She pushed the thought away.

"How long ago did they leave?" she asked.

"I dunno, maybe three hours, maybe more."

"They didn't hurt him?"

Dog shook his head.

She lowered her feet and sat forward. "We have to stop them."

Dog sighed. "And how are we supposed to do that, Billie? Huh? They're long gone. We have no idea who they are or where they went."

She bit her lip, then shook her head. "Nuh-uh. No." She rubbed clenched fingers through her blond hair rapidly, mussing it. She had to think.

"Have you got a system here?" She glanced around at the walls, looking for the telltale signs of a wall screen.

"Sorry," said Dog with a shrug. "I'm not here much. And when I am, I have better things to do." He gave her a sly little grin.

"Yeah, yeah, Dog. You're great. Where can I get access to one?"

There was the university, but as with most of the places on Utrecht, it seemed technologically backward. She shouldn't have been surprised that Dog had no system of his own.

Dog ran his fingers through his hair, frowning. "Um . . ."

"Your ship," she said.

"What about it?"

"Well, you've got a system there. I can use it to get access. If they've taken him offworld, there has to be some transport record. If they've even left yet."

"But we'd have to get up there, Billie. That will take time. I'm not even sure my ship will give you access to what you need."

"Uh-huh," said Billie, determination creeping into her voice. "You let me worry about that."

Dog bit his lip. "Hmmmm." There was something else in that expression, something he wasn't telling her, but she didn't have time to worry about that now.

"Well?"

"Well what, Billie?"

"What are you waiting for?" She stood, crossed her arms and glared at him, the challenge clear in her tone.

Dog returned her look with one of resignation, put down his now-empty glass, and got slowly to his feet.

Dog's old, beaten-up shuttle was berthed in a bay in Balance City's docks, not too far from his apartment in Algol. Billie virtually pushed him out the door and told him to lead the way.

Algol was okay, she guessed, for one of the less reputable parts of Balance City. Billie had seen far worse. In fact, even the worst areas of Balance City were a far sight better than much of what Billie had seen in her short existence. Sixteen, nearly seventeen years. But it was weird now, with this whole time thing. She didn't know what Dog had looked like before, so she couldn't judge, but seeing Jack had been a shock. It looked like he had lost about ten years. Inside, he was still the same Jack, but on the outside, he was definitely younger.

With Billie, it was the opposite. She knew she looked about twenty-seven now, maybe more. Whatever had happened with the temporal buildup had happened the other way. Jack was younger; Billie was older. If things had been different . . .

No, she couldn't even think like that. She owed a lot to Jack, but their relationship wasn't like that, *couldn't* be like that.

Now, Dog on the other hand . . .

She watched him appreciatively as he walked along in front of her, his shoulders slightly hunched, the resentment evident in his carriage.

She sniffed the sleeve of the jacket she was wearing. Yeah, there were traces of its owner impregnated in the black pseudoleather. It was only a little too large for her. Dog and Billie were roughly the same size . . . now. He had lent her some of his clothes on board the *Amaranth* after Jack and Dog had affected their rescue. A pity the clothes weren't programmable too, because she kind of liked the jacket. It would just have to do as it was, though. Same as the black pseudoleather trousers. Spacer's gear. Like Dog. Still, she wished she'd had time to get some new clothes. Nothing she had back at the university fit her anymore. She hadn't had time to do anything, really, except have a shower and rummage through her things. She'd found the white oversized T-shirt that she was wearing now, but it wasn't that oversized anymore. She hadn't grown much with the transition, but she'd grown enough, in ways she might not have expected.

Everything else would have to wait for now. There were other things she could do with getting back, but sorting out the Jack problem was more important for the present. Dog's mention of the Locality put her in mind of Outreach. Anything to do with the Locality had to do with Outreach in one way or another. If she could get some decent access from Dog's ship, then she could get into the data mines she needed, maybe even Outreach itself. Then they could identify the people who had taken Jack. At least she could find out recent or planned ship movements back toward the homeworld.

"Dog, have you got any contacts?"

There was a slight off beat in his step, but he answered back over his shoulder with nothing apparent in his voice. "Yeah, some. What do you need?"

"I don't know yet. I'll think about it."

He stopped in midstride and turned to face her. "Jesus, Billie. Ask a question. Don't half ask it. You want me to help you? Then tell me what you want."

She narrowed her eyes. "I don't know yet. It depends what I can get with your system."

He shook his head, causing his long, dark hair to fall across his face. He flicked it back out of the way before answering. "I don't like your chances. This is Utrecht. It's not exactly the most advanced planet."

"Every place has a network you can tap into," she said. "If I can get into one network, I can get into others. Information's like that. There are bridges and pathways. Otherwise it couldn't work. And where there's a bridge, there's a way in."

He looked doubtful and shrugged.

She pursed her lips and gave his arm a little shove. "Come on. Time to go."

They walked into Balance City's dock area, with all the sleek ships arranged in even lines, and Dog led her towards his own excuse for a shuttle. Dirty, banged up, it looked out of place among all the other well-maintained vehicles parked nearby. He stood looking at the ship as if waiting for something. She was just about to ask him again what he was waiting for when he spoke.

"Look, Billie, are you sure? I don't know what you think you're going to achieve."

"Let me worry about that, Dog." She looked at him, trying to work out what was forcing his reluctance. There shouldn't be any reason for him not to help her. It was almost as if he was delaying. "What's the problem?" she said.

He shrugged. "No problem. I just wanted to make sure you knew what you were doing."

"Uh-huh. Well, you can be sure," she said.

Dog keyed the sequence and the door slid open. He let her clamber in first, then took his own place at the controls, reaching up to toggle equipment and hit switches. She watched all of his moves carefully. The last time they'd been in this craft, she'd been too absorbed with talking to Jack and Hervé Antille to pay real attention. Right now, she didn't want to ask any questions to distract McCreedy, but watching close was usually enough to give her at least a start on working something out. Now she thought she had a pretty good idea what she needed to do to get the shuttle moving. Along with the stuff Dog had shown her on the *Amaranth,* if worse came to worst, she felt she would have enough of an idea to fly this thing . . . maybe. She continued watching as he touched more controls and eased the shuttle out of its berth and into the hangar, letting the parking controls draw them to the lip that led to open airspace, and the yawning gap over the chasm above which Balance City rested.

He spoke to the port controllers, seeking clearance. There was a brief back-and-forth, and then Dog sat back.

He gave her one last look. "You're sure, you're sure?"

"Shut up, Dog. Fly."

He slapped the panel and the engines roared into life, launching them out into the void and up, away from Balance City into the Utrecht skies.

Jay Caselberg is an Australian writer based in London. He grew up in Australia and has lived in the UK and Turkey. After starting life as an academic, studying the history and philosophy of science, he took a sideways step into IT consulting and moved to London in 1991. His work has taken him around the world, and to date he has traveled to more than fifty different countries. His short fiction and poetry have appeared internationally in a variety of publications, including *Interzone, The Third Alternative, Crimewave, Aurealis,* and many others. He also writes as James A. Hartley. You can find his Web site at http://www.sff.net/people/jaycaselberg.

Jay Caselberg

**Meet Jack Stein,
Psychic Investigator.**

Wyrmhole

0-451-45949-0

His specialty: Drawing clues from dreams and
psychic impressions. His assignment:
A mining crew has mysteriously disappeared.
And Jack has to sniff them out...
In his dreams.

Metal Sky

0-451-45999-7

Two years after the events of *Wyrmhole*,
Jack is tracking down a missing artifact—a
metal tablet. But Jack's investigation is about
to lead him into the clutches of a shadowy
political organization that knows the tablets
secrets—and will kill to keep them.

Available wherever books are sold or at
penguin.com

R012